Praise for A BEAUTIFUL DARK

"A BEAUTIFUL DARK has everything I love about a paranormal read. You might like A BEAUTIFUL DARK if you like: Lauren Kate, Becca Fitzpatrick, and Alyson Noël."—*The Story Siren*

"This takes the whole fallen angel thing to a completely different level! I definitely recommend this book. It will make you wish you were snowed in so no one could stop you from reading beginning to end in one sitting!"—*The YA Sisterhood*

"A BEAUTIFUL DARK brings in just enough mythology, emotion, and heart-wrenching moments to hook paranormal fans. A book just as beautiful inside as it is outside." —*Confessions of a Bookaholic*

"Author Jocelyn Davies pulls no punches with her debut novel. You'll find yourself divided between good vs. evil and which boy you'd rather follow home. Sometimes bad is the better choice!"
—*Miss Literati*

"I was so excited to find that there is a sequel already planned called A FRACTURED LIGHT. It already is on my list of books to watch out for."—*Open Book Society*

"This is a great read."—*Hopelessly Devoted Bibliophile*

Also by Jocelyn Davies

A FRACTURED LIGHT

A Beautiful DARK

JOCELYN DAVIES

An Imprint of HarperCollinsPublishers

HarperTeen is an imprint of HarperCollins Publishers.

Library of Congress Cataloging-in-Publication Data

Davies, Jocelyn.

A beautiful dark / Jocelyn Davies. — 1st ed.

　　　p.　　cm.

Summary: When Skye, who lives with her aunt in Boulder, Colorado,
turns seventeen and is suddenly pursued by two boys who are polar oppo-
sites, secrets of her true identity—and destiny—begin to emerge.

ISBN 978-0-06-199066-3

[1. Angels—Fiction. 2. Identity—Fiction. 3. Supernatural—Fiction.
4. Good and evil—Fiction. 5. Colorado—Fiction.] I. Title.

PZ7.D28392Be　2011　　　　　　　　　　　　　　2011024245

[Fic]—dc23　　　　　　　　　　　　　　　　　　　　　CIP

　　　　　　　　　　　　　　　　　　　　　　　　　　AC

Typography by Erin Fitzsimmons

12 13 14 15 16　LP/RRDH　10 9 8 7 6 5 4 3 2 1

❖

First paperback edition, 2012

For my grandparents Sandra and Mark Messler, who have been saving a place for my first novel on their coffee table since I was old enough to spell

It happened at night. I woke to the sound of the wind blowing my curtains back. I opened my eyes but saw nothing. Not even moonlight. Not even shadows.

And in the morning, the window was closed. A feather rested on the floor beneath it, the only reminder that I'd woken up in the night at all. In the shadows, I couldn't tell if it was light—or dark.

*T*he air had a brutal edge to it as I stood outside of Love the Bean, the local fair-trade coffee shop. Snow from a recent storm had frozen over in the subsequent days' chill, leaving the roads and the sidewalks in town slick and hazardous. I almost slipped four different times as I walked from my car to the front door. The wind sliced at my neck where it was exposed beneath my hat, and I scanned up and down the street for signs of life.

Welcome to Saturday night in River Springs, Colorado: downtown was dead. Eden's Gate Market, Big Mouth's Diner, Into the Woods Outdoor Co.: most of the storefronts were dark.

Cassie and Dan were waiting for me inside the coffee shop. Every year I made them promise not to throw me a party, and every year they didn't listen. It had become a tradition. So tonight, I'd planned everything. We were starting with celebratory cupcakes and lattes, courtesy of our friend Ian, who worked at the Bean and was always giving us free stuff; then when Ian ended his shift the four of us were going to see the midnight show of *Storm Enemy* at the Clark Street Cineplex, because I loved, loved, *loved* terrible disaster movies.

Struggling not to lose my balance on the icy sidewalk, I pushed through the front door.

At first, I thought I'd made a mistake. Except for the recent addition of some fairy-tale-caliber twinkle lights, the room was mostly dark, and completely empty.

"Hello?" I whispered. The door closed behind me with a light jangle of bells. I could hear a quiet, insistent sound. A soft *shhhh*ing.

"Surprise!" Cassie jumped out at me from behind a purple velvet armchair.

"Come *on*," I groaned dramatically, finding it difficult to act surprised when I really wasn't. I should have known she'd ignore my plan in favor of hers.

On cue, probably half of the junior class exploded out from behind various other velvet armchairs and overstuffed couches and from behind the coffee bar. I could see the rest of the girls from the ski team, Cassie's friends from her band, and Dan's track buddies. Northwood High School was small enough that most of the different groups got along, and apparently my birthday was enough of a reason for them to converge.

"Happy birthday!" everyone yelled.

"Cassie!" I hit her with my hat. "You promised!"

She held up her hands in surrender. "Sorry. You know I never do what you tell me to do." She laughed and shook her head. "You never learn."

Cassie grabbed my arm and maneuvered me through the crowd toward a circle of couches in the back. I could see Dan waiting for us with a mischievous smile and a glittering box.

"Okay, wait, I know you also said no presents," Cassie shouted above the music as we worked our way through the throng, "but I have no self-control."

"You better not have spent—"

"Of course not. Don't worry, it's total crap."

When we got to the table, I started to say "I hate you," but Dan interrupted me by nearly toppling me over in a bear hug. "Aw, don't be mad! Are you mad? Do you still love us? Because if not, my plan to finally have Cassie all to myself worked." He punched Cassie playfully on her arm. She rubbed the spot, and I could see the muscles in her cheeks twitch as if she was trying not to smile.

"Please, do you *see* the apocalypse? Because I'd give up on that happening until you do." She reached down to pick up a steaming mug. "And even then, it's negotiable."

"I'm holding out for a hot zombie," I added.

"Yeah, or, like, the hot scientist who finds the cure."

"Or the hot government agent who's assigned to protect you from the international terrorist who plans to wipe out the nation with the world's first zombie virus weapon of mass destruction."

"Because you carry the zombie virus antidote in your blood."

"Exactly."

"It's a recessive trait."

"What movie are we talking about?" Dan asked.

"Anyway, Skye," Cassie said, ignoring Dan's question and holding the mug out ceremoniously, "this is for you." She opened her cardigan, and a flash of metallic flask glinted at me. "Seventeen is a big year."

"It'd be bigger if the apocalypse was coming," Dan mumbled.

"Did you two start drinking before I got here?" I asked teasingly.

Cassie was decked out for the occasion in a floral mini-dress under her favorite yellow vintage cardigan, her red hair piled loosely on top of her head. She wore thick, sweatery tights and snow boots that were ubiquitous in Colorado during the winter. Dan was in his navy blue hoodie, the one he never took off. His straight brown hair flopped in his eyes, and he pushed it back. I just couldn't stay mad at them. They'd been my best friends since kindergarten, and we were still as tight a unit as ever.

"Okay, I admit it," I said. "You guys are amazing. This place looks incredible."

"Aw, she likes it!" Dan nudged Cassie. "Don't get all mushy on us now, Skye."

"It *better* look effing incredible." Cassie sighed. "It took me like two hours to finish making the paper icicles and untangle those little twinkle lights."

"You are a craft goddess," I assured her.

"Speaking of crafty," Dan said, pointing to the present on the couch behind him, "you probably don't want to hear this"—his voice dropped to a stage whisper—"but we *got you something*." He mock-ducked, as if I was going to hit him.

"Hilarious," I said. "Did you practice that?"

The present was wrapped in wrinkled silver tinfoil

with gold glitter glue looping out the words *Happy Birthday, Skye*.

"The present was totally *my* idea," Cassie said.

"But *I* was in charge of wrapping it," Dan said, jumping in.

"As if she couldn't tell." Cassie rolled her eyes at me. "But don't open it now; it might be too much for your surprise-averse heart. Do us all a favor and open it later when we don't have to painfully wait for your reaction. Okay?"

"Okay." I laughed. "Plus, I don't want to ruin this gorgeous wrapping job."

"It's harder than it looks," Dan insisted.

"I'd like to propose a toast. I know I don't usually like surprises, but . . ." They looked at me expectantly. "This one is pretty cool. Thanks."

Cassie lifted her mug. "We like doing this stuff. It makes us feel all warm and fuzzy. And we know birthdays are hard for you." I gave her a pointed look, which she pretended not to notice.

"To always having each other's backs." Dan raised his own mug.

"To seventeen," Cassie added. "The year it all falls into place."

Our mugs clinked together, echoing through the noisy coffeehouse as if it were only the three of us.

The twinkle lights cast a fuzzy glow over everything, and the music blasted full-volume out of the coffee shop speakers. More than one person had Cassie's idea to stash a flask on them. Maggie Meltzer, the captain of the girls' ski team, fed me shots of Jägermeister from her pink aluminum water bottle as the rest of the team started a dance party around us. Someone else pushed one of Dan's track friends up against me and then we were dancing, too. From somewhere I couldn't quite pinpoint, I heard Cassie's voice float up: "For someone who isn't crazy about surprises, she's really taken to this one."

Eventually I started to feel a little dizzy, like when you swim too far from shore and suddenly realize that you can't touch the bottom anymore. Pausing for breath, I tipsily made my way back to our couches, using my arms to propel myself off the furniture, swimming against the tide. Cassie was sitting next to Dan, their heads tilted toward each other, their knees almost touching as they talked.

"Hey, Skye!" I turned around to see Ian smiling and wielding a tray of multicolored cupcakes. Cassie and I liked to call him Dan's best "XY" friend. He had clean-cut sandy hair and a treasure map of freckles scattered across his face. Seeing Ian always made me happy. Not as happy as I often felt he wanted me to be, but still.

"See, we can stick to at least one part of the original plan." Ian offered me first choice. "On the house."

"How are you not already fired?" I asked as I picked out a pink-frosted vanilla cupcake with rainbow sprinkles.

"This place would fall apart without me. I'm the sexy handyman."

I pushed him lightly. "Shut up."

"Really." He nudged his shoulder against mine. "Anyway, I'd get fired for you." He set the tray on the low table in front of the couch where Cassie and Dan sat. Cassie jumped up immediately. "Oooh, sugar," she crowed, grabbing a chocolate cupcake with yellow frosting.

Ian dropped down beside me. "I've got a fifteen-minute break," he said. "So, were you surprised?"

"You mean even though you all went against my *explicit* instructions to not surprise me? Just like you did last year?"

"And every year?" He picked up a chocolate cupcake and began peeling off the wrapper, sucking some frosting off his thumb.

"Yeah. Believe it or not, I was."

Ian nodded to himself, pleased. "So what do you think

of the band?" he asked.

I glanced back to the small stage in the corner where three guys were playing indie pop. "Not bad."

"Not as good as The Somnambulists," Cassie said quickly.

"Is that what we're calling your band now?" Dan said, amused.

"But your band wasn't available tonight," Ian reminded her. "You had a surprise party to make happen."

"True." She reached for another cupcake, splitting it in half with a fork. "I have many talents." She absently passed me the other half. "I sort of outdid myself tonight, didn't I?"

"You did," I agreed. "Next year, though, when I say no surprise party, I mean no surprise party."

"Like that's going to happen," Ian said.

"If we don't throw you a party, who will?" Cassie asked, before turning her attention back to Dan.

I knew she didn't mean them to, but her words stung. I thought of my parents. I had such fuzzy memories of them because I was so young when they died, but my mom's best friend—my legal guardian, who I call Aunt Jo—had given me this whole box of photos from my childhood with them. Apparently every year on my birthday, my mom would bake me a woefully lopsided cake from Funfetti mix, and she'd let me decorate it with chocolate *and* vanilla frosting in a marble pattern. The cakes were all pretty hideous, according to the pictures, but marble-frosted Funfetti cake was still my favorite dessert. Funny the things I could suddenly miss even though I barely remembered them.

"You look really great," Ian said quietly, bringing me back to the present.

"Thanks," I said. "Must be that one-year-older thing."

"No, you always look great." He blushed, suddenly fascinated by what was left of his cupcake.

He was wearing a green polo shirt with the Bean logo over his heart. Not exactly sexy. I knew he wouldn't believe me if I told him he looked good, too. It would just be me trying to feel comfortable with his compliment. Trying to make us both feel comfortable with it.

It was getting hot in there, too loud, too crowded. I never did well with small spaces and large gatherings. I wanted to be on the slopes, skiing, with the exhilaration of the bracing wind rushing over my face. That was where I always wanted to be.

"I need air," I announced to the group.

"You mean *frostbite*?" Cassie looked up dubiously. "Have fun."

"Bundle up, dear!" Dan called in his best grandma voice.

I scanned the pile of coats on the couch for a glimpse of

mine. All I could see were my hat and scarf peeking out from under someone's parka.

"You want company?" Ian asked.

"Thanks," I said, pretending to be engrossed in searching for my outerwear, "but I'm just going to catch a few deep breaths. Not worth you getting frostbite, too."

"That's cool." He stood up. "I gotta get back to work anyway."

"The cupcakes were great."

"I didn't bake them." His voice held a strange, disappointed edge to it, and I was left with the feeling that I'd somehow done something wrong.

With a sigh, I watched him walk away. *Why didn't you just say yes, Skye? Would his joining you have been the worst thing ever?* No, but I craved the solitude, just a couple of minutes alone. He'd understand. He always did.

After snatching my hat and scarf from the couch and slipping them on, I snuck out the front door.

The cold air swallowed me whole. It felt good, revitalized me. Out here, it was quiet and peaceful. I closed my eyes and took a deep breath, enjoying the alone time. When I opened them, the full moon stared back at me, lighting up the mountains below.

"Hey."

I whipped around, embarrassed at being caught having a moment of reflection. Someone was standing against the wall of the building behind me. I could see the outline of a guy's tall, sinewy frame, but his face was obscured by the shadows cast by the awning.

"Oh," I gasped. "I'm sorry. I didn't mean to disturb you. I can—" I turned toward the door.

"No, stay," he said. "It was getting too quiet." He stepped into the light. "I'm not used to living so close to the mountains. I think they create a sound buffer, or something."

Our eyes met, and something in the way he looked at me made me pause. The blackness of his eyes was magnetic, and something strange flickered through my own in response. I had the weirdest feeling of déjà vu.

It was dark where we stood on the street, but what moonlight there was shone on his face, exaggerating the definition of his cheekbones and illuminating his smooth olive skin. His short hair was so black that it was hard to tell where he ended and the night began. "You're Skye, right?"

"Yeah," I admitted, tearing my eyes away to look back out at the mountains. I didn't want him to catch me staring. Did I know him? He didn't look familiar, but he seemed to recognize me. Maybe he'd heard someone inside say my name. "Hiding from my own party. I'm such a winner."

He sized me up. "You don't strike me as someone who would avoid a good time. So there must be more to the story. Anything—or anyone—specific that you're hiding from?"

"Nope," I said. "Nothing."

"Nothing?" His tone was playful, like we'd known each other all our lives and shared secrets.

"Or everything," I admitted, trying not to smile.

He laughed, and the low sound echoed across the empty street. My stomach twisted. *Calm yourself, Skye.* I never reacted this way to guys I'd just met. I was usually the cool and collected one. It was Cassie who was boy crazy.

"So do you make a habit of ducking out of your own parties?" he asked.

"Only when they're thrown for me against my will. Do you make a habit of lurking outside of *other* people's parties?" I shot back.

"Without question." He grinned, showing off an adorable dimple. "You never know who you'll meet."

We stood on the silent street for a while, at an impasse, just watching our breath escape in clouds of steam into the night. I wanted to keep talking to him, but my brain felt stuck.

You really need to stop letting Cassie empty her flask into your drink, I thought.

"I should go inside," I said finally. "They're going to wonder where I disappeared to."

"What'd you wish for?"

I turned to face him again. "What?"

"Your birthday wish," he said. "You know. Closing your eyes. Blowing out the candles. What did you wish for?"

For some unknown reason, warmth rushed up my spine, flooding my cheeks. Why did so innocent a question seem so intimate? "I must have forgotten to make one," I said, realizing as the words left my mouth that they were true.

"It's not too late," he said. "You've still got half an hour to change your life."

I looked at him, confused. What a strange thing to say to someone you'd just met. "Maybe I don't want to change my life."

"You wouldn't change anything at all?"

My mind flashed to my parents, of course, but wishing for a way to feel closer to them was impossible. "No," I said. "Not really."

"Well, I hope that works out for you."

I turned back toward the door, feeling like I'd missed the point of the conversation somehow.

"I'll see you around, Skye," he said as I walked back inside. "Happy birthday."

In the privacy of the fluorescent-lit bathroom, I stared at my reflection. My eyes were flashing silver in the light—true silver, not the silvery gray they appeared to be on most days. I blinked, but nothing changed. They only flashed brighter, more vibrantly. They reminded me of a movie we watched in chemistry earlier in the year. When the scientist broke an old thermometer into a petri dish, the mercury slipped from the cracks in the glass, quick and light, not nearly as thick and goopy as I'd expected it would be.

I couldn't quiet my heartbeat. What had caused my eyes to look this way? Had the effect started before I went outside? Or did it have something to do with the unexpected attraction I'd felt to the guy leaning against the wall? I realized now that I didn't even know his name.

When I heard the door to the bathroom open followed by the sound of laughter, I fled into the nearest stall and pressed my back against the cool metal door. I fought to calm my erratic heart and wild thoughts, to focus on the problem at hand. I couldn't face my friends until my eyes were normal gray again. What had I done to make it stop the *last* time this happened?

I'd been skiing in a race about two weeks before. It had been neck and neck for a while—this girl from Holy Cross Academy and I. I'd leaned into the wind, feeling for the turns, blocking out the noise, the sound, everything but the feel of the snow beneath me. At the bottom, when she congratulated me on my win, I took off my goggles. "Whoa," she'd said. "Are you wearing contacts?" And moments later, in a bathroom so much like this one, I saw it for the first time. My eyes like liquid silver coins staring back at me in shock.

I detached myself from the stall door and waited until the two girls who had interrupted me left, the door squeaking open and then shut. The bathroom was quiet. I emerged, lifting my face once again to stare into the mirror, bracing myself for what I was about to see.

But my eyes were back to the same old nickel gray.

Something my dad used to say needled its way into my thoughts. *Little silver bells. When they ring, we'll know.* It came out of nowhere. I hadn't thought about it since he'd died.

Pushing the memory aside, I took a deep breath and stood straighter, appraising the rest of me. My skin looked even paler than usual. My jeans and periwinkle sweater, which before had felt just right for a cozy night with friends, now felt frumpy. I took my sweater off. The tight T-shirt underneath was marginally better. My black waves were plastered to my neck from the dancing, and I scooped them up into a ponytail.

I glanced down at my watch. It was almost midnight. I wondered if everyone would give me a hard time for going home this early. Cassie would be disappointed. She'd been gloating all week that she'd convinced Aunt Jo to forfeit my curfew just this one night. I hated to waste it, but I'd suddenly lost all enthusiasm for partying. Why did this keep happening? Was I sick?

The bathroom door squeaked on its hinges again as I pushed my way back into the hall, reminding myself to tell Ian that he should probably get that fixed.

The light in the hall was dim, and it took my eyes a little while to adjust to the difference.

But then I saw them.

Two guys were standing with their backs to me. I could barely make out that one was blond, while the other's close-cropped hair blended into the dark background. They spoke in hushed tones. Every now and then their voices rose and then fell again, as if the conversation was heated but they were afraid of being overheard. I couldn't see their faces from where I stood, but I definitely didn't recognize them.

I could hear only a snippet of the conversation: "Not . . . yet!" The blond guy stood straight, his arms stiff by his sides and his hands balled into fists. "You are not supposed to interfere."

"Do you think I care?" the dark-haired guy whispered loudly. "Your rules mean nothing to me, Devin."

In a blur, he pushed the blond guy, sending him toppling back into a stack of wooden chairs that went crashing to the ground. At least, he must have pushed him—he moved too fast for me to see exactly what had happened. Everyone turned around to look. Someone cut the music. Devin looked stunned as he lay tangled on the floor amid a nest of chairs.

"I can see that, *Asher*."

Devin shoved himself to his feet. Asher came back at

him, and the two locked together, head to head. Some people in the crowd shouted. I tried to suppress the panic rising in my throat.

"You would have done the same thing." Asher's voice was a growl, deep and menacing.

"You know I wouldn't have."

As the crowd gathered in closer, I found myself right at the front, inside the circle. People jostled against me, striving to get a better view. I was trapped.

"Well, whose fault is that?"

Devin twisted around in Asher's grip, and Asher went flying backward—toward me. I couldn't move; the crowd was packed in too tight. Closing my eyes, I held my arms out to catch him as he hurtled into me, sending us both to the hardwood floor. Pain jolted through me as the impact knocked the wind out of my lungs, and I gasped.

"Skye!" I heard Cassie's voice rise above the ringing in my ears.

I couldn't call out to her; I could barely move. Asher weighed a ton, and I was pinned beneath him. He turned around to right himself, pressing his arms into the floor on either side of my head for balance. His face was right above mine. His eyes widened.

It was the guy I'd met on the street just a few minutes ago. The one who'd asked me what I'd wished for on my birthday. His eyes, even in all this chaos, were deep and dizzying. Looking into them was like trying to follow a penny as it falls down a well.

I caught my breath, and feeling slowly returned to my limbs.

"Get *off of me*!" I shoved as hard as I could, catching Asher off guard. He tumbled to the side, and I scrambled up. "Jerk."

I noticed the other guy, Devin, staring at me, too.

Then a loud popping noise startled me, and something began hissing loudly. I fought to push my way through the crowd toward where Cassie's voice had last emerged. Suddenly, the ground rumbled; I lost my balance and fell to my knees. Shouts grew louder, panicked screams echoed around me, and someone's hands gripped my arms from behind.

"Skye!"

I turned around to face Cassie and clutched her arm in relief. "What's going on?"

Cassie shook her head, her eyes huge. "I don't have an effing clue."

"Earthquake!" someone yelled.

Chaos erupted as though a switch had been thrown. I heard glass shattering, mugs and plates falling off shelves.

Cassie tightened her grip on my arm. "Let's get out of here!" She pulled me toward the door. "Hurry!"

The ground was quaking beneath us. As I turned toward the door, I noticed Dan and Ian running up alongside us. Dan took hold of Cassie's free arm. As Ian grabbed my other arm, he gave me a strange look.

Then he and Dan were propelling us through the door.

"Get to your cars!" Dan yelled. "Ian's on duty. I'll stay with him while he calls the police."

The two of them raced back toward the building.

Outside, people were scurrying down the street in both directions. I could feel the tremors diminishing as Cassie and I sprinted through the freezing air to where our cars were parked on the other end of the street. We stopped at her old hunter green Volvo wagon. I couldn't draw in air. It was like my lungs had locked up.

"Well, for better or for worse, everyone will be talking about your birthday on Monday," Cassie muttered as she fumbled for her keys.

I tried to stay upright, but my knees were shaking too hard. They buckled under me, and I slid to the ground. I gasped for breath again and again.

"Skye?" Cassie crouched next to me, snow seeping into her tights. "Are you okay?"

She pushed back my hair as I leaned my head against the passenger door and closed my eyes, battling to keep breathing.

"I don't know what's wrong with me," I said, my chest tightening. The street was spinning, even though the rumbling had stopped. "I feel weird. I probably had too much to drink."

"You can't drive home like this. You're shaking." She took my mittened hands in hers and squeezed.

"Just . . ." I didn't know how to explain what was wrong with me. I didn't understand what was going on. It wasn't panic. It wasn't even fear. It was like total and complete exhaustion. Like I'd pushed myself to the limit and was crashing.

"Come on, get in." She helped me up and into the passenger seat. Leaning over, she buckled me in. "I'll drive you home. We'll get your car in the morning."

As she climbed in and revved the engine, her radio played the single that had been popular all winter. Cassie began to sing along softly, automatically. She turned the wheel and glided out from the curb, down the street.

I took a deep breath, trying to steady my hands. As the

music and Cassie's voice washed over me, I happened to glance in the side-view mirror. On the street, a lone figure stood in the shadows, getting smaller and smaller as the car pulled away.

The next morning was gray and heavy with the promise of more snow. When I opened my eyes, the weak light filtered into my room through the bay window. As it washed over my pale blue walls, I felt almost like I was outside, just floating in the sky. I buried myself deeper under my cream-colored jersey comforter, letting the soft cotton surround me. I pulled it tight to me like a cocoon, blocking out the world. I had a slamming headache.

I didn't feel any older on the day after my birthday than I had on the day before it.

I wanted to stay under the covers all morning, but my cell phone rang, forcing me to get out of bed and walk all the way across my room to where it was charging on my dresser.

"Hey, Ian," I said after I saw who was calling. Shivering in my boxers and T-shirt, I ran to get into bed with the phone. I closed the window on my way back. I didn't remember leaving it open, and now the room was freezing. I glanced outside before pulling the curtain closed. The sky looked dark, like the storm headed our way was about to blow down some serious power lines.

"Hey," he said. "How are *you* feeling this morning?"

I laughed. "I'm fine. I got up, answered the phone, and now I'm back in bed."

"Don't tempt a guy, Skye; I'm only human. Are you wearing pajamas?"

"*Ian!*"

"Kidding! Kidding." Only I had a feeling he wasn't. He made jokes like that a lot, but he was a good friend and I'd never thought of him as more. "I really did call to see how you're doing. It was kind of scary there toward the end."

Absently, I pulled the covers over my head, watching for cracks where the light shone through. "Yeah, you guys really put the 'surprise' in surprise party." I yawned. "I've never heard of an earthquake hitting this area before."

"Is that what you heard?"

"What do you mean?"

"It wasn't an earthquake. The boiler in the basement exploded."

I chewed on the inside of my cheek. "Wasn't that thing brand-new?" I remembered last year when Ian was going on and on about how the installation was messing up his whole shift schedule. Ian's job at the Bean included all kinds of odd fix-it jobs, and he'd been there before school some mornings to help oversee the installation.

"Yup. Apparently it just overheated. It got so hot it even melted in places—that's what caused the explosion."

"Whoa," I said, bringing the blanket down from over my head. The cool air hit my face. "Weird."

"I know."

"Was anyone hurt?"

"Not that I've heard. We were really lucky."

"Skye?" Aunt Jo knocked on my open bedroom door. "Babe, if I'm gonna drive you into town to get your car, we'd better do it now. It looks like snow; I don't want it to get stuck."

I nodded at her. "Ian?" I said into the phone.

"Yeah," he said. "I heard her. Stop by the Bean if you get a sec when you're in town. I'm here cleaning up the mess."

"That sucks."

"Tell me about it."

"They couldn't get anyone else to help?"

"Rub it in, please?"

I laughed. "See you in a bit." I heard the sound of shattered glass being kicked, then Ian sighed into the phone.

"I'll be here."

I hung up, but the phone immediately started ringing again. Cassie.

"We're going to get a blizzard!" she sang. "How are you feeling?"

"Head. Car. Snow. Town," I moaned.

"Got it. Call me when you get back and are feeling better."

The line clicked dead.

We drove in silence for most of the way there. I just didn't feel much like talking. When I'd gotten home the night before, Aunt Jo had been waiting up for me, so Cassie and I had to tell her all about the un-surprise party and what I'd thought was an earthquake. Cassie had explained that I'd been so shaken up that she'd had to drive me home. I didn't want Aunt Jo to worry, but how could I explain what had really happened to me when even *I* wasn't sure?

Aunt Jo's eyes kept shifting nervously from the road to look at me. I had filled her in on what Ian had just told me about the boiler exploding. It was scary to think that the night before could have been a way bigger mess than just a bunch of shattered glass.

I let my head fall against the headrest and watched the trees flash by.

Aunt Jo stopped in front of my black Subaru. I hopped out of the passenger side of her car, my boots crunching loudly in the snow. She got out, too, and came around to the curb. She slapped her left hand uneasily against the side of the SUV, and some grayish blond wisps swung loose from her ponytail. Her cheeks were just shy of burned, the result of last week's mountaineering trek with Into the Woods Outdoor Company, the outdoor sporting goods and adventure company she owned and managed.

She'd always been happy running the show from behind the scenes, until two weeks ago when her head trip leader, Jenn Spratt, had taken a terrible fall. Her carabiner hadn't been secured during an ice-climbing trip. Jenn had broken her left leg and dislocated a shoulder. Aunt Jo had her office staff working on finding a temporary replacement, but until then, she was the only one qualified enough to take groups out into the backcountry. Lucky for me, growing up with Aunt Jo had taught me to be pretty self-sufficient. The past couple of weeks, she'd been away for long stretches of time, coming home sunburned, wind-burned, scratched, and bruised. But all of it just made her look pretty—outdoorsy and alive and younger than she was. It was weird to think that my mother's best friend was the same age my mom would have been if she were still alive. I couldn't imagine my mom doing the active and strenuous things Aunt Jo did. I imagined her as fragile, ethereal. Perfect.

"Listen, before I head home, I'm going to pop into the Bean to see Ian," I told her.

"Don't stay out too long." She frowned upward at the heavy clouds. "We're in for some major weather."

"I'll be fine," I said. "Seriously. See?" I knocked on one of the tires. "Snow tires. It's all good."

She looked at me a moment longer. "Okay," she said, entirely unconvinced. You'd think for someone who spent 99.9 percent of her time trekking through the mountains avoiding bears and rattlesnakes, she'd put more faith in things like snow tires. "Be careful." She mussed her hand through my dark, wavy hair.

"It's just a little snow," I insisted. "We get it, oh, twice a week?"

She gave me a warning look. "I'm serious, Skye."

"I'll be fine. What's with the gloom and doom?"

"Oh, this whole explosion thing just has me shaken up,

that's all. Thank god I was home and not out on a trip. I hate my new schedule; I wish I didn't have to be away from you for so long. What if you'd been hurt and I wasn't here?"

I didn't want to admit that, secretly, I was kind of thinking the same thing. She had enough to worry over with all the extra work she'd taken on after Jenn's fall. I gave her a reassuring smile. "But I wasn't hurt *and* you were here."

"Promise me you'll be home soon, and I'll make you dinner tonight or something."

"A real home-cooked meal—from scratch?" I widened my eyes in mock surprise and batted my eyelashes. Aunt Jo had become the queen of stocking our freezer with frozen dinners. The "healthy" kind that had ingredients like wild brown rice, organic kale, and quinoa—this totally bizarre little grain that Aunt Jo had instructed me was pronounced "keen-wha." The meals couldn't possibly be as healthy as the manufacturers claimed. Anything that came in a little plastic dish you had to heat in the microwave couldn't be that good for you. When Aunt Jo was home, though, she cooked real meals good enough to dream about the whole time she was away. "I want lasagna!"

"Don't push your luck," she said dryly. "But if you hurry

home, I'll bake you some cookies."

"I'm glad to see you're not above bribery."

"You can't be above anything when raising a teenager."

I stuck my tongue out at her. "Love you!"

"Yeah, yeah," she said, shooing me away. "Love you, too. Say hey to Ian from me."

I pulled away, watching as she got back into her car and drove off. Something wet stuck to my forehead, and I looked up to find it was already snowing—thick, heavy white flakes. *Perfect*. After the point I'd made about overreacting, Aunt Jo would kill me if I got stuck in the snow. I pulled my hood up to cover my neck and started walking down the street. The sidewalk outside the Bean was charred and black. Standing in front of the empty wooden frames that had once held windows, I stared at the destruction.

Glass had shattered all over the floor along the walls where the picture frames had fallen. Chairs were over-turned; couches were torn and bleeding upholstery. The glass in the pastry display case under the cash register had blown out.

Every single sheet of glass in the entire place had been splintered into tiny shards; a fine, prismatic dust covered everything. The afternoon light glinting off the shattered glass was almost blinding. I shielded my eyes.

"Ian?" I called.

I heard a clatter in the back.

"Who's there?" he shouted.

"It's Skye." The clattering stopped. Silence.

Ian emerged from the back looking completely harassed. His short sandy hair was sticking up as if he hadn't even brushed it, and his eyes were bloodshot.

"Do you see?" he asked, shrugging and dropping his arms to his sides. "Do you see what I have to do? This may be too big a job for even the Sexy Handyman."

"I'm so sorry," I said. "This is unreal." I didn't bother with the door—just stepped through where one of the huge storefront windows had been. I forged a path through the debris to the counter. "Are you okay?"

He picked up the broom leaning against the wall behind him and began to sweep the floor with it. "I'm fine. But are *you*?"

"I'm okay. I'm a little shaken up, but—"

"No," he pressed. "I mean, are you *okay*?"

I stared at him. "Ian. I'm fine."

"So you're, like . . . feeling . . . normal?"

"Like I just said." Why was everyone suddenly freaking out on me? "It was just a boiler."

"Yeah, it *was* just a boiler," he said, his eyes boring into mine. What was going on? "But that's not what I'm talking about."

"So what are you talking about? I promised my aunt I'd be home before next Tuesday, so . . ."

"You really don't know?"

"Ian," I said, getting annoyed. "Come on. What is it?"

"Okay." He put down his broom and came around the side of the counter. He had an excited glint in his eye, and his brow was furrowed with intensity. "Your eyes are gray."

"Yes," I said. "Is that your big revelation?"

"Come on, just listen. Last night they were silver."

My heart skipped a beat. He had noticed?

"They can look that way sometimes," I said casually. "Trick of the light."

"Skye," he said, putting both hands on my shoulders. "Silver. Metallic. Like the stuff that's inside those old thermometers."

I shivered as he brought up the exact imagery I'd thought of.

"Can you put something over the window?" I said. "It's freezing in here."

"Did you hear me?"

"Yeah, I did. I just don't think it's that big a deal. My

eyes can look silver in certain light. I don't know why you're freaking out about it."

"I've never seen anything like it. I've seen your eyes in all kinds of light. I mean, they're beautiful." He paused, his cheeks flushing red. "But that's not the point."

"Look, I really appreciate you letting me know." I didn't like where this conversation was going. I broke away from his hold and took a few steps backward. "But I'm fine. Do they look silver now?"

Ian's face fell. "No. . . ."

I shrugged in response.

"Yeah, you're right," he said, looking away. "I guess I sound crazy. It was probably just glass flying or something. It was some insane chaos in here. Forget I said anything, okay?" But his eyes still held that same intensity. I backed away. I had to get out of here.

"I'd offer to stay and help," I said, "but I have to go finish up some reading before the semester starts. See you tomorrow."

"You're unbelievable. It's still vacation! You are the only person I know who catches up on reading she's not even behind on."

I smiled. "I want to go to Columbia. And that's how you do it."

"Whatever works, Skye, whatever works."

"Good luck with the place."

"Thanks," he said, still standing in the same spot, unmoving.

"Later, Ian."

As I walked outside, I glanced over my shoulder, through the window. He was back to sweeping up the glass. He looked so alone. Guilt nudged at me.

What was I running from, anyway? So my eyes had been wonky last night. And Ian had seen them. It didn't necessarily mean anything bad. Maybe I was overreacting. Maybe, like I'd told Ian, it really was just a trick of the light. Just because I always immediately thought the worst, didn't mean I needed to stop being a friend.

I took out my cell phone and called Cassie. When she answered, I got straight to the point. "I'm at the Bean, planning a little surprise of my own. You and Dan need to get over here."

"Um," she said. "Doesn't the Bean kind of look like an earthquake hit it?"

"Cassie."

"Sorry."

"Are you going to make quips all day or are you going to help me?"

"Make quips. . . ."

I coughed loudly into the phone.

"Fine." She sighed. "I'm coming to help you. It's not easy being so selfless, you know."

I snapped my phone closed, and stepped back through the gaping hole where the front window used to be. Glass crunched beneath my boots, and Ian turned to look at me. I smiled. "So, are there any extra brooms around here?"

With Dan and Cassie helping, we had the glass swept up and the broken furniture hauled out to the Dumpster by the time the crew from Wylie's Windows had arrived.

Cassie broke out a thermos of her special hot chocolate sprinkled with chili powder. Then we sat on the couches and watched as repair people sealed the new plate glass windows into place. Beyond them, the dark clouds were rolling nearer. I guessed karma had kept them at bay until we were done.

"I can't believe you guys helped me clean up this mess," Ian said as he surveyed the work. "I was getting paid for it."

"I mean, we're *really* good friends," said Cassie.

I tipped my mug in his direction. "You probably do owe us. Don't worry, we'll collect on it soon."

"There's still a lot left to be done," Dan said as he glanced around at the buckled floor and splintered walls.

"The construction crew will be in tomorrow," Ian told him.

We sat in silence for several moments simply enjoying watching someone else work. The Bean's general manager, Burt, had come through earlier with the insurance adjuster to assess the damage and was in his office now making phone calls.

"So what was with those guys last night?" Cassie asked, a glint in her eye. "The two who were fighting."

Dan shrugged. "I don't know. I didn't even see them until the crowd formed. Were they there the whole time?"

"They were arguing about something," I said.

Cassie sat up. "You saw them? Did you get a good look? What did they look like?"

I took a sip of the spicy hot chocolate and suddenly wished I hadn't said anything. I'd sort of wanted to keep my private conversation with Asher outside, well, private. "Yeah, when I came back inside. I sort of heard the beginning of their fight."

"What were they arguing about?" Dan asked. "Had to be pretty serious, the way they were going after each other."

Everyone looked at me like I was going to spill some

huge juicy piece of gossip. "Honestly, guys, I don't know. Something about rules. Whatever. I didn't really hear."

Ian snorted. "How about the Respect Skye's Birthday rule?"

"That *is* an important one," I said, giving his shoulder a nudge. He smiled and turned away, but I could see a blush creeping up the back of his neck.

"But who were they?" Cassie asked. "Anybody know?"

"Why are you, like, *so* interested?" Dan said, kicking her foot lightly.

"Dan," Cassie said, addressing him like you would a visitor from another planet. "If they are new in town and they are hot, I'm interested."

"They've never been in here before," said Ian. "At least not while I was working. They're probably just tourists. Here for ski season."

Only I wasn't so sure. I thought about the guy who'd been leaning against the wall outside. Asher. The sense of déjà vu I'd felt when he'd looked at me. But I couldn't tell my friends that. I couldn't even explain the feeling to myself.

I remembered the lone figure standing in the street, watching us as we drove off. Even now the memory gave me chills. I tried to brush it off, but the scene clung to me.

Why did I know that it had been Asher? And why had he been watching me? Had he felt the same giddy attraction I'd felt? Or was it something more?

"Just so you know, Skye, we did not invite them," Cassie said.

"Yeah, but we didn't close down the Bean, either," Ian said. "Burt nixed that request, so we couldn't exactly control who was at the party. Anyone could have come in off the street."

"Next year, I'll convince him to close it down," Cassie promised.

"Next year, no surprise party," I insisted. "Please? For my senior year, you have to grant me that one wish."

"Yeah, sure, whatever you say, Skye." Cassie put her hand in front of her face and shook her head at Dan and Ian as though I couldn't see. Another surprise party was inevitable.

"Well, since you're ignoring all my requests anyway"—I got to my feet—"I promised Aunt Jo I'd be home before the storm hit, and it's been way longer than an hour."

Ian stood up. "Thanks again. You saved my life today." He awkwardly pulled my hood down over my face before shoving his hands into his pockets and saying he needed to go talk to the manager. He walked off.

"He's so cute," Cassie said. "I don't know why you don't just go out with him already."

"You think all guys are cute," Dan muttered.

"No, I don't, Daniel. I think some are *hot*."

I left them to their squabbling and headed out to my car. I didn't know why I had a sense that someone was watching me. I glanced around. People were trudging up and down the street, wandering in and out of the shops. But I was looking for someone in particular. Asher.

Only I didn't see him. Instead, I was climbing into my car when something else caught the corner of my eye. I jerked my head around, but it was gone. I could have sworn I'd seen a shock of blond hair, blue eyes.

I turned the key in the ignition, promising myself I would officially banish all thoughts of the two guys from last night the second the car roared to life. They were probably just what Ian had said they were: tourists. I'd never see them again.

On the drive home, I kept the windows open. I hoped the freezing air would make everything vanish into the white sky.

The next morning, I woke up floating.

My eyes were closed, even though it didn't feel like I was asleep anymore. It was hard to tell. I must have been in that weird state between dreaming and waking, where dreams could be memories and the real world could be a dream.

It felt like my body was suspended above the mattress, though how far above it I couldn't tell. And suddenly, I didn't want to open my eyes at all. I stiffened in panic.

I was floating?

I counted backward, still unsure if the counting was happening in my head or if I was saying the words out loud.

Three. Two. One.

I opened my eyes.

But I wasn't floating at all. The sensation of being in midair had vanished, and I lay in bed, the comforter tangled tightly around my body as if I'd been tossing and turning the whole night. It was morning. The only thing that floated in the air was the occasional dust particle caught by the weak winter sun. The window was open, and the cold air blew my curtains back to let in the gray light of the early day. Was the clasp broken?

The alarm on my nightstand buzzed loudly, and I fumbled to snooze it. When I saw what time it was, I froze. Seven thirty. School started in forty minutes. I was late. I was never late. How many times had I hit Snooze?

I forgot everything as I scrambled to pull myself together. I burned through my morning routine, pulling on a pair of dark jeans, a couple of long tanks, a chunky cardigan, and a long necklace or two. In the bathroom, I washed my face and rubbed in some tinted moisturizer, brushing my teeth as I frantically scrambled to apply two coats of mascara with my left hand. I swept my hair back into a loose knot, stepped into my boots, grabbed my backpack, and pounded down the stairs.

By the time I blew through the kitchen, Aunt Jo was already sitting at the table, a mug of coffee in her hands. "I'm leaving on a mountaineering trip to the Collegiates this morning," she said offhandedly, narrowing her eyes to study me. I really wished I didn't look so harried. It ruined the image I wanted to project: that I was fully capable of taking care of myself.

"I'll be back late Saturday," she continued. "I'll have my cell, but if you can't get in touch, call the office. They can connect with satellite."

"I know the routine." It was always the same whenever she took a group out. I poured coffee and about half a box of sugar into a travel mug. The Collegiate Peaks were a spectacular section of the Rocky Mountains. Looking at her small, wiry frame, you'd never picture her trudging up the side of a mountain underneath a forty-pound back-pack, but she was deceptively strong. And, as she liked to remind me when the question of breaking curfew came up, a pro with an ice pick.

"I'm trusting you to behave while I'm gone," she said.

"I'm trusting you to come back and bake me some cookies."

She laughed. I knew she felt guilty about leaving me alone so much, so I always tried to make it seem like it was no big deal. But the truth was I really missed her when she was away. But then she'd probably miss me when I went off to college, and I didn't want her making me feel guilty then. So I was paying forward.

I grabbed a cereal bar from a box in the cabinet and kissed her on the top of her head. "See you soon," I said. "I love you."

"Love you, too," she replied, smiling after me. "Don't forget. Call the office if you need anything!"

And then I was in my car and flying to school. The snow hadn't stuck very much, aside from forming some weak piles along the side of the road, and the roads themselves were already clear. The trees were a green-and-brown blur on both sides of me. I had a perfect, tardy-free record—there was no way was I going to start off the semester being late for homeroom.

Just as I pulled in to the parking lot, my cell phone rang in my backpack. I pulled it out while maneuvering the wheel with one hand. Cassie's number blinked up at me.

"Lady," she said breathlessly into my ear. Cass always said everything breathlessly, as if she couldn't wait to tell you. "Are you ready for second semester?"

"I'm ready for my coffee."

"What? I don't think I quite heard that."

"I *said*," I repeated, louder this time, "let me drink my coffee in peace, woman."

"You're no fun. See you in homeroom; this gossip isn't going to spill itself."

Cassie's favorite thing in life was gossip. And it was almost always about guys, which was Cassie's favorite subject.

I glanced at the clock on the dashboard. 8:01. Nine minutes to make it to homeroom before I was officially late.

On my way up the front steps of the school, I stopped. I felt a prickling sensation that caused the fine hairs to rise on the nape of my neck.

I knew no one was behind me—I had been alone in the parking lot when I got out of my car—but I turned around anyway.

"Morning, Skye." It was Asher, looking up at me from the bottom step. His short black hair ruffled faintly in the breeze.

He looked guarded, one leg on a lower step, the other tensed on the step just above it. But beneath his serious exterior, it looked like he was trying hard not to smile.

"So," he said, clearing his throat, "I'm sorry for fighting at your party. I didn't mean for you to see what you did, and . . . hear what you did. It wasn't because of you, Skye. Devin and I have a long-standing history. . . ." He paused. "I was really glad we got to meet outside. What did you end up wishing for?"

"I—" I'd forgotten to make a wish after all. But what he was saying made no sense. Why would I think the fight had anything to do with me? I didn't even know these guys. I wondered if maybe he was just nervous about seeing me again. I knew I was.

"Oh," he said. "I forgot my opener. Sorry. I'm Asher." But I already knew that.

He held out a hand. I eyed him suspiciously. Slowly I reached my hand out as well. He met me halfway. When our hands touched, a tiny wave of goose bumps trailed up my arm. I quickly pulled away.

"See?" Asher smiled. "Not so bad, right? Anyway, look, aren't you going to be late for homeroom? Want me to walk you?"

"Inside?" I said. "But I . . . There's a pretty strict security policy. . . ."

"Well, it's good to know my new school has at least one leg up on my old one," Asher said casually as he gestured for me to go ahead.

"Your *new* school?"

"Yep. Looks like you're stuck with me for a while. But don't worry, I'll try not to start any more fights."

"You'd better not," I told him lightly, trying to hide my

shock. "I can't be associated with a known troublemaker."

Asher's face broke out into a wide, wicked grin. "That's a shame, because my cousin would tell you that trouble-making is something I was born to do," he said. His eyes flickered between mischief and seriousness.

"Your cousin?"

"The guy I was fighting. But I'd advise you not to believe anything he tells you."

Something about his sudden, intense gaze made my cheeks burn. Quickly I walked on ahead through the school's big front doors, and Asher jogged a few steps to catch up.

"Ah . . ." he began, fumbling with a sheet of paper in his back pocket. "Maybe you can help me find *my* homeroom. Where is room two-eighteen, exactly?"

I smiled in spite of myself. "This way, come on."

As we walked down the hall and up the stairs, I got that same prickly, being-watched feeling as before. The girls all stared at Asher—and glared at me. The bell was going to ring any second, and most people had already filtered out of the halls to their classrooms. But the stragglers turned as we passed, parting for us like the Red Sea. Their whispers followed us down the hall. I slid my eyes sideways as we walked in relative silence. I had to admit, it wasn't just his eyes that were alluring; it was as if all of him radiated this magnetized power, drawing people in toward him.

"It's just up here," I said, snapping myself out of it.

When we reached the open door to the room, I waved my hand like a magician unveiling something that had been hidden. "Here you go."

"After you," he said.

I blinked at him, my heart pounding suddenly. I hadn't told him that I was in this class, too.

"What's wrong, Skye?"

He could have just assumed, a small voice whispered inside my head.

The sharp sound of metal against metal made me look around.

The blond guy from the party—Devin—was standing by a locker on the far side of the hallway.

And he was staring at me.

His face was expressionless, but the temperature in the hallway seemed to plummet.

He hefted his backpack onto one shoulder and approached. I wanted to head into the room, but I was rooted to the spot. He stopped in front of me.

"I'm sorry about ruining your party Saturday night."

His voice was quiet, calm, shy. But also seemed sincere. I

hadn't been this close to him yet, and now I could see that his eyes were a tranquil blue. Peaceful. It was something I'd longed for since my parents had died—a place with no troubles.

When I glanced back at Asher, I could sense the animosity rolling off him in waves. I looked back and forth between them, unsure of what was going on. Standing there, I felt closed in—trapped—like I had Saturday night during the fight.

"You should both talk to Dr. Schneider," I said. "The guidance counselor. I hear she's great with conflict resolution."

The bell rang.

"Thanks, guys. Now I'm late to class."

"First time for everything," Asher said.

How had he known?

I hesitated at the door. Ms. Manning was already pacing the front of the classroom, going through the day's announcements.

I heard something drop in the row of seats by the window where Cassie and I had been sitting since the beginning of the school year. She was already seated there, bending over to pick up her calculator from the floor. She turned her head, and I could just see her eyebrow rise through the messy red-blond wisps of hair that had fallen in her face. She shot a pointed look at the two guys standing near me, winked, righted herself, and began to scribble in the notebook in front of her.

"Skye?"

Ms. Manning was standing in front of her desk, staring

at me as if she was waiting for an answer to a question I hadn't heard.

"Sorry, Ms. Manning," I said, humiliated. I'd never before had to do the tardy walk of shame. I hurried to my desk and slipped quietly into my seat beside Cassie. She kicked my ankle lightly with the toe of her gray vintage suede boot.

"Nice entrance," she whispered. "Drama queen."

"It wasn't her fault we're late, Ms. Manning," Asher announced. "My cousin and I got lost, and Skye helped us find our way. It's our first day here. New school. You know how it is. I'm Asher. I've heard great things about you." He flashed a dazzling smile, focused only on her. She actually blushed and patted her mousy brown hair that frizzed out in a crown around her face. I almost laughed as I remembered the note Cassie had sent me last semester: *Why doesn't she use conditioner?*

I figured that now, Ms. Manning was wishing she had. She looked past Asher to his cousin. "And you are?"

"Devin." He looked uncomfortable, as though he didn't relish being in the spotlight as much as Asher apparently did.

"Welcome to homeroom. You'll find empty seats in the back, boys. Make yourselves comfortable there."

As they walked to the back of the room, Asher winked at me. My heart kicked up, and I fought not to smooth my hair like Ms. Manning had. I couldn't help but be impressed by how he'd effectively diffused the situation with Ms. Manning more easily than I'd ever seen anyone do it. I had a feeling the three of us wouldn't be marked as tardy. My perfect attendance record would remain unmarred.

I stole a glance over my shoulder. Asher slumped low in his chair, splaying his legs out in front of him. Devin sat up straight, tucking his legs beneath his desk. Not stiff, exactly. It was more that he was perfectly controlled, like in yoga. I could almost envision him meditating, a low hum playing inside his head.

"Well, now that we've had our excitement for the morning," Ms. Manning began, drawing my attention away from the guys, "let's look in the packet that you should have taken from my desk when you came in."

Everyone just stared blankly at her.

"Really, guys? Come on, vacation's over. Let's get those heads back in the game. Cassandra." Ms. Manning looked sharply at Cassie as a stack of packets passed back to Cassie's desk. Glaring at her, Cassie took one and gave them to me.

She has it in for me, she scribbled in tiny script at the bottom of her packet.

I pretended not to see and looked down at mine. I had Ms. Manning not only for homeroom but for history as well. It was important that I stayed on her good side. Ms. Manning liked me, probably because I actually paid attention in class, and I was banking on her to write me a letter of recommendation for Columbia. I wasn't about to screw it up now.

The packet on my desk was a detailed itinerary for the junior class ski trip, a Northwood High School institution that we'd been talking about since freshman year. It was going to be a nice break from competitive skiing, which I'd been doing all winter.

". . . leaving next Thursday, at eight thirty a.m. sharp. On page three is the packing list, please stick to it. . . ."

As Ms. Manning's voice faded into the background like a cloud of chalk dust, I became acutely aware of Asher and Devin sitting behind me. I casually glanced over my shoulder again at the back row. Asher was studying me with a lazy smile. Almost like he was challenging me to hold his gaze.

Beside him, Devin's calm had dissipated as he glared at his cousin. Together these guys were like this force of energy that constantly seemed to be adding up to trouble. But separately—I stole a glance at Asher again—I was a little intrigued by what they might be like.

Devin was a puzzle, though.

As though reading my thoughts, he shifted his gaze over to me. The warmth in his eyes made me wonder if I wanted to spend some time figuring him out. I whipped back around and discovered a note on my desk. I recognized Cassie's loopy, artistic scrawl.

Goner was all it said.

For the rest of the period, I felt eyes on the back of my neck. The clock above the blackboard ticked slower than normal. Cassie's pen scritch-scratched music notes across her paper. She tapped her foot against the side of her chair in rhythm. I was dying for the bell to ring.

And then suddenly it did.

"Catch you later," Cassie said with a wink toward the boys as she slipped past me. She had Music Theory after homeroom on Mondays, Wednesdays, and Fridays, so she never stuck around to chat on those days. Today, I knew there was a reason why she wanted to leave me alone.

"So I think your reputation for never being late to class is safe." I glanced up from slipping the ski itinerary packet between the covers of my notebook. Asher looked as though he'd accomplished world peace. Behind him, Devin was hovering warily, like he was expecting to have to jump his cousin at any moment. I wasn't used to so much animosity and distrust. It seemed particularly odd that two guys who were related to each other would so openly dislike each other.

"Yeah, so how did you know about that?" I asked.

Devin stiffened, his zen totally gone now. Apparently he wasn't comfortable with the direction the conversation was going. Or maybe he just didn't like that I was talking to his cousin.

Asher just gave me a conspiratorial wink. "Like I said. A reputation is something that everybody knows."

I narrowed my eyes.

So kids at school were talking about my never-tardy record? I was pretty sure that wasn't happening. "Yeah, well, in keeping with my reputation, I need to get to my next class. And, guys, seriously, see someone about your anger issues. Even when you're just sitting next to each other, I can tell that you're battling something out. It's not healthy."

I stuffed my notebook into my backpack and walked away.

I thought I'd have at least a class or two to think about my reaction to the new guys before I could run everything by Cassie at lunch—but just seconds after I walked through the door to Spanish, Devin did, too. He parked himself two seats behind me and the next row over. Which, as everyone knows, is the perfect spot for covert flirting: passing a note down the row, "accidental" pencil-dropping with the casual glance behind you, piling your hair on top of your head and then letting it cascade in seductive tangles down your back. I'd seen Cassie run through the entire arsenal. But I stayed rock-still in my seat, not daring to turn around, hardly even daring to *breathe*. I could tell, just tell, that he was watching me. It bugged me. I wasn't that fascinating.

If this was some weird kind of cousin rivalry—see who could get the girl first at the new school—I wasn't playing the game. Let them fight it out. It seemed to be something they liked to do anyway.

Of course, Asher showed up to third-period history. He said and did nothing, but his mere presence at the back of the classroom prevented me from absorbing any of the important dates of World War I. And in fourth-period chemistry, I got so distracted by *not* paying attention to Devin at the next lab table that I let my glucose solution bubble over the top of my test tube and spill all over the place.

By lunchtime, if you'd asked me to recount the event that started World War I or balance the equation for the solution that I'd spilled in chem, I'd have had no clue what you were talking about. These distractions were going to have to stop.

I spotted Dan at our usual table, a slice of pizza just visible under a Jenga tower of French fries on his plate. I hurried through the lunch line—grabbing along the way a plastic-wrapped turkey sandwich and an apple—and weaved through a maze of tables to get to him. When I dropped into the seat across from him, I felt like I pulled the weight of the world down with me.

"Whoa," he said through a mouthful of fry. "You okay?"

"Just tired," I said. "I guess I still haven't recovered from the weekend."

"Still, best party ever." Dan swallowed and grinned.

"Best party ever," I agreed. "It really *rocked*."

"Well, sometimes it's nice to just *shake things up*." He laughed his slow, raspy laugh, dipping a French fry into a blob of ketchup. "The boiler exploding? Definitely not a part of the surprise, by the way."

Cassie came over with her tray of juice and organic

veggies—Northwood is top-ranked in a national survey of high school cafeteria food—and scootched in next to Dan, scrunching her nose at his French fry tower. She unpacked her lunch tray slowly, fully aware that we were watching her. With dramatic flair, she unscrewed the cap of her Odwalla juice, took a bite of steamed butternut squash, and looked up at us.

"Skye has a crush," she announced.

"What? I do not!" I cried. "What are you even talking about?"

"Please, do you think I'm an amateur? This is what I *do*, Skye. This is what I live for. Besides, I've been your friend for how long? You don't think I'd recognize the signs?"

Dan shot me a wry grin. "Do you need me to ask who it is, or is Cassie about to tell us that anyway?"

"I do not have a crush!"

Ian slid into the chair beside me. "Hey, guys. What's up?"

"Apparently Skye has a crush," Dan informed him.

Ian brightened slightly. "Oh, yeah? Anyone I know?"

"The guys from the Bean," Cassie said. "The ones who were fighting."

"*What?*" I scoffed, trying not to notice how Ian suddenly looked deflated. "You've totally lost your powers of observation."

Cassie took a sip of juice and cleared her throat. "Prepare to be proven wrong. Clue number one: You were late for homeroom. You're never late for homeroom. Clue number two: Your arrival to homeroom happened to coincide with the arrival of two hot new guys—who you apparently rescued. Saving them from the horrific fate of being lost and having to wander these halls for all eternity."

"It was only Asher. Devin found his own way. Besides, Asher wasn't lost. He just asked where the room was."

"And you volunteered to be tour guide? Perhaps allowing for a little chitchat along the way, your little heart fluttering like a butterfly—"

"Cassie, I will shove this French fry in your ear—"

"Clue number three: You're getting flustered and defensive. This is really a textbook case. But let's press on, shall we? Clue number four: You couldn't stop turning around to look behind you, though you tried to make it look like you weren't by rooting around in your backpack—"

"But I—"

"Shh. This brings us to the final and most important clue: You haven't touched your lunch."

I looked down at my tray—it was true. I hadn't even taken the turkey sandwich out of its cellophane wrapping.

Warmth crept up my neck and bloomed across my face in what I could only imagine was a completely incriminating blush.

"Ah!" Cassie cried, pointing her index finger at my face. "Witness the defendant's telling facial color! Skye *never* eats when she's nervous. Sensitive stomach. And why should she be nervous," Cassie said, slamming her hand on the table as if she was auditioning for *Law & Order*, "if she doesn't have a crush?"

Ian studied me as though he didn't know who I was anymore. Dan clapped, in his amused, disinterested way. "Brilliantly deduced, Holmes."

"Thank you, Watson." Cassie beamed. "So which one is it? I have the dirt on both of them, so it doesn't really matter, to be honest."

"I hate to break it to you, Holmes," I said to Cassie, "but you're wrong this time." I unwrapped my sandwich, noisily, and took an insanely large bite. With my mouth full, I said, "They just happen to be in all of my classes. No crush." I swallowed hard. "If you ask me, they're actually a little creepy."

At that moment, Asher walked by, a small group of sophomore girls surrounding him like a swarm of bees. As he passed, he caught my eye and shot me a half grin. I felt the incriminating blush deepen and looked down at my sandwich. My appetite had deserted me, and I wasn't sure I'd be able to force any more food in my mouth in order to fool Cassie.

"Right." Dan rolled his eyes. "Totally creepy."

"Well," Cassie continued, "I'm going to give you all the details anyway. That one over there is Asher. He and his cousin Devin, the blond one, just transferred this term from Whitehall Academy, that private school in Denver that burned down last semester. You know Emily Redwood, in my art class? She's friends with Alison Coles, whose mom is on the admissions board, and apparently they both had perfect scores on their entrance exams. The story is that they were so freaked out by the fire that their family moved them out to River Springs to clear their minds. You can totally tell, too. They have that haunted look." I followed her eyes to where Devin was sitting in the corner, scowling into a book, an untouched slice of pizza on the tray in front of him. She raised an eyebrow at me. "I bet he's locking all the pain away deep inside. So tortured. You should go for the other one."

"How come no cute girls ever transfer here?" Dan mumbled.

Cassie frowned. "Don't be a pig. We're talking about Skye."

"Could have fooled me."

Cassie smacked him on the arm.

"Whichever one you do like," she said, "how about you save me the other one, because the guys at this school are hopeless." She glared at Dan, picked up her tray, and marched off.

Dan shrugged and took a bite of pizza. "So," he said with his mouth full, "what's the real story?"

I sighed. "I have absolutely no idea."

"Yeah," he said, shaking his head as he watched Cassie walk away. "Tell me about it."

he rest of the week passed entirely within my own head. When anyone spoke to me, I had to force myself out of a fog before I could respond—and even then, I'm not sure I was making any sense at all.

I couldn't seem to shake off the feeling that Asher and Devin were trouble, and that their particular brand of trouble was directed specifically at me. I vowed to avoid them as much as possible. It's not like it was easy, though. It seemed that everywhere I went, Devin was lurking behind a locker or Asher was bumping into me in the stairwell. It almost seemed as though they were following me, but what could I do? I couldn't exactly accuse them of it—how conceited would that have sounded? But still, I ran into them too often for me to believe it was just coincidence.

When Friday night finally arrived, I was more than ready for a little distraction. The Bean was reopening. Cassie and Dan were meeting me there.

When I walked through the door, the smell of coffee instantly put me in a better mood. A local singer-songwriter sat at a piano on the stage, singing something soft and sweet. The place was packed. I saw Ian behind the coffee bar and saluted him in what I hoped was a strictly platonic way. He waved back. Things had been a little awkward between us since Cassie had sold me out at lunch, and I felt like I needed to go out of my way to make things okay between us.

I searched the dimly lit room. Every table and seating area was occupied. I finally spotted Cassie and Dan on a sofa, nodding their heads in time to the music. Cassie's vintage leather shoulder bag and gray peacoat were flung across the armchair beside them.

I headed to the bar to grab a latte. Ian was now occupied at the other end, serving two freshman girls, so I waited around and fiddled with the sweetener packets. Suddenly Asher was leaning on the counter next to me, blocking my view of Ian. I jerked back slightly and found myself looking into his eyes.

"See, I figured if I stood between you and your latte, you

couldn't ignore me anymore," he said cheerfully.

"I haven't been ignoring you," I said casually, widening my eyes in an innocent "Who, me?" kind of way. "And who said I'm getting a latte? I could be getting anything. An iced tea, for all you know."

"Skye," Asher said, grinning. "I'm not an idiot." He glanced at my hat and puffer jacket. "An iced tea? At least a latte is in the right seasonal ballpark."

"I never said you were an idiot," I said quietly.

"Yeah? Then do you honestly expect me to believe that every time I tried to talk to you this week, you legitimately had something pressing to do in the opposite direction?"

I couldn't exactly argue with that.

We stood there for a moment, looking at each other, at an impasse. I wasn't sure how it happened—maybe because of the people crowding the counter—but somehow it was like he was almost curled around me. I could feel the heat his body generated being absorbed by mine. I imagined how it might feel to be snuggled up against him on a snowy afternoon. Suddenly I was way too warm, like I'd been at the party Saturday. I could only hope that my eyes weren't turning silver. He didn't strike me as someone who would accept my flimsy explanation as easily as Ian had.

"What happened at your old school?" I finally broke

the silence, needing the distraction as much as anything. "Cassie said it burned down."

Asher's face clouded over. "Something like that."

"How can it be something *like* that? Either it is or it isn't."

"Skye Parker, when are you going to stop looking at the world in black and white?" Suddenly Asher stopped, like he'd just heard himself say something stupid. His eyes seemed to get darker as we stood there. "It's complicated."

"Okay," I said, confused. "Never mind."

He scuffed a foot against the recently replaced floor. "Things can change really quickly. You're not always ready for it."

"What are you talking about?" I said, propping an elbow on the counter. "Are you a Magic Eight Ball now?"

He looked up from his shoes and gave me a sheepish smile.

"Sorry," he said. "That was weird. I was just talking about moving here. It's all just really . . . I don't know, different, I guess. Lots to figure out." He picked up a complimentary mint from a small bowl on the counter, studied it as though it held the answer to all life's dilemmas, then popped it into his mouth.

If I kissed him right now, he'd taste like mint, I thought—and then immediately wished I hadn't. I watched the shape of his lips move, drawing upward into a small grin. When I looked back up, I realized he'd caught me staring. I looked back down at the sweetener packets.

"It'll get easier," I said. "It takes time, but it happens."

"Haven't you lived here your whole life?"

Something he apparently didn't know about me. I found comfort in that.

"Yeah, but change doesn't always involve moving."

"Look," he said. "What are we doing here anyway?"

"Here in the coffee shop or here in the universe?"

"Cute, Skye. Here in the coffee shop. Want to go to a movie? *Storm Enemy* is still showing. I have a thing for bad disaster movies."

"What? Now?" I asked, taken off guard both by his suggestion and the fact that he'd tapped into the one movie I'd been dying to see. I was back to wondering how he knew so much about me. It could have just been coincidence, but I'd watched too many police dramas to believe in coincidence. The girl who believed in coincidence almost always ended up dead.

He smiled, the playfulness returning. "Yes, now."

"I'm . . ." Was he asking me out? On an official date? "Um, I'm actually here to meet my friends," I said, pointing to the sofa in the back. Why did this feel so awkward? It was the truth, but it felt like I was making up an excuse somehow.

He looked past me. "About that. I don't really think she's going to notice if you're not there."

I twisted around. Cassie and Dan were still sitting next to each other on the couch, but their head nodding had evolved into a battle of dance moves.

"Here you go, Skye. One latte."

I spun back around to find that Ian had set a steaming mug in front of me. He was eyeing Asher as though he expected him to steal the silverware—or start another fight. I couldn't blame him.

"She didn't even order," Asher pointed out. "She could have wanted an iced tea."

"I've known her for years. I know what she likes." I could almost hear Ian adding, *"And it's not you."*

"Thanks, Ian." I started digging around in my bag for my money.

"On the house," Ian said at the same time that Asher said, "I've got it," and tossed a ten dollar bill onto the counter.

Ian didn't move. He just stared at Asher, who held his gaze. Confrontation made me uneasy. This was like something from the nature channel: wolves trying to mark their territory. Finally Ian picked up the crumpled bill and begrudgingly made change.

Well, I'd never asked to be marked.

I picked up my latte. "Thanks. I'll see you both around." I glanced at Asher. "Sorry about the movie."

That broke the spell. Asher opened his mouth as if he was going to say more, but then he closed it again. A look passed across his face. Disappointment? Indifference? I couldn't tell. "No worries," he said. "Sure. Another time."

And then before I could say anything else, he turned quickly and wove his way through the crowd, without so much as a backward glance at me.

"I don't trust that guy," Ian said. "You don't seriously like him, do you?"

I have no idea, I thought. I wasn't sure what I felt toward Asher. Confusion mostly.

"No," I said firmly, turning around to face Ian. "He's new. I was the first person he met at school so he sort of imprinted on me. Like a baby duck."

I was trying to get him to smile. It didn't work.

"Look," I continued, "he doesn't really know anyone—"

He shot me a pointed look, and I sighed a little. He was right. There were all those sophomore girls at lunch. "I was being friendly. That's all."

Why did I feel the need to justify myself?

"Just watch out," he warned before heading off to see to a customer.

I turned and came up short. Cassie was watching me from her spot on the couch next to Dan.

As I walked over, she dragged her jacket and bag off the chair next to them and onto the floor.

"Is it hot in here?" she asked, fanning herself.

"Kindly shut up," I replied.

"So is Asher *The One*? Does that mean I get Devin? You know I like them emotionally unavailable." She rubbed her hands together like an evil villain. "It's more of a challenge."

"There's nothing to choose, Cass. You can have them both. Seriously. I'm not interested. Plus, he's weirdly mysterious."

"So he's hot *and* enigmatic," Cassie purred. "So far I'm not seeing the bad in this. I wonder what dark secrets he's hiding behind those gorgeous eyes."

"That he's a serial dater," Dan offered.

Cassie looked at him. "Seriously, Dan? That's the best you can come up with?"

"I just don't understand all the interest in the guy. Girls

latch on to him like he's Velcro."

"Jealous?" she prodded.

Dan scowled. "No."

"I like the music tonight," I said, trying to steer us back to less volatile ground.

"Oh, yeah," Cassie said. "Stella is awesome. She writes all her own songs."

The music stopped, and everyone clapped.

"Thanks," Stella said into the microphone. "I'm going to take fifteen."

"Oh, good," Cassie said, hopping to her feet. "I want to talk with her about her music. Get some tips. Come on, Dan. Pretend I'm Velcro."

Laughing, he got up and took her hand as they weaved through the crowd.

"Watch our stuff, will you?" Cassie asked. "And save our seats. We won't be long."

"Sure," I said, knowing she'd be gone the full fifteen. Once she started talking music with another musician, she lost all track of time.

I leaned my head back, closed my eyes, and sipped my latte, trying to expel the stress of the week with each quiet breath. Devin had looked so calm in class the other day, his posture straight, his face so tranquil. I shifted now to reach the same pose, straightening my back and relaxing the muscles in my face. For a minute or two, it seemed to be working. I let my shoulders drop. Maybe I needed to look into yoga. Then the old leather of the couch creaked, and I felt a knee brush against mine as someone sat down next to me. "Sorry," I said, opening my eyes. "That seat's—"

I froze at the sight of Devin sitting there. What was I all of a sudden, the Welcome Wagon?

"How's your couples counseling going?" I asked casually.

"My what?" He looked confused.

"Your fight with Asher?"

His face clouded over. "Oh," he said. "That."

"I take it not that well?"

"It's more complicated than that," he said, looking away. I took that as a signal that our conversation was over, so I closed my eyes again. I felt mildly snubbed. Cassie could chase him away in order to reclaim her seat. Or flirt with him. Whatever she wanted to do.

"I'm sorry," he said beside me.

"What?" I opened my eyes, surprised.

"You shouldn't worry about Asher and me." He appeared almost apologetic, and something inside me softened a little. "It's been like this all our lives. Listen," he said, shifting a little on the couch to face me. "I feel like we haven't gotten off to the best start. I usually like to kick things off with a fight to break the ice, but I guess this time it didn't work, huh?"

I stared at him blankly.

"Sorry," he said with a small smile, "I'm not very good at small talk. I don't often find myself starting over in a new place, getting to know strangers." Asher had alluded to the same thing, but I somehow got the feeling it wasn't as hard for him. I wondered at Devin's lack of the same kind of brazen confidence. He was so classically attractive, with the hair, skin, and features of a fairy-tale prince. Everything about him was just so . . . *perfect*. How could he not see that in himself?

"You're doing okay," I said, a smile coming easily and naturally. "Maybe you just need to give people a chance to get to know you."

He lifted his gaze to me. His eyes were really incredible. Soft and hard at the same time, water and ice, and the bluest blue I'd ever seen. They almost didn't look real.

"I saw Asher talking to you over at the coffee bar," he said, and I could see the tempest forming in his eyes. There was a slight lilt to his cadence, almost as if he'd worked hard to banish an accent. I couldn't place where it might have come from. "He's trying to win you over."

Even when Asher wasn't here, the argument was still triangulated. It was like they were programmed to interfere in each other's lives.

"Is that what he was doing?" I asked, not bothering to hide my annoyance.

"It's what he always does. Whatever he wants. He doesn't care at all——" He stopped abruptly and glanced at me. Hesitation flickered across his face.

"About the rules?" I finished for him.

I almost laughed at the shock that passed over his features, as though I'd reached out and slapped him. I sipped calmly on my latte and studied him over the rim of the mug. "I overheard you guys on Saturday," I said. "Before you knocked me over."

He furrowed his brow. "What . . . what exactly did you hear?"

I shrugged noncommittally. "Something about your rules. I got the impression he wasn't too impressed with them. So what are they exactly?"

Devin looked away. "It's a code that I . . . Look, it's nothing." He sighed. "We don't have to get into it here."

I laughed. "Well, based upon what I saw—you know, trying to destroy each other in a crowded coffee shop where anyone could have gotten hurt—I'd say your code isn't working too well."

"Asher doesn't understand. Rules exist for a reason. He doesn't grasp"—he glanced at me—"why they're important." With that, he seemed to run out of steam. "It's our problem to resolve. I shouldn't have bothered you with it."

"No, really, it's okay," I said. "It's interesting. And hey, I think you mastered the art of small talk."

A corner of his mouth curled up, and the tranquility returned to his eyes. "Maybe. Not really. I just knew you'd understand. You seem very precise."

Precise. I did sometimes have control-freak tendencies, but it was an odd thing to say—and an odder way to phrase it.

Devin may have been beautiful, but it was no use denying there was something strange about him.

"Ahem." Cassie cleared her throat. She and Dan were standing above us, grinning, clearly waiting for an introduction.

"Devin, these are my friends Cassie and Dan."

"Hey, man," Dan said, doing that chin-nod thing guys always do.

"Hey, man," Devin repeated, but the way he said it sounded unnatural, slightly foreign—more formal in its casualness than if he'd simply said hello. He stood up. "I should go."

"Oh, no," Cassie said quickly. "Don't let us kick you out."

"Thank you, but I really do have to go. It was a pleasure to meet you." He looked down at me, the half smile once again playing on his lips. "It was nice talking to you, Skye. Thank you for the small-talk lesson."

"You're doing great," I said, again feeling how easy it was to smile at him. With Asher, I'd begun to feel like conversation was a game, a skill, and I couldn't show my hand. I had to hide my smile, make him work for it. With Devin, things just seemed so easy. "See you at school."

He strode away, and Cassie plopped down on the cushion he'd occupied. "Definitely a tormented soul there."

"How do you figure that?" Dan asked.

"You only have to look into his eyes to know."

Dan snorted. "I didn't see anything." He stretched. "I'm going to see if the pool tables are open."

When Dan was out of earshot, Cassie shifted around to face me squarely. "So both mysterious cousins hitting on you in the same night? Please divulge all, immediately. Spare no boring detail."

"I don't know if I would characterize that encounter with Devin as *hitting* on me."

She gave me a sly grin. "But the encounter with Asher . . . ?"

"I'm not sure if he knows how to talk to a female *without* hitting on her. I mean, even Ms. Manning went all gaga for him that first day."

"True. But it must be nice to have two guys interested in you."

"I wouldn't go that far. We just talked."

"Here you go," Ian said, suddenly standing next to us.

I looked up, startled, as he removed my empty mug and replaced it with another filled to the brim.

"*This* one's on me," he said. Before I could even thank him, he was heading back to the counter.

"Hmm," Cassie murmured. "Make that three guys."

At the moment, I felt like it was three too many.

*C*assie has always been prone to hyperbole, but the weather reports supported her theory that it was the coldest month on record in River Springs.

Even at home, our house felt too big and drafty, the cold seeping in through the cracks at the base of the big plate glass windows overlooking our backyard—the mountains looming up dark and aloof in the distance. The house was built into the side of a hill, so the side that faced out was made up of lots of windows. When you looked out, it felt like you were suspended in the sky, with no ground beneath your feet and the mountains stretching out before you. I used to love that feeling of weightlessness. Now, after the floating dream, I found it unsettling. It didn't help that I was periodically experiencing waves of nausea mixed with images of Asher's dark eyes and Devin's blue ones.

Aunt Jo was home from the backcountry and tried to keep things cozy by baking. I, being kitchen-averse, just stalked around in a hat and scarf and kept turning up the thermostat.

"Cut it out, Skye; it's not that cold." She laughed as she scooted a tray of cinnamon spice cookies into the oven.

"But I'm fa-fa-fa-reezing." I shivered dramatically, huddling up on one of the stools that surrounded the cherrywood and marble kitchen island.

"I think the thermostat can stay at seventy. Put on another sweater."

"I'm already wearing, like, five."

Aunt Jo exaggerated an eye roll. "You'll live. Here. Taste."

I took the wooden spoon from her and bit off a chunk of raw cookie dough. It was delicious, spicy. I missed Aunt Jo's cooking when she was gone. She'd been too tired last night after getting in, but today the kitchen was filled with the aroma of vanilla and cinnamon.

"It would be better fresh out of the oven," I pointed out hopefully.

"Well, then you're just going to have to wait another fifteen minutes." She turned around and patted down her apron. "Do me a favor and get my *Barefoot Contessa* off the credenza in the hall, okay? Maybe I'll make apple turnovers for dessert tomorrow."

"'Kay," I said, hopping off the stool and padding down the hall in my wool socks. I slowed as I passed the thermostat on the wall. I didn't care what Aunt Jo said—even though it said seventy degrees, it seriously felt like negative fifty.

I shivered and reached to adjust the thermostat to eighty. But as my hand neared the digital display, my heart began to race. I couldn't believe what I was seeing.

Without my touching the controls, the numbers began rolling upward at a scary-fast rate. When the display reached a hundred and one degrees, the small white box sizzled and shorted out. The screen went black.

"Shit!" I whispered. What had I just done? I hadn't even touched it. I stared at my fingers. I was too afraid to look in the mirror, afraid I'd see that my eyes had morphed again into that weird, mercurial silver.

Had I just caused the thermostat to short-circuit . . . without even touching it? No, it was ridiculous even to think it.

"Skye?" Aunt Jo called. "Everything okay?"

I grabbed the cookbook off the credenza and trotted back into the kitchen.

"Yep!" I said, dropping the book onto the counter and looking away. "I think the thermostat's broken. We should get that thing looked at."

"Keeping the house at subtropical temperatures doesn't mean it's broken," she said with a snort. "Can you toss me the egg timer?"

"Sure." I extracted the neon green egg timer from the drawer in the island and tossed it to her. "Hey, I think it might actually be warmer outside. I'm going to take a walk. Mind if I disappear till the cookies are done?"

"Are you really that cold? Hope you're not coming down with the flu." She came toward me with her hand outstretched as if to feel my forehead.

I ducked away, grabbing my heavy coat, mittens, and knit cap. "I'm fine. I won't be out too long anyway."

Once I was outside, I stuffed my hands in my pockets and started trudging through the snow. My fingers still stung. I couldn't explain what had happened with the thermostat. Maybe I'd simply built up a charge of static electricity and when I'd gotten near enough—*Pop! Bang!*

I should have had the courage to look in the mirror, but

even if my eyes were silver, what did it mean? Everything was getting so weird lately. My eyes. The sensation of floating when I woke up. The boiler explosion. The thermostat short-circuiting. Two—no, three—guys showing an interest in me. In my whole life, I'd only ever had one boyfriend. And that had been a disaster.

I wended my way through the trees until I reached my favorite thinking spot. I felt like I was standing at the edge of the world. Below me was a vast expanse of white dotted with evergreens.

I inhaled deeply, filling my lungs with the sharp scent of pine. I was obviously searching for connections where none existed. The boiler had been defective. The thermostat, old. Devin and Asher were doing that whole cousin-rivalry thing. I doubted that I meant anything to either of them—I was just another thing to fight over. Ian and I had always hung out together so I should expect him to feel protective of me. My eyes—I couldn't explain them away so easily. It was more than the way light hit them. They were a molten silver color that scared me.

I was sure now that I'd even blown the floating incident out of proportion. It was common for people to dream about flying. It symbolized breaking free from something that was holding you back. I was seventeen now. I was getting ready to apply to colleges. To leave Aunt Jo and River Springs. I was ready to be out on my own. That was all.

I spread my arms out. Felt the wind rushing past from the gorge below. This was a great place for flying kites in the summer because of the updraft. I tilted my head toward the sky, closed my eyes, and did what I'd done since I was six: I imagined myself soaring to wherever my parents were, being reunited with them once again.

Suddenly my foot hit an icy patch on the ledge, and my legs flew out from under me. My eyes flew open. I screamed, felt myself drop . . . and stop.

Standing on solid ground again, my heart thundering, I stared into familiar blue eyes.

Devin's arms were wrapped tightly around me. I couldn't feel his warmth through our coats, but for a minute, I imagined I could. It was an icy heat, like the combination I felt whenever I ate a mint. Sharp but sweet. Cool and hot at the same time.

"You shouldn't stand so close to the edge when it's so icy."

His voice was incredibly calm. He could have been commenting on my selection of a coat, not saving my life. Where had he come from? How had he gotten here? And what were the odds that he'd be right where I needed him to be *when* I needed him to be there?

"What are you doing here?" I asked. I was breathless, not certain any longer if it was my nearly plummeting to my death or his nearness that was making it so hard to draw in air.

"Protecting you. What does it look like I'm doing?"

"No, I mean why are you *here*? You just happen to be at the same place I am? The girl who believes in coincidence always ends up dead, Devin."

"What?" His voice faltered. "I was exploring the trails. It was . . . fate."

"So you're saying it was your destiny to find me here?"

"Is that so hard to believe?" He released his hold on me and stepped back. "I've explored a lot of the trails in this area since moving here, but this one is my favorite. It's so calm here. So different from the halls at school." Devin looked up at the gray sky, thick with clouds.

Maybe we were more similar than I'd imagined. "I know what you mean."

He smiled, and his eyes seemed to change color. From crystal clear shallows to the depths of the ocean.

We looked at each other, neither of us speaking. I was struck again by how easy it was to be with Devin. With

Asher, our connection was quick, immediate—a fire flashing through my veins. When I was with Devin, the burn was a slow one. I almost didn't realize it was happening until I felt the heat reach my cheeks.

"How do you do that?" I asked, swallowing hard.

"Do what?"

"Give the impression that you're in some sort of zenlike place. My heart is still racing, but you look like nothing happened."

"Nothing did happen. You're fine, right?"

Nothing catastrophic, but something was definitely happening.

I walked over to a boulder closer to the trail, brushed off the snow with my mittens, and sat down. Devin stood there hesitantly.

"Sorry," I said. "I'm still a little shaky. Do you mind if we sit for a minute?"

"No." He wandered over and settled down beside me. The view was breathtaking. As silence eased in between us, I thought of what Cassie had said about Devin being tormented.

"Did you lose someone you cared about in that school fire?"

He seemed to hesitate, then shook his head. "No."

"You don't seem as comfortable here as Asher."

"This place . . . it isn't *home*," he said quietly.

"What was home like?"

He waved his hand out to encompass everything. "Like this. Not the snow and the cold. But the quiet. The beauty. The tranquility."

"In Denver?"

"When you're home, everything is easier. It's all laid out for you." A corner of his mouth inched upward. "No anger management was necessary."

I laughed. "So you talked to the counselor?"

"No. It's pointless. Asher is going to break rules . . . no matter what. Again and again. That's who he is. And as long as he does . . . it just makes things harder for me."

"He's a real rebel," I said, smiling.

The peacefulness in Devin's features momentarily slipped away, and I wished I'd never brought up Asher. Finally he said, "Yeah, a real rebel."

He grew silent again. I could see the tranquility easing back into him. I wondered if he was chanting in his head, *I will not let Asher upset me. I will not let Asher upset me.*

Of course it was also possible that he was chanting, *Asher, die!* But I didn't think so. Even though they'd gotten into the fight, he hadn't delivered the first blow. He just didn't strike me as the type who would hurt some-one or wish him ill. He was more of a dove. Asher was the hawk.

The wind whistled through the gorge. As we sat there, the clouds were growing heavier, darker, and more twisted.

"I think we're going to get more snow," I said, glad that there would be a fresh layer for the ski trip in a few days.

"Why do *you* come here?" Devin asked suddenly.

I brought my feet up to the boulder and wrapped my arms around my legs. "It makes me feel closer to my par-ents. They died when I was six." I paused. It was so easy to talk to him that I felt like I could just keep going, spill-ing all kinds of secrets without thinking twice. "Do you promise you won't laugh if I tell you something?"

"Of course," he said. His lips were serious, but his eyes were encouraging.

"Sometimes I have this insane thought that if I con-centrated hard enough I could fly to wherever they are." I hesitated, wondering if I should have said anything. "Which I know is ridiculous, because all I'd do is fall flat on the ground below, but still. Here I just feel a sense of . . . lightness."

He was staring at me.

I laughed self-consciously. "But it's one of the reasons I like to ski. Just that rush of motion, it's almost like flying. Or what I think flying would feel like."

Devin looked like he was choosing his words carefully. "No, it makes sense. A lot of sense. Do you ever dream about it? That you're flying, I mean?"

I smiled. "Yeah, actually. The other morning, I woke up thinking that I actually *was*. Like I was floating." I laughed. "It was really unnerving."

Why was I telling him this? He might not be as funny or confident as Asher, but he was a good listener. And accepting.

"Flying," Devin said, kicking a pebble across the frosted trail with his foot. "It's sort of a strange sensation if you think about it. Nothing above you. Nothing below you."

A gust of wind rushed up, hitting us suddenly, hard.

"It's definitely going to snow." I hopped off the boulder. "I'm cold, and I have warm cookies waiting for me. I should get home."

"I need to head back, too."

He slid off the boulder and fell into step beside me as we began to make our way back down the trail. I was careful to look out for icy patches this time, and I noticed Devin watching my steps closely. Several times when the slope got too steep and I'd start to lose my footing, he'd grab my arm and steady me. Protecting me again.

When my house came into view, an awkward silence hung between us. I felt so much closer to him now than I had before today, but that didn't mean I was ready to invite him in for cookies.

"I have to go." His gaze met mine. "Be careful around Asher. I know he's charming, but he's also very dangerous."

"Because he doesn't like to follow the rules," I said lightly.

"Because he can get you killed."

I opened the front door to the smell of cinnamon cookies wafting from the kitchen.

"Skye!" Aunt Jo called. "Where have you been? They're getting cold!"

"Sorry!" I hung up my jacket and hat in the hall and ambled in. Aunt Jo was sitting at the table doing a crossword.

"Did the walk warm you up?" she asked.

I thought about Devin's final words and shivered.

"Not remotely."

She laughed.

"It'll teach you a lesson about being thankful for the heat we *do* have, won't it?"

"That's for sure," I said. "Cookies?"

"On the counter."

"Milk?"

"In the fridge. Skye, seriously, did you just move here? Where's your head right now?" *Good question. Somewhere in the clouds by the trail where I left it, probably.*

I bit into a cookie and chewed it quietly.

"Aunt Jo, have you ever been in love?" I asked.

"Of course. I love you."

I scowled. "You know what I mean. In love with a guy." She dated from time to time, but there had never been anyone serious.

Chewing slowly, she stared at the ceiling. I wondered if she'd stored the answer up there so it would be readily available when she needed it.

"I've been crazy about some guys," she finally said, "but the timing of our lives wasn't right for anything permanent." She gave me a speculative glance. "Why? Are you feeling something for someone?"

"Mostly confusion."

"That's usually how it starts."

I laughed, licked the crumbs off my fingers, and reached

for another cookie. "We have a couple of new guys at school."

"New is good."

"I don't know. Our paths cross at the oddest times, in the strangest places." I didn't tell her about running into Devin during my walk. It just felt like a secret I wanted to hold close for the moment. "They're a little strange. Like they're competing with each other to get my attention—not because they're necessarily interested in *me* but because they don't want me to be interested in the other guy." I shook my head. "And now that I've said that out loud, it makes no sense."

"I have no doubt that if they are showing interest, it's because they find you as amazing as I do."

"You're biased." I sipped my milk.

"Just because I'm biased doesn't mean it's not true."

By the time we'd finished eating our cookies and I'd gone up to my room to tackle some homework, I'd convinced myself that Devin was just being overdramatic with his warning about Asher. For whatever reason, he and his cousin weren't close and they didn't like each other. Some families were like that, I guessed. I didn't really know. All I'd ever had were my parents—no grandparents, uncles, aunts, cousins, or siblings—and Aunt Jo.

Sighing, I dropped onto my bed, flipped onto my stomach, and pulled out my American History notebook, figuring I could distract myself by actually learning a thing or two. But dark thoughts tiptoed through my brain for the rest of the night. I'd always been so good, not wanting to disappoint my parents—even though they were no longer here to know—not wanting to be a burden to Aunt Jo. I followed the rules. Got to class before the late-bell rang. Always turned in my homework on time. Asher was a little bit wild. Alluring, maybe, in a bad boy sort of way. What would it feel like to be with someone like that? To not follow the rules?

Devin, on the other hand, was a rule follower. Rules created order. It was the reason every civilized society lived by them. A set of codes, moral and ethical. But what really appealed to me about Devin was the tranquility I could see on his face. He possessed that calmness that I had yet to achieve. Rules created order—*and order created calm.* I always strove for calm.

Hours of fruitless studying passed. I made sure the window was closed and locked before I got into bed. I lay wide awake, counting the fake stars on my ceiling till I couldn't remember what number came next.

In my dreams, Devin was forgotten. Asher's face was close to mine, his lips almost touching me as he whispered in my ear.

The moment I saw Asher in homeroom on Monday, my face flushed embarrassingly and goose bumps trailed all the way down my arms. I looked away quickly. After my dream, I just couldn't face him. I didn't remember what he had whispered to me—only the feeling that had lingered afterward. Only the memory of his lips as they barely grazed my skin.

In American History, he tossed his backpack down and sat in the empty chair next to me.

"That's Ellie's seat," I said, perhaps a little too sharply. Ellie and I were two of only three juniors on the ski team, and she'd kill me if I gave up her seat. "She always sits there."

He crossed his arms and leaned way back in his chair,

looking at me. "From what I understand, you need someone to keep you on task. There are a lot of dates to memorize in American History. And it doesn't look like you're doing too hot as far as World War One is concerned."

I grimaced. He was right, of course. Since he'd arrived, I was having a difficult time concentrating in all of my classes, but for some reason, history, with its rote memorization, had been the hardest. Having him sit next to me was like sabotage.

"Hey, Skye," Ellie said, appearing behind us. "Ready for practice today? I heard . . ." She trailed off as she noticed Asher. Her hand immediately went to her blond corkscrew curls, and she began twirling one around her index finger.

"Sorry," I said. "He was just leaving."

Ellie's eyes grew wide.

"No!" she said quickly. "Really, don't worry about it." She smiled at Asher. "You take it. I forgot my glasses today anyway, so I should sit closer to the blackboard." The flirtation in her voice was a little sickening. "Enjoy my seat. Keep it warm for me."

She sashayed up the rows of desks to a seat closer to the front, eyeing us the whole time.

I turned to Asher, dumbfounded. He laughed.

"Hey, don't look at me," he said, hands up in surrender.

"I can't help it if I have that effect on people."

"On girls, you mean," I shot back.

"If you say so," he said with a grin.

"I'd rather not."

He leaned in, bringing his earthy scent with him. There was something primal and familiar about it, but with him leaning so close to me, I couldn't concentrate hard enough to place it. "I know you've been spending some time with my cousin. Really not a good idea. You might want to avoid him in the future."

"Funny. He said the same thing about you."

His eyes widened slightly at that. "Yeah, I'll bet he did."

"What is it with you two anyway?"

He settled back in his chair. "We just have different philosophies on life."

"I'm not sure that statement would hold up in court. You do know that most people who break the rules eventually end up in prison, right?"

"Right," Asher said, grinning again as if we had some kind of secret between us. "Or they discover lifesaving medical procedures, or invent machines that make our life easier, or win Nobel Prizes for advances in world peace and get written up in history books. Rule-breakers color outside the lines. They change the world."

I stared at him, trying to formulate a cutting retort—and failing.

He smiled smugly and leaned back in his chair.

We sat in silence for the rest of the period. Every time I glanced over at him, the look on his face made it clear that he thought he'd won the argument.

As I got into line in the cafeteria during lunch that Wednesday, Devin fell into place behind me.

"Hi," he said. "How were the cookies?"

"Delicious. You should have come in for some." I immediately wanted to slap my hand over my mouth. Why had I said that? Was I flirting with him?

"Maybe next time. Is your aunt back from her trip?"

"Yeah," I said. "She got back a few days ago. She's actually not my aunt, she's my legal guardian. I just call her that."

"Oh," he replied. "Right."

"She was my mom's best friend. She adopted me when they died."

"I'm sorry about your parents. That had to be hard." His eyes met mine, and I saw sympathy and understanding there. Had he lost someone, too? If not in the fire then in some other way?

"Yeah," I said. "It was. Is, I mean." I wished we were back on the quiet trail in the woods. Maybe I could have talked more easily there, but in the bustling cafeteria, it was nearly impossible to get the words out. We were at the front of the line, and I turned from Devin to Greta, the lunch lady. "Turkey sandwich and an apple, please."

"Enjoy your lunch," he said.

I almost invited him to join me but stopped myself. "Thanks," I said. "You, too."

I spotted Cassie and Dan at our usual table, smiling and watching as I wove through the rows toward them. I smiled back, but an uneasy feeling was creeping up on me.

I had never mentioned anything to Devin about Aunt Jo—especially not that she'd been away.

"Now usually I'm not one to say I told you so. . . ." Cassie cooed as I sat down. "But that is what I told you. So."

"Laugh it up," I said.

"And the timing couldn't be more perfect!" Cassie clasped her hands together.

We were leaving for our ski trip the next day, and as Cassie made sure to remind me, it was known for being hookup central. Apparently it was some rare combination of coming in from the cold, the endorphins produced by steaming mugs of hot chocolate, and the effect that cute ski outfits had on teenage guys. Cassie had it down to an exact science.

But I wasn't so sure hooking up was what Devin and Asher wanted.

"Although you may have some competition," she said. I followed her gaze across the cafeteria, where Asher was sitting at the end of one of the long tables—surrounded by girls. "Looks like he's having no trouble fitting in." I saw Maggie and Ellie on either side of him; Ellie was twirling her hair and batting her eyelashes at Asher, and Asher was eating it up, leaning in to whisper in her ear, making her throw her head back in a fit of laughter.

I wasn't sure if I was disgusted—or disappointed.

Devin sat at the far end of the same table. A few of the girls tried talking to him, but he avoided eye contact and appeared vaguely uncomfortable the whole time. I smiled a little to myself and felt mildly better.

Asher looked up, caught my eye, and winked. As though, even while he was sitting in the middle of that huge group of girls, I was the only one that mattered.

I looked away, my blood boiling. It's not that I was jealous—because I wasn't, not at all—but it drove me crazy that he thought he could wink at me and I'd suddenly swoon like all the other girls at school. How could he put me in the same category as them? No way would I fall to pieces over someone so easily. I shot him a dark glare, and he just smiled, resting both arms on the table, his eyes challenging.

"Not interested," I said, turning back to my friends.

Dan frowned. "Now what does that guy have that I don't?"

"You can ask him yourself," Cassie said, perking up. "He's on his way."

"Hey." Asher smiled at us. "Can I sit here?"

"What? No!" I cried, just as Cassie squealed, "Sure!"

Asher sat down next to me and threw an infuriatingly cocky grin my way. I shot Cassie a death glare.

"What's going on, guys?" he asked, nipping a French fry from Dan's plate and popping it into his mouth. Dan looked pissed. Cassie looked delighted. I wasn't sure how I looked. "Not much," Cassie trilled. "How are you adjusting to Northwood?"

"It's not bad." Asher jerked his chin at the table of sophomores he'd left behind, all of whom were now watching us like hawks. "I actually stopped by to see what Skye was doing after school today."

"Why?" I asked suspiciously.

"Because I wanted to see if you were free to hang out tonight."

Cassie whipped around to face me, her eyes just daring me to say no. Her vicarious interest in my love life suddenly made me anxious.

I swallowed. They were all staring at me. The side of my arm was brushing up against Asher's, and my mind raced at the possibility of more than just our arms touching.

"I can't tonight," I lied. "Tomorrow's the ski trip, and I take my skiing very seriously."

"Oh, so do I," he said in mock seriousness. "How right you are." He stood up and stretched, and when his sweater rode up, I caught a peek of his flat lower abdomen, tan, even though it was winter. I looked away. Ellie sauntered by, and Asher winked at us. "Gotta go," he said, and he was off.

"Ugh." I turned back to Cassie. "Gross. Can't he stay focused for like two minutes?"

"Skye!" she cried, and threw a fry at me. "What is wrong with you? He is clearly *so* into you!"

"No, he isn't!" I could hear my voice creeping up the octaves. "He just thinks I'm like the other girls who fawn all over him the minute he winks at them."

"Do girls like winking?" Dan asked no one in particular.

"Fine," Cassie continued. "But it's obvious you want

him bad, so don't get all moody and upset when he starts dating someone else."

"I won't get moody and upset," I insisted, but Cassie was too busy snorting to come up with a witty reply.

I glanced over to where Devin was sitting. He was watching us, the corners of his mouth tilted up in a strange smile. It wasn't a sweet smile, or a shy one like that day on the trail. It was almost smug.

The sky was still black and the house was silent when I woke up the next morning. I had packed for the trip the night before, sticking carefully to the list that Ms. Manning had sent home with us on the first day of the semester.

I spent a few minutes rechecking the list to make sure I hadn't missed anything. Wool socks, check. Long underwear, gross, but check. Parka, ski pants, goggles, check, check, check. The list had recommended Gore-Tex gloves, but when I had dug mine out of my ski team gym bag, I realized that I'd ripped one during an intense moment in my last race and a long gash now ran down the thumb, rendering them totally useless. I'd thrown them into my overnight bag, along with an extra pair of fleece gloves, just in case. The fleece wouldn't keep my hands dry, but since this was my weekend *off* from racing, I'd just do an easy run or two and then hang out in the lodge by the fire with my friends.

I put on a pot of coffee. While I waited for it to brew, I stared out the picture windows into the backyard as the rich, earthy smell bloomed into the kitchen. The sky faded from velvety black to inky navy to the color of my favorite jeans and, finally, what those jeans would look like if I rubbed them down with sandpaper, stretching out frayed and raw above the mountains.

When the coffee was ready, Aunt Jo joined me for breakfast. I poured a bowl of cereal and topped it with sliced bananas.

"For once, our schedules are in sync," she said. "You have this ski weekend, and I'll be taking a group trekking through the Presidential Peaks."

"Still no luck finding a temporary replacement for Jenn?" I asked between bites.

"None at all. I'm not even sure it's worth the trouble of looking now. She'll be back on her feet in a few more weeks, and life will return to normal." I didn't want to admit how happy that made me.

When the sky was light and I was fully caffeinated, I

gave her a huge hug good-bye, loaded my bag into my car, flicked on the radio, and drove to school. As I pulled my car into the lot, Cassie, Dan, and Ian were huddled together by the front steps. Cassie waved.

"Hey!" she said gleefully as I flung my duffel onto the pile of students' bags waiting to be loaded into the bus. Cassie's excitement was so obvious that she was literally vibrating when I hugged her. She was wearing an outfit I could describe only as Ski-Bunny-Chic-meets-Elmer-Fudd: a huge fake-fur hunting hat with earflaps, black thermal leggings, and huge snow boots. Dan wore his Chilean knit hat from the hippie store in town, and Ian had on a beanie with some kind of skater logo on it, like a Martian or devil clown or something.

"Exactly how much coffee have you had this morning?" I asked, eyeing Cassie suspiciously.

"Oh, shut up, you know I don't touch that crap," she said.

"But you did have two Mountain Dews on the way over here," Dan said, grinning.

Cassie pulled the knit strings dangling from his earflaps.

Ian smiled at me, which was a relief. I hadn't really talked to him alone since he and Asher had been trying to mark their territory at the coffee shop Friday night.

I smiled back. "Ready for a weekend of fun in the snow?"

"You bet. I've been looking forward to this for years."

I eased a little closer to him. I felt like I owed him an apology or something. "We missed you at lunch this week."

"Yeah, I had a project in Woodshop I needed to get done."

"Oh," I said. "I thought maybe you were mad at me or something."

"No," he said, his face softening into a smile. "Come on, Skye. Never."

"Okay. Just wanted to make sure we're good. You've been my friend forever."

"Yeah," he said softly. "Your friend."

Dan punched Ian's shoulder to get his attention, and they started talking.

I did a quick scan of the parking lot, waving at a few girls who were standing near us. I couldn't help bristling a little at the sight of Ellie, remembering how Asher had jetted off after her the day before. Then I chastised myself for the pettiness. I'd turned him down, after all. Had I expected him to mope around with a broken heart?

Just about our entire class was there, standing in small groups like ours, waiting for the driver to put us out of our misery and open the doors of the bus.

I actually couldn't find Asher—or Devin for that

matter—among the sea of hats and scarves, and for a brief moment, I felt my stomach sink in disappointment.

The bus doors finally opened. "Come on," Cassie urged. "Let's grab some seats together before everyone else gets on."

It was the same temperature on the bus as it was outside. Cassie and I slid into a seat toward the back, near Cassie's bandmates Trey and Evan—cute boys with scruffy hair and plaid shirts. She immediately turned in her seat to talk to them about a new song she'd been working on. "I have it on my iPod," I heard her say. "I recorded it on my computer the other day."

Dan and Ian were two rows in front of us.

"Turn the heat on!" Josh Brooks called from the back row.

"It's not magic, it takes time!" The bus driver shouted back. I could hear the clink of the yellow school bus's old heating system lurch into gear. I was shivering, trying to generate my own body heat.

"Crap," Cassie muttered, swinging back around and rummaging through her backpack. "I left it in my overnight bag. Hold on, I'm going to see if they've loaded our bags on yet." She popped up and I watched her red waves bouncing down the aisle as she hurried off the bus.

Absently I waved my hand across the heater duct along the base of the wall, near my boots. Nothing. Great. It was going to be a long, cold ride.

The heater clanked again, and all of a sudden, a blast of hot steam shot out at my hand. "Ow!" I cried out, pulling it away.

"Are you all right?"

I jumped, startled to find Devin standing in the aisle by my seat.

"Y-yeah," I faltered. "It was just the heat. It came on really quickly." I held up my hand to show that it had burned me, but there was no mark, no redness anywhere on it. Devin just stared at it. Then he shook his head slightly. His eyes found mine.

"Is someone sitting . . . ?" He gestured toward the empty space next to me. "I got here late." He looked around. Barely any empty seats were left.

"Yeah," I said. "I mean—"

"She means yes, there is," Asher said, sliding into the seat from out of nowhere. He didn't look at me; he just kept staring at Devin. Like he was sitting there more to piss him off than to be near me.

Devin's face clouded over.

"Ooh, it's warm, too." Asher rubbed his gloved hands

together. "Feel how warm it is, Dev? Too bad you'll have to find another seat."

Devin frowned. "Fluke," I barely heard him utter, and Asher shot him a triumphant look.

"It's just a seat," I said, growing tired of their game.

"Oh, it's more than that," Asher said, his voice low but gleeful.

"Hey, boys," Cassie trilled as she made her way back down the aisle, her cheeks pink and her eyes shining playfully as they caught mine. "You're in my seat, Asher. Scram." Asher glanced from me to Devin, whose expression was now turning smug. He got up slowly, nodding his head politely and allowing Cassie to pass.

"See you on the mountain," he promised me before walking away. Like we'd agreed to meet up there and he had something special planned.

Devin gave me a pointed look, as though trying to remind me about his warning. I smiled back at him reassuringly, hoping he'd interpret it correctly: I would be okay.

"Found it!" Cassie held up her iPod as she slid in next to me. "Ooh, it's toasty here; it's freezing everywhere else on the bus."

"You mean the heat's still not on?" I asked, a chill creeping up my spine.

"Nope," she said brightly. "How did you get our vent to work so quickly?"

I thought of short-circuiting the thermostat in our house and how quickly the hot air had blasted out of the bus's air duct when I'd run my hand across it. How *had* I gotten it to work?

All I could do in response was shrug.

"So that was interesting." She jutted her chin to where Devin and Asher had just been standing.

"It's weird." I groaned, falling so that my forehead rested against the cushioned seat back in front of us. "I don't understand either of them. One minute I think Devin really likes me, is going out of his way to talk with me, but then it's like he changes his mind or something because he'll keep his distance. And Asher gets this kick out of pushing my buttons, but then he flirts with every girl in school. It's not like they're really interested in me. It's more like what they're really trying to do is force me to choose between them or something."

Cassie's mischievous grin widened. "Let me put this in simple terms. They want what every guy in this school has always wanted. You're usually just too wrapped up in other things to notice. I've never seen you respond to any of them this way." She paused thoughtfully. "Actually this is the first time I've seen you respond at all. Since Jordan, I mean." She looked away guiltily at the mention of my first and only boyfriend.

"I don't think that's it, though," I said quietly, making sure they couldn't hear us. "I don't know *what* they want."

"Okay," Cassie said, patting my knee with her mittened hand. "But what do *you* want?"

I leaned back in my seat and stared out the window at the icy parking lot as the bus engine groaned to life.

What did *I* want?

That was a much harder question to answer.

I slept for most of the trip, leaning on Cassie's shoulder as she scribbled away in her notebook. At some point, the heat was working for the entire bus, and when I woke up, it was starting to verge on uncomfortably warm.

By the time we got to the resort, checked in, and got our room assignments, dinner was being served. The sun was already beginning to fade into dusk, and a sharp wind was picking up. The dining room had wide windows that looked out over the mountain, where tiny lights were just beginning to blink on, illuminating the trails. Nothing was more beautiful than the sun setting over the peaks and painting the slopes in shadows. I ate quickly; I hadn't realized how ravenous I was.

As the servers were clearing away our plates, Ian suggested night skiing—but our faculty advisers, Ms. Manning and Mr. DeNardo, the head of the English department, quickly nixed that idea. Instead they announced free time before bed, then went off to a deserted corner of the dining room to go over the schedule for the following day.

We all congregated by the huge fireplace in the main room of the lodge, where the fire was crackling and we could order hot chocolate from the bar at the far end of the room. As a group of us settled into a long banquette, Cassie nudged me and covertly opened her fleece; a hint of silver flask flashed up at me.

"You are insane," I whispered. "That is, like, breaking the first rule of any class trip! Do you want to get suspended?"

"Do you want to be boring and predictable and get straight A's and get into Columbia without breaking a sweat?" Cassie whispered back. "Or do you want to have a memorable ski trip?" Glancing over her shoulder to make sure the coast was clear, she poured a little into her hot chocolate.

I was stung, but it wasn't the first time she'd gotten on my case about it. I weighed the options. Was I really so uptight?

"Okay, fine," I whispered, closing my eyes and waving

her on before I had a chance to change my mind.

Soon Trey and Evan had joined us, and Ian and Dan pulled up another couch.

"Ooh, let's play Never Have I Ever," Ellie cooed, climbing over Ian's side of the couch and sitting with us. Ian got up to make room for her, squeezing in next to me. We formed a little circle by the fire. Cassie was totally in her element as she passed the flask around.

While Ellie explained the rules to anyone who didn't already know how to play, I made a silent vow to myself not to think about Asher or Devin, or Columbia, or my grades, or the thermostat, but just to enjoy the ski trip. Cassie was right—I was starting to get too uptight, and I needed to relax and have fun. So what if Asher was intriguing, or Devin was mysterious, or that they seemed to follow me everywhere? Come to think of it, I hadn't seen either of them since dinner. I looked around. Devin was sitting in an armchair at the other end of the room, reading a thick paperback. I didn't see Asher anywhere.

"Skye. Skye. *Skye?*"

"What?" Blood rushed to my cheeks. Everyone was staring at me. Cassie giggled.

"It's your turn," Ian mock-whispered into my ear, nudging my arm.

I couldn't help it—the whispering in my ear reminded me of Asher. My mind went blank as I remembered my dream.

"Never have I ever . . . gotten drunk on a ski trip," I finished lamely.

"Not *yet*," Ellie said, and Cassie gave me a pseudo scowl.

"Do-over," she sang.

"Um, okay." I bit my lip. "Never have I ever wanted to hook up with someone on a ski trip."

Cassie grinned. "Do they have to be on the same ski trip as you?"

"Just drink your hot chocolate, woman!" Dan shouted from across the circle. Cassie lifted her mug, toasted the group, and took a long sip. On the couch opposite me, Ellie drank quickly from her mug. Sitting beside me, Ian shot me a sidelong glance. I didn't meet his gaze.

"Who do you want to hook up with?" I whispered to Cassie.

"Uh-uh." She wagged a finger, smiling mysteriously. "You'll have to get me drunker than that."

Over the course of the next two hours, various people wandered away, and several more joined in. Ian was sitting next to me, his pinky grazing my knee. I wasn't sure he even realized he was doing it.

Devin stayed glued to his chair on the other side of the room, glancing over the top of his book every now and then to scrutinize us. I wondered what he was thinking. I considered inviting him to join the group. It was obvious he wasn't as comfortable here as Asher. But would he be embarrassed to be put on the spot? I just didn't know him well enough to know if he wanted or dreaded an invitation.

I went to take a sip of my hot chocolate and realized my mug was empty. "Anyone else want another?" I asked, standing up.

"Sure," Ian said, leaning back against the couch and linking his hands behind his head. "Nice to be the one waited on for a change. Thanks."

I walked past Devin——who looked up from his book to smile at me——and over to the bar, where I ordered two hot chocolates. Suddenly I heard a familiar voice——warm and scratchy, with just a hint of a sly smile——coming from the vestibule around the corner, where the ice and vending machines were. My heart thumped loudly.

The woman behind the bar looked tired as she placed two steaming mugs on the counter. I picked them up, but one handle was unusually scalding. I put it down, then gingerly I picked it up again. A blinding heat seared through my hand, and I let the mug fall back on the counter, some hot chocolate sloshing over the side. "Sorry," I mumbled.

The woman's face fell as she went to get a rag from the kitchen. It occurred to me that I should get some ice to cool down the hot drinks—but that would mean walking toward Asher's voice. I slowed as I got closer. Did I even want to *see* him?

I turned to face the vestibule.

Asher's back was to me. A breathy giggle escaped from somewhere between him and the wall. *Ellie.*

"*What* are you doing?" I blurted out before I could stop myself.

"Skye!" Ellie cried, breaking away from him. "What are you doing here?"

"Hey, Skye." Asher turned around and smiled, leaning back against the side of the ice machine as if nothing was wrong. "How's the game?"

"It's good, um . . ." Suddenly I felt stupid. "I just came in for some ice. I didn't mean to crash the party."

Asher eyed me skeptically. "Ice? For your hot chocolate?"

My face burned. "It's really hot, okay?"

I stepped between them, noisily grabbing a handful of ice from the ice machine. Asher watched me speculatively while Ellie crossed her arms over her chest and looked away.

"Skye?" Ian stood in the doorway of the vestibule, holding our mugs. When he saw me with the ice, he smiled. "Too hot?"

"Why is this such surprising news to everyone?" I said, my voice rising. "It's called *hot* chocolate!" I walked over to Ian to plunk the ice into the mugs, but before I had a chance to take more than a step, the ice melted in my hands, dripping sadly through my fingers and onto the carpet. "What the hell!" I could feel tears beginning to prick my eyes, and I had no idea why. I vowed I wouldn't lose it right here in front of everyone.

"Um, you were taking a long time, so I came to see if you needed help." Ian's eyes flicked from Asher to Ellie and back to me. "Whoa, your eyes just did that silver thing again," he said quietly.

Asher looked at me sharply.

My heart pounded.

"Is everything okay?" Ian asked.

"Oh, everything's *fine*." Asher jumped in, his eyes flicking back and forth between us. "So are you two . . . ?"

"What? No!" I cried, noticing too late that Ian had stayed quiet.

An awkward silence hung in the air.

"Yeah, so I'm going to bring our mugs back to the table," Ian said, not bothering to hide his discomfort as he turned around and left. I had to do something about this.

"Sorry to interrupt," I said pointedly, looking from Asher to Ellie. "Feel free to go back to whatever it is you were doing." I walked out of the vestibule to follow Ian. As I neared the end of the hallway, I heard, "Skye, wait!"

"What?" I wheeled around. Asher jogged to catch up with me.

"What's going on?" He shoved his hands in his pockets.

"What do you mean?"

"What was that back there?"

"Nothing."

"Skye, seriously. Why are you so upset?"

"I'm not upset." I said it too quickly. Asher looked at me strangely, and I knew I'd been caught in a lie.

"Could have fooled me. You know, if you don't tell me, I'm going to have to make my own assumptions." He gave me an evil grin. "And they won't be good."

"Well . . ." How was I going to explain myself out of this one? Even *I* didn't know why I was upset.

"Yes?" he prodded.

"Well, I just—I don't understand. I thought you

were . . . you know . . . but now you're flirting with Ellie—" I stopped and looked up at him. His eyes were soft and brown and warm, and I was more confused than ever. "Look, I don't know what I thought, never mind. I'm just tired."

"You slept the whole way here."

"You noticed?"

"I notice everything about you."

My breath caught in my throat.

"Don't try to distract me," I muttered. "I'm still mad."

"Wait—that didn't make you *jealous* back there, did it?" His eyes were twinkling.

"Are you doing this on purpose?"

"Huh," he mused. "Imagine that."

I had to get out of there or I was going to truly make a fool of myself.

"I have to leave. Go back to Ellie." I pushed past him and headed down the hall.

"Skye, come on!" He shouted after me. "I'm kidding!"

But I was already on my way back to the seating area. Ian was in his spot, his elbows on his thighs, his hands clasped around a mug as though it was a life preserver, his eyes on the floor like he had laser vision and could create a hole to fall through. I tapped his shoulder. When he looked up, I could tell that he wasn't happy to see me.

"Let's go get some air," I said. I was relieved when he didn't make an excuse not to come with me.

We grabbed our jackets and headed out to the wooden deck. I could feel Devin watching me with curiosity as we walked past.

Once outside, I inhaled deeply. The sky was dark now, and the tiny lights flickered across the face of the mountain, a mirror image of the stars above. The lights from the lodge reflected off the snow, creating a halo around the deck. Beyond that, shadows and moonlight cast a blue glow.

"Ian—"

"Don't say anything."

"We're friends—"

"Please don't give me the 'let's be friends' talk. Guys hate that, and all it does is make us feel stupid that we wanted more."

My heart felt as though it was going to cave in on itself. "But we *are* friends, and I need to make sure that we're going to stay friends. Next to Cassie and Dan, you're the best friend I have. I don't know what I'd do without you."

He shoved his hands into his pockets. "You like Asher, don't you?"

"I don't know. It doesn't make any sense, but something about him . . . I can't explain it."

"He's a player. He's going to hurt you."

"Are we okay?" I asked. I didn't want to talk about Asher.

He shook his head and smiled. "Yeah, we're okay."

I leaned forward, folded my arms on the railing, and gazed out on the snow glistening in the moonlight. "It's going to be a good day for skiing tomorrow."

Ian joined me, our shoulders touching. It was comfortable, standing so close like that.

Then something snagged my gaze. Devin was trudging toward the trees. Alone. He was always alone. I had this insane desire to join him, to escape the confines of the lodge. Ian's eyes followed mine.

"Unless . . . ?" Ian said, his voice trailing up at the end. He shook his head. "I'll never get girls."

"Have you ever noticed how tranquil he seems whenever Asher isn't around? He stays so calm. I wonder how he does it."

"I think I'd get bored being that calm."

"Maybe I wish DeNardo and Manning hadn't vetoed your idea for night skiing," I said. "Think we could sneak off and do it anyway?"

Ian laughed. "Not really wanting to get into trouble here. Cassie's flask is only about as far as I'm willing to go. If it was a group out there, I'd do it. But just you and me . . . If one of us got hurt . . . I don't want to think about what would happen."

Asher would do it, I thought. He'd go with me. He'd break the rules. But he was with Ellie.

Ian and I stood out there for a while longer, until I couldn't feel my toes. Then I had to say good night.

Cassie and Dan were still with the group gathered near the fireplace, but I was no longer in the mood for a crowd.

I took the stairs two at a time up to the room I was sharing with Cassie, where I crawled under the covers and lay there, staring into the darkness. Even when she came in and called my name softly, I didn't answer. I just listened to her getting ready for bed as I lay there, stiff, unable to move, unable to sleep, unable to think about anything but Asher, and how much I hated seeing him with Ellie. *Why do I care so much? Didn't I already learn my lesson with Jordan?*

Somewhere, at some point, I must have fallen asleep, because the next thing I knew it was morning and Cassie was nudging me awake.

*B*reakfast was torture.

Ian was distant again, and I wouldn't even make eye contact with Asher, though it didn't stop him from trying. Devin avoided all of us. I wondered if Asher had told him what had happened. They were cousins, right? Didn't cousins tell each other things?

Maybe soon the whole school would find out how I'd made a fool of myself in the stupid ice vestibule.

All I wanted was to put on my skis and fly away.

After breakfast, we went outside and Mr. DeNardo organized us into groups based on skill. Cassie was in the bunny slope group. She'd worn a special hat with little bunny ears on it in honor of the occasion. I couldn't help laughing. Despite the fact that Dan was a great skier, he opted to be in her group.

I was grouped with the advanced skiers, along with Ian—who looked surprisingly serious in a pair of dark goggles and a helmet—Ellie, Maggie, Asher, and Devin. The moment we were grouped together, Asher scooted around to stand next to me. "Skye," he whispered. I moved away.

Ian eyed me doubtfully as we made our way to the chair-lift.

"You and me today?" I asked.

"Sure," he replied.

I stuck by his side, making sure to sit with him on the way up. There was no way I was sitting with Ellie after the whole debacle from the night before. And if Asher thought I was going to ride up the mountain with him, he was crazy. They could sit together for all I cared.

It was cold and white at the top of the slope. Looking down from where I stood, the people below resembled the multicolored pixels of a TV screen arranging and rearranging themselves into all kinds of strange shapes. Standing there, I tilted my head back and stared at the blue-gray sky, pretending I was the only one around for miles.

Ian and I positioned ourselves in the middle of the group,

teetering on the edge of the double black-diamond trail known as Jacob's Ladder. The girl standing on his other side caught his attention, and he began talking with her. Past his shoulder, I could see Devin waiting patiently at the far end of the line.

The sharp swoosh of someone coming to a stop behind me was startling. I glanced back.

"Good day for this, no?" Asher shaded his eyes with his hand as he squinted into the sky. "I hope the weather holds up."

I didn't say anything.

"Look, about last night—"

"Forget it, okay?" I turned to face him. "It happened. It's over. We're moving on."

"We are?" His voice was serious, but his eyes, as always, were smiling. It felt like he was making fun of me, and, annoyed, I pulled my goggles down and faced the slope.

"Are you a good skier?"

"Haven't lost a race this season," I replied without looking at him.

"Wow," he said. "You must have amazing control." Steady on his skis, he swooped a slow, graceful arc behind me, coming up on my other side, forcing the guy who had been beside me to make room for him. Asher's voice was low in my ear. "But it's something else for you, too, I'm guessing."

"And what would that be?" I stood up straight again, eyeing the edge. We were standing too close to it. One slip, and we'd be soaring down the mountain. I backed up.

"*Losing* control. That's why you like to ski, isn't it? The feeling of falling but still knowing you can catch yourself. You're a control freak because you know that if pushed, you would topple too far in the other direction."

"I'm not a control freak," I challenged. What did he know? Once we got going, I was going to wipe that cocky smile right off his face.

Asher pulled his goggles down over his eyes, secured his grip on his poles.

"My mistake," he said. "Let's race."

And he took off, body leaning into the wind, poles straight back and tucked under his arms. Seconds later, I was right behind him, my plan to ski with Ian abandoned. Asher had presented a challenge I couldn't ignore.

"I'll win!" I called, my blood boiling.

"Prove it!" he yelled back. His voice was remarkably clear above the wind.

I kept my focus on Asher—I wasn't aware of anyone else on the mountain. If he swooped left, so did I. If he cut a sharp turn right over a bump, I followed. It became a game, a challenge. I'm not sure why I felt the sudden need to prove myself to him, but my body kept pace almost involuntarily. He knew I was watching him, like he'd been watching me since we'd met outside the Bean. Well, now he'd know what it felt like. And *damn*, he was an amazing skier. In his black parka and ski pants, he was like a dark star, hurtling forward. And I was his shadow, furtive and quick. Asher's movements were sure, controlled, and he flew with seemingly no effort at all. I didn't see him stumble once. I could feel the earth rippling and moving underneath me as I surged ahead.

And suddenly I was passing him. His crouching figure pulled alongside me, and then he slipped back until I couldn't see him anymore. Every bump, every notch, every roiling swell of snow and rock and earth beneath me seemed to fall away like sand in an hourglass. And then it really *did*. The snow underneath my skis really *was* moving, falling away. My footing faltered, and on the verge of pitching forward, I glanced back.

Blind panic shot through my veins. Snow was ripping down the slope, balling up like boulders and thundering toward me with breathtaking speed. My heart was beating fast, and my breath came in sharp, ragged gasps. The snow drove down harder. I looked around wildly for some kind of sheltering rock or overhang. Anything at all to hold on to. But I was moving too fast. No one was behind me anymore—no one, not even Asher. I was alone. I was alone, and I was falling.

I hit the side of the mountain hard, the wind sucked out of my lungs like a vacuum. I felt a sharp twist of pain as my ankle buckled and snapped beneath me, and I went down.

I'd gone from calculated control to being completely helpless in the blink of an eye.

The sensation of falling: the fear, the elation.

The ground fell out from underneath me, and I dropped away. To someplace darker.

12

Someone was saying my name. It sounded beautiful, like a song from somewhere otherworldly. Had I died? Was I in heaven?

Was I someplace . . . else?

"Skye!"

My eyes shot open.

I was in a cave of some kind. As I sat up, slowly, with one hand out to steady myself, my surroundings came into focus. Wherever I was, it was dark, but a pale light shone through the seemingly translucent walls. Was I trapped under the snow? The walls around me shimmered and swayed slightly. What I was sure of, though, was the excruciating cold. The snow had soaked completely through the rip in my Gore-Tex gloves and through the fleece I wore underneath them.

Crouched on his knees in front of me was Asher.

"What are you doing here?" I forced out, my voice thick. My tongue felt like some kind of foreign object in my mouth.

"You're awake!" He exhaled loudly, and relief shone in his eyes. He put his hand on my arm. "Are you okay? How do you feel?"

"My head . . ." I began, trying to cut through the fog pressing down on my brain. I realized that my ankle was throbbing in pain. "And my ankle. It's twisted or broken or something."

Asher furrowed his eyebrows, glancing down at it.

"Where are we?" I asked.

"I think we fell into some sort of snow cave." Snow surrounded us, but we sat safely in the makeshift shelter.

"How did you . . . ?"

"I saw you falling, but I couldn't reach you in time. You disappeared into the snow, so I jumped in after you." Asher was feeling around my ankle with his hands. I winced, and he saw me. His face fell. "Sorry. I can't . . ." He cleared his throat. "I don't know how to fix it, Skye. I called for help while you were out." His eyes flicked upward, presumably toward the outside world. I wondered what kind of cell reception we had down here. It's not like I could climb out with a maybe-broken ankle. "I didn't want to leave you here, alone," he said, not meeting my eyes as he packed snow around my foot.

"It was weird." I took a breath, grimacing as he steadied my ankle. "I was feeling this rush of power as I passed you. And it's like—it's almost as if the snow and ice started crumbling because of it. Because of how I felt. And then the more I started to panic, the more helpless I was . . . the harder it came." I glanced up, afraid to meet his eyes. He was staring at me. Not in disbelief, exactly. More like he was contemplating something impossible. I hoped my eyes weren't silver. I looked away. "It sounds crazy, I know."

He didn't say anything, and in the icy silence of the cave, I shivered. My fingers were beyond numb—they burned.

"Are you cold?" Asher asked quietly.

"Freezing." I took off one Gore-Tex glove and poked a finger through the hole. Then I took off my fleece glove and held it up with a sad smile; it flopped over, soaking wet.

"Here." He unzipped his black parka and wrapped it around me. I could feel the heat from his body still trapped inside as I drew it closer. It smelled earthy and warm.

"No," I protested weakly. "You need it."

"I naturally run hot," he said with a grin. "I'll be fine.

How about you? Better?"

"Mmm. Thanks." I drew my hands inside the sleeves. He was looking at me strangely.

"If I show you something, will you promise not to tell anyone?"

"Are you going to keep me entertained until we get rescued?"

"Something like that, but you have to promise."

"Promise. Anything to distract me from the possibility of us dying."

"You're not going to die. I won't let that happen."

He sounded so certain, I could almost believe him. But I also wondered how anyone would ever find us before we became human popsicles.

He moved around so that he was sitting behind me. I could feel his chest against my back, his breath trace across my neck. I tried in vain to keep my own breathing steady, but the combination of the pain, the cold, and being so close to Asher made it come unevenly, shallow.

Asher reached both arms around me. "Take your hands out of the sleeves," he murmured. I did, slowly—and he took both of my hands in his and brought them in close. He cupped them together, our palms facing upward. "Okay," he whispered into my hair. "Don't freak out."

I stared at our hands, resting on top of each other. How could I possibly feel more freaked out than I already was?

And then.

A small flame bloomed between my palms. It didn't hurt—all I could feel was a gentle warmth as the flames licked my fingers, circulation returning to them. The whole snow cave filled with a soft orange glow, firelight flickering shadows on the walls like they were telling a story.

I was holding fire in the palm of my hand.

"Asher?" My voice was getting higher, my heart beating much too fast. "How are you doing this?"

"If I told you, it would ruin the fun," he said, and even though he was behind me, I could tell he was smiling. "A magician never gives away his secrets."

"What is it with you and secrets?"

The flame flickered in my hand, and then flared up, toward the ceiling. When it died out, a circle of snow had melted, exposing the sky above.

"Whoa." Asher whistled softly to himself. "That wasn't supposed to happen." He pulled away, inching around so that he was facing me again. His eyebrows were scrunched together in confusion. "I'm usually better at controlling that. I don't know why . . ." He looked at me. He put his hand on my cheek. His fingers were still warm, and my shivering quieted.

"Look," he said. "About last night."

I sighed. "I really don't want to talk about it."

"No, listen. You were right—I have been trying to get your attention. But not for the reason you think."

"Okay," I said dubiously. "Then why?"

He smiled warmly, running his thumb softly over my cheekbone.

"Skye," he murmured. "It's . . . complicated."

"I don't understand," I said, the words sounding stuck in my throat. I was vaguely aware that he'd used this line before, but I was slipping off into sleep and couldn't focus.

"Listen, we don't have to decide the fate of the world right this minute." He cupped his hand under my head as it came to rest against his shoulder. "Skye, can you stay awake for me? Talk to me. Keep yourself talking."

"What should I say?" I was so drowsy.

"Say anything. Say what you're thinking about right now."

I don't know why I was thinking about this, but the words came tumbling out of my mouth before I had a chance to second-guess myself. "My parents died," I said hazily, the fog wrapping itself around my head again. "In a car accident. When I was six." I yawned.

"I'm sorry," Asher said softly, positioning himself next to me. I felt him take my hand in his. It was warm. I moved myself so that I was leaning against him, burying my head in his warmth. I could feel his breath rising and falling.

"I don't really remember the accident very well. I don't know why I survived and they didn't." It felt good to talk about it. I never talked about that with anyone. "I could have died." I didn't like the way it sounded out loud.

He brushed the hair away from my face. "But you didn't. Don't worry, okay? Help will come."

I could feel myself growing heavier, the world darker again. I almost thought I could feel the feathery touch of his lips on my forehead.

Almost.

I opened my eyes again in a much different kind
of place.

The walls were just walls, about as opaque as
walls can get, and I was toasty warm beneath the wool
camp-style blanket draped over me. I wore flannel pajamas that I didn't recognize, and I was lying on my back
in a narrow bed. I was, it appeared, in the ski lodge infirmary. A place noticeably lacking in magic. On the ceiling
above me, the various cracks and watermarks had been
whitewashed over not very adeptly with a coat of paint.
I felt okay—much better than earlier—except for the
shooting pain in my ankle.

Had I really just been trapped in a makeshift snow cave
with Asher? And had he really created . . . fire? Out of

thin air? I felt like I was waking up from a vivid dream and confronting the harsh light of the real world. For all I knew, I was.

Where was Asher now? Feeling stiff and immobile in the infirmary bed, I turned my head on the pillow, hoping he'd be sitting there beside me, waiting to tell me that what I had seen was only my imagination. Or at least explain the neat trick and how he'd hidden the lighter.

Instead my eyes landed on Devin. He was sitting in a chair pushed up against the wall, staring out the window to the slopes beyond. He wasn't looking at me.

"What are you doing here?" I asked, confused. "Where's Asher?"

Devin turned to me, his expression placid. "You're awake."

My pulse quickened. "How long have I been out?"

He looked at his hands. "A while."

"Am I okay?"

"You don't have a concussion, which was their biggest concern. Everything else is . . . fixable."

"Everything else?" I tried to sit up, but Devin reached a hand out gently to stop me. A wave of dizziness overcame me, and I leaned back against the pillow. "Where are my friends? What are you even doing here?"

"Did your fall also make you forget that we're friends,

too?" He looked around. "Nurse? I think she has some memory loss after all!"

"Stop it!" I swatted his hand down.

"How do you feel?"

"Why are you here?" I repeated.

"I was worried."

"But where's Asher?"

"Asher," Devin repeated, his eyes frosting over. "Who knows? Changing his clothes, warming up, amassing more groupies. What am I, his guardian?" He pursed his lips.

"He's your cousin," I said, bristling at the word *groupies*. "Shouldn't you be more worried about him? We both could have died out there."

Devin grimaced. "Asher can take care of himself. He doesn't need me to worry about him."

"Well, *I'm* worried about him—"

"He didn't have a scratch on him, Skye—"

"Who rescued us, anyway? I—ow!" I'd tried sitting up too quickly, and pain sliced its way up my leg. I grabbed my ankle, which, despite being tightly wrapped in ACE bandages, still throbbed with pain.

Devin shook his head. It was as if he'd forgotten that I was hurt. "Oh," he said, glancing at my ankle and then back to me. "Are you okay?"

"I'm *fine*," I said. "It's just my—ow—ankle."

"It hurts?" he asked.

I nodded. "Pretty bad. It must be a sprain or a torn ligament or something."

Devin stood up and moved to the side of the bed. He put his hands gently on my ankle.

"Here?" he asked.

I closed my eyes, wincing, and nodded. "Yeah."

My eyes still closed, I could now feel his two hands pressing against my ankle. His touch was remarkably gentle, and I let myself sink deeper into the pillow as a sense of calm washed over me.

He pressed his hands against me, slightly harder. The pain in my ankle flared from sharp to incredible—and then, just like that, it subsided. I opened my eyes in disbelief. Devin took his hands away, eyeing me hesitantly.

"It should be fine now," he said.

I turned my foot one way and then the other. There wasn't even a twinge of discomfort. Staring at him, I tried to make sense of what had just happened. "I don't understand. How did you—" I was interrupted by the door to the room flinging open, and Cassie, Dan, and Ian tumbling in. Cassie's bunny hat was askew, and her eyes were wide and questioning. Dan's goggles were around his neck, his knit hat clutched in his gloved hand. Ian looked lost—like he wished he had a latte to offer me.

"Skye! Are you all right? What happened?" Cassie rushed to my side in a dramatic gust of fluttering hair. "We heard you were in an avalanche and—oh, you look okay. Are any parts of you broken? Will you ever walk again?"

"I'm fine, I think," I said, smiling at Dan and Ian, who hung back along the wall.

"Cool," Dan said, and noticed Devin. "Hey, man." He nodded.

"Hey," Devin said stiffly.

Cassie looked up at Devin, noticing him for the first time and turned, wide-eyed, back to me.

"Oh!" she exclaimed, surprised. Then a slow grin spread across her face. "Oh." She bent low to my ear. "Are you in the *middle* of something?" she whispered. "I mean, we can go. . . ."

"Cassie, I'm fine—"

"Actually, *I* need to go," Devin suddenly announced.

I didn't want him to leave. I still had questions. Was it just me, or was he trying to avoid giving me the chance to ask them?

"Devin—"

"I'm glad you're okay."

He stood up and nodded curtly to Dan and Ian.

And then he was gone. The door slammed behind him, and the room echoed and then went still.

"Ooookay," Cassie finally said into the silence. "So I heard this rumor that Asher was *ve*-ry heroic when you were rescued."

"Is he okay?" I asked, sitting up quickly at the mention of Asher. "Was he hurt? Devin didn't seem to know." *Or care*, I thought.

"He's fine," Ian said. The muscles in his jaw tightened. "The guy has all the luck."

"Was anyone else caught in the avalanche?" I asked.

"No, you guys were so far ahead, no one could catch up," Ian explained. "We were all able to avoid it. It was unreal, how fast you were going. You guys were a blur."

"I got caught up with the challenge. Sorry I left you behind."

"Hey, you did me a favor!" He grinned reassuringly. "I'm going to see if I can scrounge up some hot chocolate or something for you."

That was Ian. Always wanting to provide comfort food and drinks. He headed for the door.

"I'll go with you," Dan said. "Let Manning and DeNardo know Skye's okay."

After they left, Cassie leaned in. "So what's the real story?"

"I don't know what you're talking about."

"Come on, Skye. I'm your best friend. You have to give me *something*."

I gulped. Could I tell her about the strange events? If I told anyone, it would be Cassie. But how could I begin to explain creating . . . *holding* . . . fire in my bare hands? And the way Devin had seemingly healed my ankle with just a touch?

Before I could decide what to do, the door opened and a nurse walked in.

And I wasn't sure why, but I suddenly felt as though it was the second time I'd been rescued that day.

"So let me get this straight," Cassie said. She caught my eye in the mirror and turned around, mid-blush stroke. "You fainted in Asher's arms, but you woke up in . . . Devin's?"

The sun had long since set behind the mountain, and we were back in our room at the lodge, getting ready for the campfire later that night. The nurse had discharged me from the infirmary a few hours earlier. When I didn't show signs of anything worse than boredom, they'd sent me on my way.

"I guess you could twist what I said so it sounds like that." I grinned.

Now I sat propped up by pillows on the bed, in softly worn jeans and a black zip-up fleece, watching Cassie line her eyes with deep brown liner. I didn't know who she could possibly be getting so glammed up for—she hadn't told me about any new crushes lately, and she was the worst secret keeper I knew. If Cassie liked a guy, we all knew it.

"So?" she prodded. "Details?"

I had hoped after the nurse had interrupted her that Cassie would forget she had questions. But I wasn't so lucky. I thought of the snow falling away beneath my skis, the terrifying speed at which it had come toward me. Asher and our cave. The fire. Devin—healing my ankle with no more than a touch. It would sound totally insane to say all of this out loud. It was totally insane just to *think* it. I wondered if the trauma of the ordeal had made me hallucinate.

I needed to find Devin and Asher. I wanted them to explain what was going on. But Cassie had morphed into a mother hen and hadn't left my side since I was discharged.

I smiled impishly. "There's nothing to tell! I just blacked out when I fell, that's all. I don't even remember it, just that Asher was there with me."

"I'm calling your bluff," Cassie said with a swipe of lip gloss for emphasis. "I'll get it out of you, one way or another." She laughed an evil-villain laugh, then giggled at her own ridiculousness. Cassie's giggle was addictive—it had gotten us into trouble way too many times to count (in the library, in the back of class, during last year's guest lecture on the evils of social networking). I was powerless to resist it—soon we were both laughing so hard it hurt. We were still laughing when we heard a knock at the door.

Cassie got up to get it. Dan and Ian stood on the other side.

"Oh, sorry, is this the wrong room?" Dan teased. "We're looking for our other, cooler, sane friends." His hair flopped into his face, and he brushed it back out again. Dan needed a haircut so badly it was comical, but something like that would never occur to him on his own. His mom would probably kidnap him in a week or so and whisk him off to Supercuts. Cassie sniffed and wiped away a tear, smudging her eyeliner.

"Who gave you a black eye?" Dan asked.

"Shut up, you're one to talk. You look like a shaggy dog." Cassie laughed, her eyes gleaming. She fixed the smudge as I grabbed our jackets from where we'd flung them on the edge of the bed and tossed Cassie's at her. I was still ginger on my ankle even though it didn't hurt anymore. Unbelievably, when I'd first left the infirmary it had felt fine—like I'd never sprained it in the first place. But it had been hurt. I knew it had.

"So word on the street is that Asher saved your life," Ian said.

"I wouldn't go that far." Or maybe I would. Without him, they might have never found me. He and Devin both seemed to have an uncanny ability to sense when I was in trouble and come to my rescue. But then again, I never used to get into so much trouble before they arrived.

Cassie shooed the guys away from the door. "Come on, come on. Let the invalid pass."

To the left of the lodge, a dirt path snaked downhill through the woods. As I followed it through the dark, Cassie's flashlight bouncing off the pine trees, the motion reminded me of the snow slipping out from under me. My vision swam, and for a moment, I felt dizzy. I stopped abruptly, waiting for the forest to stop spinning.

"You okay?" Ian whispered, coming up next to me.

"Fine," I said, shaking my head to clear it. "I'm fine."

"Maybe hanging out tonight is too much, too soon after your fall? Do you want me to walk you back to the room?"

But going back to the room would accomplish nothing. I didn't need a night to rest. What I needed were answers. I had to discover if I was going insane or if there was even the smallest possibility that the strange things that had been happening to me were real.

The path opened into a clearing, where a fire was already crackling away and Ms. Manning was just finishing up laying out the rules for the restless crowd.

"Remember, no alcohol, of course, and no smoking. Keep the area clean; put the fire out when you're done." She smiled and held up a plastic grocery store bag filled with marshmallows, graham crackers, and chocolate. "Because we had an exciting day," she said, eyeing me.

As Dan, Ian, Cassie, and I spotted a log on the far side of the fire and headed toward it, I was bombarded with questions from my classmates. Apparently the rumors had been raging out of control. Though I was happy to be safe, happy even to be *alive*, how could I explain to them what had happened on the mountain or in the infirmary? I would have to be convincing about whatever lie I told. I had no idea what I was going to say, but I opened my mouth, about to make something up.

"She was incredible." Asher's voice cut in from behind me, and all eyes focused on him as he walked up next to me. "You should have seen it. A huge chunk of ice broke off the side of the mountain and gathered this momentum of snow. Yet Skye was totally outmaneuvering it," he said, shooting me a sideways grin.

"Until I fell," I added.

"But even then," Asher told the group. "Heroic. No wonder she wins all those medals."

I groaned at the melodrama. "It wasn't heroic."

"Well, you hit your head pretty hard. You might not remember it all exactly how it happened." He gave me a pointed look, and I shut up. I had promised to keep his secret. It *had* happened. So the only question left was, How?

Playing along, I pinned him with a fake smile. "You must be right," I said lightly. "I don't even remember how we got back. Maybe after the campfire, you can fill me in."

Then Ellie was there, grabbing Asher's arm. "Glad you're okay, Skye," she said over her shoulder as she pushed him toward the other side of the fire. I caught his eye, but he just shrugged and gave me a what-can-I-do? look.

"Looks like you've totally lost out with Asher," Cassie said under her breath as I sat down next to her.

"Cass, it really doesn't bother me."

But secretly I was seething. What was wrong with him? How could he be the way he was with me in the cave and then, the next minute, scamper off with Ellie like nothing had happened between us? Maybe the chemistry between us was all in my head.

I settled onto the log next to Cassie, and Ian sat beside me. Within a few minutes, we were roasting marshmallows and making s'mores.

"So I guess we have you to thank for this," Ian said, licking chocolate from his fingers. "Maybe you should try getting sent to the infirmary more often."

"I think Ms. Manning was just trying to make me feel better." She'd been the one handling all the paperwork for me at the infirmary, and had tried Aunt Jo's cell but hadn't gotten through. Finally, I called the office; they'd been in regular touch with her via satellite and promised to let her know what had happened. I was exhausted just thinking about how hard it was to track her down.

After all the s'mores had been devoured, Devin showed up at the edge of the group. I watched as he strolled over and joined Asher on the other side of the fire.

Cassie clapped her hands, drawing everyone's attention. Her eyes took on a mischievous glint. "Let's tell campfire stories. . . ." She picked up a gnarled piece of kindling from next to the fire and tossed it to Dan. "Dan, tell us about that time you snowboarded off the mountain and it turned out the ski patrol who saved you was dead."

"She wasn't dead," Dan huffed. "She had no face, okay? And now there's not much left to tell."

"Okay, then, I have one." Asher spoke up from across the fire. Next to him, Devin's eyes barely reflected the dancing flames as he stared at them.

Dan passed the stick to Asher.

"Stage is yours, man," he said. "Though beating the faceless ski patrol story? I dunno. . . ."

Asher gave him a cocky grin. "Shouldn't be too hard."

I watched him carefully. The firelight flickered across his face, catching a dimple near the left side of his mouth. His eyes held a spark of excitement. "It's a legend we tell in my family," he said carefully. Devin's jaw clenched, but he kept his eyes trained on the fire and didn't say a word.

"Once upon a time," Asher said with a flourish, "there was an all-important council that ruled over the people of Earth. It was higher than the president of the United States, higher than the powers of all the world. It was called the Order. Older than time itself, the Order was responsible for one thing: to keep the world in check.

"Its members fell into ranks. The highest were gifted with the Sight. The ability to foresee people's destinies. And the Gifted saw it as their duty to guide the lives of those who roamed Earth. While the lower rank"—his eyes flashed with controlled fury—"were forced to carry out the orders of the Gifted. They were known as the

Guardians of the Natural Order. Or Guardians, for short." Asher took a breath. "They had no free will. They were essentially slaves to the Gifteds' commands."

The faces of those surrounding the campfire were rapt, their eyes unblinking. Asher had that kind of power. Devin avoided everyone's gaze, but I saw his hands clench into fists as his cousin continued.

"A small group began to emerge who refused to adhere to the Way of Things. They believed the world would be better if those gifted with the Sight didn't meddle in the fragile balance of Earth and its people. The world would be better if chaos was allowed to bloom every now and then. If people could make mistakes and live a life that was messy and beautiful. The group formed, fought, lost, and left the Order. But as punishment, the rebels, banished from the Paradise in which they lived, were forced to walk among the people whose lives they used to control."

"The rebels spent their time on Earth harnessing their own powers. To counter the Sight of the Gifted, they honed their control of the elements. They learned to create chaos."

Asher poked his stick into the flames, and sparks fanned out into the darkness. Devin flinched, something I'm sure no one else noticed. Slowly he lifted his gaze to me. His eyes were unreadable but definitely not tranquil. I realized I'd been watching the two of them too closely. I looked away.

"That was how things were, anyway," Asher continued, regaining his command of the circle, "until something unprecedented occurred that rocked the natural order of things." His voice hooked on to the word *rocked*, sounding almost like a growl. "Upsetting both sides, the Order and the Rebellion." He looked right at me, and I heard myself take a sharp, involuntary breath. "*Love.* The great destroyer of worlds."

Cassie gripped my arm. She was the biggest sucker for epic love stories.

"Eighteen years ago, a Rebel fell in love with a beautiful, lonely Guardian. The Guardian had a predestined soul mate chosen for her by the Gifted. Like all Guardians, she had been raised to hate the Rebellion and everyone in it. But in spite of everything, what she felt for this Rebel went deeper. Maybe he had sexy eyes, I don't know. Or a great smile." Asher winked at me, and my stomach dropped away. He had a great smile, and he knew it. "Unable to act on her feelings, she tried in vain to hate him. But she soon realized that she had a choice to make: stay in Paradise and allow her destiny to unfold as the Gifted had planned—or forge a new path. One that was unscripted. She didn't know what would happen. Only that she would be walking into the unknown if she left the Order.

"It turned out the Rebel Elders were as angered by this love as the Gifted. And so, a council of the highest order was held: seven of the Gifted and seven Rebel Elders. The couple was tried."

Everyone around the campfire was silent. Cassie had her head resting against Dan's shoulder as she stared at Asher, their faces glowing amber in the firelight. Dark shadows flickered across Asher's face. His story was clawing at my memory. I had heard it before, somewhere, hadn't I? Parts of it? But where? And how could that be? I struggled to remember.

Asher captured my gaze and held it as he said, "The Rebel and the Guardian stood together waiting for the tribunal's final verdict. The price for their love was banishment—they would belong to neither faction. They would be nomads, forced to walk among the people of Earth, stripped of their otherworldly powers. And, going forward, their days would be numbered, like the very people among whom they were forced to live. Their punishment was mortality.

"When the couple settled in a small town and gave birth

to a daughter, both sides took note. What would a baby born of the Order and the Rebellion be like?

"The Gifted and the Rebels worried that such a child could be dangerous. But they reminded themselves that this child would be human. She might not have any powers at all. . . .

"And so the vigil began. Agents from both sides were sent to guide and protect her. And to determine what, exactly, was in store for her future."

The sounds of the fire snapping and popping echoed through the trees. Asher looked up at us, as if finished with the story.

"What ended up happening?" Cassie asked breathlessly.

Asher hesitated, glancing at Devin before continuing.

"That's all we know. The legend is supposed to be open to interpretation." He swept his gaze around the circle, giving us all a devilish grin. "It's just a legend, after all."

I clapped along with everyone else, but I was flooded with disappointment. Why had the story ended so abruptly? Some pull deep inside me didn't want to leave the girl's life open to interpretation. I wanted to know who she was, what she became.

"It's so romantic!" Cassie sighed. "Oh, Skye, can you even imagine? It's like a celestial *Romeo and Juliet*!"

"If you like that kind of thing," Dan grumbled, faking a yawn. "I'd rather hear about a ski patrol with no face."

"What about you, Skye?" Asher asked quietly, squeezing himself onto the log next to me. He stretched his legs out toward the fire, and the flames exploded in a leap of spark and ash. I thought about the fire in the cave. "What did you think?"

Honestly I didn't know what to think. The story sounded so familiar, but my mind was struggling to place where I'd heard it before.

And suddenly, without warning, it came to me. All these memories came pouring back, moments long forgotten. My father holding me up to the bathroom mirror before bedtime, telling me something I couldn't quite remember. Both of us studying my reflection and laughing. He and my mother tucking me into bed. My mother's soft, clear voice singing to me as I drifted off to sleep. What was the melody of her favorite song? What were the words to her lullaby? Something about the Ancient Gifted Ones, and the Rebellion, and the love of a thousand lifetimes.

I scanned the others sitting around the fire, my eyes resting momentarily on Devin. His jaw was clenched, and I could tell he was upset. By the story? Why?

The fire popped loudly. He looked at me. And I could

see in his ice-blue eyes the warning he'd given me about Asher.

Dangerous.

I looked away from Devin. My heart was pounding.

One phrase kept replaying in my mind.

Love. The great destroyer of worlds.

How could Devin and Asher know about the songs, the stories my parents made up for me? Who *were* they? Was I just looking for connections?

"Skye?" Asher whispered into my ear. "Are you okay?"

Suddenly I was furious with him for telling the story—and at myself for letting it get to me.

Destroyer of worlds.

"Leave her alone, Asher," Devin said quietly, sternly, from his place by the fire. "You've done enough."

It was all connected in some way. It had to be. The fire. The story. The two of them, staring.

The boiler explosion.

The avalanche.

The songs.

My parents.

And the axis that brought them all together. Me.

15

Nothing was as formidable as Aunt Jo on a rampage.

She was waiting for us when we got back to the lodge near midnight, and not at all happy that Ms. Manning was allowing me to "run wild in the woods at night" after my brush with death.

"I wasn't running wild!" I insisted. Everyone was watching as they filtered back in from the campfire, and I tried to keep my voice down to avoid an even bigger scene. It was humiliating. "I was sitting. On a log. By a fire. It was very *un*-wild! It was the dictionary definition of *un*-wild. If you looked up *un*-wild on Wikipedia, you'd get a picture—"

"Get your things," she said. "I'm taking you home."

There was nothing I could do to argue.

Half an hour later, I found myself in her silver SUV, snaking down the road that led away from the lodge.

The mountain roads were dark and winding, scarier at night than they'd been in the early morning the day before. Aunt Jo drove in tense silence; I leaned my head against the window and tried to push out all the thoughts that were encroaching on my sanity.

After Asher's legend, as he'd called it, no one had been willing to compete with another story. I had hoped to catch up with Asher and Devin alone, but as the circle around the fire dissolved, Asher slipped away with Ellie and Devin simply slipped away. They were so elusive, the two of them. One minute, I felt I had a handle on each—the next, they were evaporating into the night and I was left staring into the fire, wondering what had just happened.

As I stared out the window at the night shadows, Aunt Jo muttered every now and then under her breath. I caught snippets of "almost killed," "incompetent teacher," and "if your mother were here. . . ."

"Aunt Jo," I said finally, "you don't have to worry so much about me. I'm okay. I wasn't even hurt."

"When we get back to town, we're running by the

emergency room to make sure."

The emergency room. I shuddered. I hated hospitals. I hadn't been since . . . well, since I was six. And I wasn't about to go now.

I groaned. "The medics already checked me out. I'm *fine*." And Devin had taken care of the one injury I'd had. How had he done that? Did he have some kind of hippie, voodoo medical training, where all he had to do was apply pressure to the right points, and, voilà, no more pain? Maybe I'd just been in shock from the fall and had exaggerated the pain in my ankle to begin with. It's possible that the injury hadn't even been as bad as I'd thought.

But the fire Asher had created. The way the campfire seemed to respond to him as if he were able to control it. I couldn't explain that one away.

Aunt Jo sighed. "Fine," she conceded. "But you're staying in for the rest of the weekend. And if you're walking even the slightest bit unevenly on Monday, I'm taking you to the hospital."

"What about your trip?"

"What about it, Skye? Come on. I ended it early so I could take care of you." She paused, and I could feel the whole car sigh under the weight of her thoughts. "It's not going to be for that much longer. I'm going to start looking for Jenn's replacement on Monday. I promise." Her eyes were trained on the road.

It was nearly dawn when we pulled in to the parking lot to pick up my car. When we got home, I crashed on my bed and slept the sleep of the dead. When I finally opened my eyes, the afternoon sun was streaming in. I threw on the faded maroon River Springs Community College sweatshirt that had once belonged to my dad, and padded down into the kitchen. The aroma of Aunt Jo's ancho chili rub spiked the air. Cooking was her zen; maybe this afternoon she was in a better mood.

She was at the counter next to the sink, dipping pork medallions into the spicy mix.

"How are you feeling?" she asked without turning around.

"I'm fine," I said, hopping onto a stool by the island. She turned around, her hands covered in meat and spices.

"I know you are, but it scared me, okay? I don't know what I'd do if I lost you."

"You're not going to lose me," I said quietly.

"That's what I thought about your mom," Aunt Jo said, turning back to the counter.

We were silent for a while after that.

Since I'd slept so late, the rest of the day went by quickly. We ate the pork medallions for dinner, with carrots and ginger mashed potatoes, and afterward we held a disaster movie marathon. It was nice to have this time with Aunt Jo, munching popcorn and laughing. Even if she had over-reacted. But that was kind of nice, too—to be reminded how much I meant to her.

That night I had strange dreams. In one of them Asher and I were running from a volcano. I tripped and fell in the street, and Devin was the one who saved me. Aunt Jo was there, angry that I could be stupid enough to trip. Cassie and Dan were buried under the hot, molten lava. They didn't make it.

I woke up the next morning gasping. I was once again unable to shake the feeling that I was floating above my mattress. I couldn't handle any other strange things happening to me this weekend. I didn't open my eyes until the dizziness subsided.

And that's when I realized how cold the room was.

Peeking my head out of the covers, I felt a frigid breeze brush against my face. I looked around my room, and my eyes rested on the curtains flapping gently against the wall. The window was open, though I'd been making sure to lock it every night before bed—ever since the morning after my birthday.

My heart pounding, I scrambled out of bed to close it. But I stopped short before I ever reached the window.

An inky black feather was dancing along the floorboards in the icy breeze. I had never seen anything like it before. Its length spanned at least from my elbow to wrist, and the color wasn't just black, like the crows that stalked the fields behind our house—it had an iridescence to it.

I bent to pick it up, examine it, but another gust blew the curtains into my face and before I knew it the feather was swept up by the wind and twirling through the open window, back out into the morning sky.

What kind of bird has feathers like that?

I shook my head. Too many strange things had been happening lately. Maybe on my birthday when I stepped out of the Bean, I stepped into an alternate universe.

I spent the morning reading. In the afternoon, I hiked the fields near our house. I was hoping I'd cross paths with Devin, even though I knew that was impossible. He would be at the ski lodge until the bus brought everyone home late that afternoon.

At one point along the trail, I thought I heard a branch

snap behind me. I had the unmistakable feeling that someone was watching me—but when I turned around, time after time, no one was there. I was alone, the sound of my breath echoing into the gorge.

That night I dreamed about my parents, and in my dream, they told me the story that Asher had told us around the campfire, and soon my memories became dreams and my dreams were memories. The connections were slipping from me as fast as I'd made them.

On Monday, Cassie was waiting for me in the parking lot when I drove up. Her arms were around me as soon as I got out of the car.

"Are you okay?" she cried. "Did Jo rush you off to the hospital?"

"I somehow convinced her not to," I said. "But let me know if I can't remember how to get to homeroom or suddenly start falling over in the middle of conversations, okay?"

Cassie smirked. "So you're telling me that if you start acting *weird*, to let you know?"

I nodded.

"Um, Skye?" she said, tapping me on the shoulder.

"You've been acting weird for days."

I laughed lightly and tried to play it off. "I've just been distracted, that's all."

Cassie smiled at me knowingly but didn't say anything else on the subject.

We started walking toward the main building. "How did the rest of the weekend go?" I asked.

"Not as much fun without you there, but I persevered. I can ski the bunny slope without falling now, at least. So yay me."

"Gold star!" I smiled at her.

So far, I was doing a pretty good job of pretending not to have anything pressing on my mind. But I had to ask. I took my phone out of my pocket and pretended to scroll through a few texts. "Uh, how were things with Devin and Asher?"

"Weird. They had some kind of family emergency and left a few hours after you did. At least that's what I heard."

I stopped, grabbed her arm, and spun her around to face me. "You mean they weren't there?"

"Yep. That's what 'left' means. What's wrong with you?"

"How did they leave? They came on the bus."

She rolled her shoulder in a lazy shrug. "I guess someone came to get them. It was the middle of the night.

What's the big deal?"

I wasn't sure, but something told me it was a big deal. I intended to get the answer very soon when I confronted them.

Unfortunately they were conveniently late to homeroom. Ms. Manning had already begun her morning announcements when Asher sauntered in with a you-gotta-forgive-me grin. Devin trailed in after him, avoiding her accusatory stare.

As they walked past me, Asher's grin disappeared. His gaze wandered over me as though he was searching for something. I felt my blood blaze through my cheeks. Then before I knew it, his eyes flicked away from me as he took his seat.

Devin sat down next to him, and caught my eye. *"You okay?"* he mouthed as he pushed his backpack under his chair.

I shook my head slightly. *"After class,"* I mouthed back.

But class dragged on longer than usual, just to torture me, it seemed. The clock ticked away, every second stretching into five. I sat in my seat, tearing tiny bits of paper out of my notebook and balling them up into mountains of paper snow on my desk. By the time the bell rang, I was a time bomb ready to explode.

I couldn't reach them in the swarm to leave the room. Cassie was trying to talk to me about getting tickets to a show on Thursday at Red Rocks, and when I turned away for a second, they'd disappeared.

Out in the hall, I thought I caught a glimpse of Asher's hair as he turned the corner and down a staircase. I followed, maneuvering my way through the between-classes crowd.

On the first floor, the hallways had begun to thin out. He was at the end of the hall, by my locker. He turned around. Our eyes met.

He was waiting for me.

I grabbed him by the arm and dragged him into the nearest empty classroom.

"Ooh, Skye," he said, grinning as I slammed the door behind us and pushed him up against it. "I want this, too, but not here! Not now!"

"Look, I have to talk to you," I said, ignoring him. But standing there staring into his dark eyes, it was hard to ignore how it felt to be so close to him, to be touching him. Part of me wished, just for a second, that I had pulled him in here for another reason.

I pushed that thought out of my head and pressed on.

"My ankle is healed. Completely healed, after Devin touched it. And *you* created fire, out of thin air. And before that, there was an avalanche, and before *that*, a brand-new boiler exploded in the middle of my party—when you and Devin were fighting. And you know a story that my parents used to sing to me at night as they put me to bed. How do you know it? How do you know the stories they made up just for me?"

The smile melted away from Asher's face, and his eyes grew serious. I loosened my grip on him, and he slipped away from the door, moving farther into the empty classroom.

"Look, Skye—"

"They were bedtime lullabies. Stories. That's all they were supposed to be. *Stories.* Something to help me fall asleep." As I said it out loud, I felt the adrenaline I'd been holding inside all morning begin to seep out. I sat down in an empty chair.

Asher ran a hand through his dark hair, watching me. "I'm sorry," he said, clearly agitated.

"Just tell me," I choked out. "If this involves my parents, I have a right to know."

"Look, I know how you feel. I want to, I really do. But not here." He glanced over my head toward the door. "If Devin sees us—"

"I don't care about Devin!" I yelled, my temper rising. "I want to know, Asher. Tell me." I steeled my voice, quieted it. "Does this have anything to do with my parents?"

He looked torn, his jaw working like he was grappling with something.

"Okay," he finally decided. "Meet me on the roof after school. I *will* tell you everything. I promise. Maybe not all at once, but . . ." I leveled him with my gaze, and he faltered. "It's still being worked out, a lot of it. We don't know . . ." I waited for him to finish, but it seemed like he'd said everything he was going to say.

"'We' as in . . . you and Devin?"

He rested both hands against the desk, then stood up again and paced the room restlessly.

"That's all I can tell you right now," he said. "Until it's time. It's . . . it's the one rule I promised I'd follow."

"Fine. You'd better be there." I stood to leave, but he grabbed my hand.

"I'm sorry," he said again, softer this time. I lifted my eyes from our hands and looked up into his face. I could tell that he meant it. I just wish I knew what he was sorry about.

I didn't know what to say. It was hard to remain mad when what I really felt was confused.

I pulled my hand away from his and walked into the hall. As I glanced back, I could see Asher standing there, just watching me.

The remainder of the day was a meaningless haze of random equations, dates, and other things to memorize. I couldn't stop thinking about what Asher knew—what he promised he would tell me. Part of me was nervous, but part of me, a small part, dared to hope that whatever it was did have something to do with my parents. That it would give me some clues about their life. The connection between the stories they used to tell me and his similar story at the campfire was too strong. I had to know, or I would drown in the not-knowing.

At lunch, Cassie rattled on about the weekend.

"You know Trey, from my band? He's kind of a babe, isn't he, Skye? I love that whole rumpled plaid thing. So hipster. Mmm."

"*Trey?*" Dan's face scrunched up. "Now we're on to Trey? Do you ever rest? What about the two brooding arsonists from Denver?"

Cassie stole a French fry from his plate.

"Devin and Asher? Old news," she said as she dipped it in ketchup. "Besides, I heard Ellie has the market cornered as far as Asher is concerned."

My attention snapped to her.

"What?"

"I told you to act faster," Cassie said matter-of-factly. "But I think you snoozed on this one. Ellie told some of the girls on the trip that she and Asher are together. I guess they hooked up a bunch of times or something." She swallowed. "She says he's a good kisser."

Intense heat radiated from my chest to my cheeks. I glanced over to the table where Asher usually sat surrounded by girls. Today the table was empty.

I felt like an idiot. While I'd been brooding about my dead parents and stupid lullabies from my childhood that I barely remembered, Asher had been off hooking up with her. And I didn't even know why I cared so much.

Cassie glanced at Dan then back at me.

"Sorry," she said quietly. "I know you haven't really liked someone since the whole thing with Jordan last year—"

"I don't like Asher," I cut in. "And I'm over that whole Jordan thing."

"Skye." She put her hand on my arm. "Yeah, okay. It was hard when he cheated on you with Megan Birch. It was an incredibly dick thing to do, and we all hated him for it. We still do. But you can't blame Asher for this one. You walked away from him every chance you got. Not all guys are going to totally screw you the way Jordan did. Sometimes you have to risk a little bit of pride to fall in love."

"Cassie." I sighed. "You've never been in love. How do you know what you're talking about?"

"I read it in *Cosmo*," she said. "When you like someone, you have to allow yourself to be vulnerable enough to let them in. Love is messy." She bit into a carrot. "Like the Rebels in Asher's story."

"Oh my god, stop, okay? I don't like Asher!" My voice sounded hollow.

"Devin then? I noticed him talking to you as he walked by in homeroom."

"Two words is not exactly *talking*."

"It's gotta be one of them. You should have seen the relief on your face when they strolled in."

"I was just glad that whatever their emergency was— it was okay now." I kept spinning the lies and my guilt increased with each one. I'd always been totally honest with Cassie.

Dan mentioned something about her band, and thankfully the conversation veered away from me.

As soon as the bell rang at three fifteen, I took the stairs two at a time to the roof. As I opened the fire door, the fear struck me that the roof might be empty. What would I do if Asher had been lying?

But he was there when I pushed through the heavy metal door. Waiting for me.

And so was Devin.

evin stood with his back against the water tower, his lips drawn into a tight line, arms folded across his chest. There was nothing tranquil in his expression or stance. He was all hard lines and edges.

Just a couple of feet away from him, Asher balanced on the edge of the roof, his arms spread wide. Just picturing him with Ellie after everything that had happened that weekend made my stomach churn.

I hesitated before I spoke. I was going to be cool. Controlled. I was going to pretend that what they were about to tell me didn't mean the world to me and maybe even more than that.

"Planning to jump?" I asked, placing a hand casually on my hip.

They both whipped around. Asher hopped down and grinned. "Not now."

"Did he tell you anything else?" Devin asked, shooting an accusing glare at Asher before taking a step toward me. His voice softened. "What do you know?"

"Uh, nothing," I replied, with a glance at Asher. "That's why I'm here."

"Told you," Asher said smugly. "Should we show her?"

"Show me what?"

Devin frowned. "I don't know if she's ready," he said. "It might be too much of a shock."

"In case you've forgotten, I survived an avalanche," I said, doing a relatively decent job of sounding like I wasn't terrified. "Whatever it is, I can handle it."

A look passed between them. I just stood there watching, my heart in my throat. Now that I was here, I was beginning to think that maybe it was better not to know.

Devin nodded. "Look, whatever happens, just remain calm."

I started to say okay, but then I felt the heat.

It was like the old school bus heater clanging to life, but noiseless and expanding out all around me. Then light burst in front of me like a star exploding, so bright that I had to shield my eyes and turn away.

Through my closed eyelids, I could sense the glow fade back to the dull gray sky and feel the heat melt into the bitter winter cold. I tugged my jacket tighter around me and opened my eyes.

The first thing I saw was Asher and Devin, side by side, facing me.

And then I saw the wings.

Giant wings rose from their backs in a blaze of feathers. Devin's were pure white, and light bounced off them so that the feathers resembled waves: peaking and capping, rolling, alive. Asher's were black, inky, dark, drawing the heat of the day and the light of the sun and my breath into their feathery folds.

Asher caught my eye. "Well?" he said tentatively. "What do you think?"

What did I think? That it wasn't possible. And yet, I was staring at the proof that it was. The wings were mesmerizing, the most beautiful things I'd ever seen.

I reached my fingers out involuntarily to touch one of Devin's wings. But before I could get too close, I lost my nerve and drew my hand away quickly.

Devin laughed. Seeing his face light up like that seemed odd. I'd never heard him laugh before, but the sound filled me with a sudden, inexplicable joy. It was nice to see him happy. It made him seem less reserved, and more beautiful.

"I told you it was a shock," he said, his smile lingering.

"I'm—I'm fine," I said, gulping.

The truth? I wasn't fine, not by a long shot.

I wanted to sit down, to find something to lean on. I felt dizzy, strange, out of breath. But I needed to be tensed and ready—just in case I had to run.

"What *are* you?"

Asher laughed. "You asked me to tell you how I knew the story your parents used to tell."

"Still a little confused over here," I managed.

"I know it because it's my story, too."

"It's our story," Devin added.

"What? But how . . . ?"

"It's a creation myth," Asher explained. "Your creation myth."

His words made no sense. "But it's not a creation myth," I said. "It doesn't explain how the world was created."

Asher gave me a pointed look. "Not the world, Skye. *You.*"

The sky twisted and shifted above me.

"I don't understand," I said. "Is that supposed to be a joke?"

Devin looked livid as he turned to Asher. "I knew you'd screw this up," he said, seething. "You had to be all dramatic and get a rise out of her."

"Stop it! Stop trying to freak me out! Can't you see this isn't funny for me?" I said.

"It's—it's not supposed to be funny," Asher insisted, taking several steps toward me. "It's your heritage." He said the last bit quietly, almost as if I'd offended him.

My knees buckled beneath me and gave way. I felt dehydrated, dizzy; the roof tilted and pitched as I grabbed desperately at the concrete, trying to get it to stay still.

"Shh," Asher murmured, taking the last few steps and kneeling next to me. I felt his hand on my back. "Hey."

"Are you saying that the Rebel and the Guardian in the story—they're my parents?" My voice sounded far away, as if those were someone else's words, not mine.

Asher looked up at Devin for support. Devin nodded somberly. His wings folded gracefully behind him, crisscrossing each other before melting seamlessly into his back. My chest tightened and I fought for air. The sky was caving in around me, and I lay back against the freezing concrete and closed my eyes. "I c-can't breathe," I said, wheezing. "Asher?"

"I'm here," he said. "You're okay."

"I—I need to go home."

Devin stepped in. "I'll take you." He reached a hand down to me, and I took it as he pulled me up. He glared at Asher. "I knew I shouldn't trust you. Of course you'd find a way to mess this up."

I wanted to say that it wasn't Asher's fault, but I had no idea what Devin meant. What was "this"? What were they trying to tell me? That the myth was true? I tried to remember what else Asher had told us that night around the campfire. Something about Paradise? I stumbled, and Devin caught me in his sturdy arms.

Asher looked like he wanted to say more—but for once,

he didn't. I was grateful. It made it easier to leave.

Devin led me toward the fire door. Just before I started down the stairs, I turned. Asher's own black wings were folding behind him, glittering in the final moments of daylight and disappearing into some part of him I couldn't see.

My mind was tugged in a thousand different directions as we walked through the parking lot. I barely noticed all the remaining cars that belonged to the students involved in after-school practices and meetings.

Even before these guys showed up in my life, I'd felt like I was different from everyone else I knew. How would I fit in with Cassie, Dan, and Ian? Holding this secret—a secret so big that it felt like it would consume me.

I must have shivered, because Devin took his jacket off and hung it across my shoulders lightly, almost as if he was afraid to touch me. I hoped he didn't realize that it wasn't just the cold I was shivering from.

"Thanks."

He was quiet, leaving me to my own thoughts. And there were lots of them. Every now and then I would begin a sentence and leave it unfinished, trailing off into the bitter night air.

Finally Devin turned to me, his face illuminated as we passed under a streetlight. "That happened very quickly, much more suddenly than I would have liked." Then we were back in the dark, his face hidden again. I saw him relax and realized he preferred if I couldn't see him. "If you have questions, you can ask me." We were almost at my car; I could see it a couple of rows away.

"What are you?" It was the question I'd asked before that they'd managed to avoid answering.

"I'm a Guardian. A messenger."

My head spun. "Okay, you know what? *So* not ready to know any more right now."

Devin seemed to take me seriously, because he didn't say anything else. We reached the row my car was in and started down it.

"So was there a school in Denver that burned down?" I asked.

"Yes," he confirmed. "But we weren't students there. Our paperwork is forged. It was Asher's idea to use that story." Devin grimaced. "We needed an excuse to transfer in the middle of the year."

"Why now?"

"Because you turned seventeen, and the Elders have always believed that if anything was going to happen, it would happen now. When you're on the verge of adulthood.

"Wait, what do you mean, 'happen'? Like what?"

"That's just it, Skye. We don't know. So I was sent to watch you. And of course, the Rebels didn't trust me to report honestly to them, so they sent Asher." He took a breath. "It's like in the story Asher told. There needed to be agents from both sides."

So that explained their animosity toward each other. "So you're not really cousins."

"Only in the same way that you would be related to Cassie through Adam and Eve. Somewhere in our genealogy we share a common ancestor. But that's about it."

I suddenly realized just how utterly exhausted I was. The excitement of the past few days was really catching up to me. I stopped a few feet away from my car and leaned on a steel-blue Saab. "It's all so much."

"It's okay," he said. "You don't have to say anything right now. You have time to process all this. I've, uh—what do they say?" He turned to me and smiled awkwardly. "I've got your back?"

I laughed—or at least I started out laughing, but before I knew it, my laughter turned into choking, and I turned away so that Devin couldn't see the tears streaming down my face. He must have noticed anyway, because he put his arm around me gently, as though he could infuse me with the tranquility he always seemed to emit when we were alone. When Asher wasn't there.

"It's all right, Skye," he said softly. "That's the reason I'm here. To watch over you, to protect you."

I surprised myself. I melted into him and buried my face in his chest. I could feel his breathing hitch in his throat. Slowly his other arm wrapped around me.

"The fight . . . that night at the Bean . . . during my birthday . . . was that about me?"

I felt him stiffen, hesitate, then relax. "Yes. Asher made contact with you before we were supposed to. It upset the balance of things and has been causing chaos ever since. It's like I've tried to tell you. He's dangerous."

There was that word again. *Dangerous*. But it meant so many different things. Dangerous because of his effect on Devin? Dangerous because I had no idea who—or what— Asher truly was? Or maybe— Could I even let myself think it? Maybe he was dangerous because of the effect he had on me.

"Are you all right?" Devin asked after several moments. He was holding me so close that I could feel him swallow.

"No." I sobbed. "I'm the opposite of all right." He brushed his hand over my back, and I started to feel calmer. "I didn't really get a chance to know my parents that well. I was so young when they died. I have no idea if the memories I have of them are real or . . . if I, you know, made them up. And now you're messing with all that. All the memories I thought were one thing. Now you're telling me . . ." But I couldn't finish. I didn't know how.

I pulled away from his chest and looked into his eyes. Something flashed in them. Confusion? Something more? As though he was only just seeing me for the first time. He touched my cheek. "You're so special. In ways . . . I wasn't expecting."

He tensed and abruptly released me. "I have to go," he said with an unexpected icy demeanor, and my heart sank at the abrupt change. "I'll see you at school tomorrow."

"Okay."

He seemed to have second thoughts. "Skye," he said almost tenderly. "Tonight you're tired. I know. But soon you're going to have to meet your destiny."

"And if I don't want to meet it?"

He didn't smile. This was all so serious for him. He was on a mission even if I didn't completely understand it.

"It'll be easier if you embrace it," he said.

"For whom?"

"Everyone. Trust me, Skye. I . . . care about you. Probably

more than I should. I only want what's best for you."

"How can you know what's best for me?" I asked. "You just met me."

"The Order can see our destiny. It guides us. It allows us to exist in a place with no fear."

Maybe that was why he always looked so calm. I wondered what it would be like to live in a place where there was no fear. Maybe, I thought, that was some kind of Paradise after all.

He nodded at my car. "Are you okay to drive home?"

I was upset, but I wasn't dizzy anymore. I could drive.

"Barring any unforeseen disasters, I think I can manage."

Devin reached as though to touch my cheek and then dropped his hand to his side. "I know all of this is overwhelming, scary. But think of that afternoon when we sat on the boulders. How peaceful it all was. The Order is like that, only much, much more so. It's beautiful, Skye. You shouldn't fear it."

I swallowed. "I'll see you at school tomorrow?"

He nodded and, with a slight smile, trudged away. I didn't want to admit that I was sorry to see him go. I walked up to my car and unlocked the door. As I got in, I had that same prickly feeling I'd had when I felt Asher watching me on the first day of the new semester. I whipped around, wondering if Asher had followed me.

But it wasn't Asher.

Several rows away, I caught a glimmer of blond hair. A stunning girl stood glaring at me. I'd never seen her before. But something in her shocking blue eyes was familiar and cold. Instinctively I slammed my door, locking it behind me. But when I looked out the window, the girl was gone.

I fought my way out of bed the next morning and, legs shaky, somehow managed to get in the shower. I turned the water up as hot as possible without scalding myself, letting the steam billow in clouds. I tilted my head back and opened my eyes; the beads of water clinging to the ceiling reflected lots of little me's, all staring back down. Had the night before really happened? And the night before that? In the new light of morning, everything they'd told me seemed impossible. Even in the steamy bathroom, I shivered as the next logical question snaked its way into my brain. If my parents were a Guardian of the Order and a member of the Rebellion—what did that make me?

Could I really have lived seventeen years knowing

nothing about who I really was?

It struck me that I could simply choose not to believe them. Maybe if I ignored Devin and Asher and just kept moving forward, not letting myself get tripped up over any of this, it would all just go away. I could go back to being Skye Parker, star of the Northwood High ski team and Columbia University shoo-in. Even as I pictured it, I doubted that I could live with so many questions ignored. So many left unanswered.

I turned the hot and cold knobs at the same time, and the water shut off with a sharp squeak.

Now that Asher and Devin had opened the floodgates—whatever they led to—I wondered if it was even possible to go back to the way things were.

I grabbed Devin's jacket off my desk chair once I was dressed and ready to leave. It was no longer warm, but it did smell like him: crisp, clean, like the air at the top of a mountain.

There was a note from Aunt Jo on the kitchen table.

> *Hey Rock Star,*
> *At the office late tonight. Planning a trip out at the*
> *end of the week. You'll be okay for dinner, right? There's*

lots of frozen stuff in the freezer.

Love, Aunt Jo

A warm, unexpected surge of relief flooded me. Aunt Jo was the one person I couldn't keep secrets from. With her out of the house, I wouldn't have to worry about how to avoid telling her that the girl she'd known for the past seventeen years, the girl she'd raised, might not be who she seemed to be.

My goal was to swing by Devin's locker and drop off his jacket on my way to homeroom. But when I approached the north corridor, my heart dropped into my stomach. Devin was standing at his locker, engaged in a heated conversation with the blond girl who'd been standing in the parking lot the night before. As I stood there, an image from one of my nightmares suddenly came rushing back: a pair of scorching blue eyes boring a hole in the atmosphere, all of the oxygen seeping out of it into the blackness of outer space, the air sucked out of my lungs and swirling among the stars.

I almost turned around—I'd give him his jacket in homeroom—but something stopped me. Instinct told me to stay out of sight. That I'd want to hear what they were talking about. Taking a breath, I ducked behind the nearest row of lockers and tried not to make a sound.

"I can't believe you're here," I heard Devin whisper fiercely. "It's so incredibly risky, Raven. What if they find out? You're being . . . rebellious." He said it with the same tone someone might use if accusing a person of being a serial killer.

"Pardon me for *looking out for you*," she spat. Then her voice got softer. "Besides, they know I'm here. They're worried about you, too. Please, Devin, you have to come back. Tell the Gifted to give this mission to someone else. Maybe they'll do it this time. If you really beg—"

"Someone else?" Devin's voice cut in, sharp. "Beg? What makes you think this time will be any different from the last? Or the time before that? I do what they tell me. I have no choice. Look, we talked about this before I left. You knew I would be gone for a while. I'll see you soon, okay? You just have to—"

"You can't know how soon it will be." Her voice dropped, and I had to hold my breath and strain my ears to hear what she said next. "You know what kind of mission this is. It's different from the ones before."

"But I've been training for it for so long. All of my other missions were simply training for this one."

"What about us? We are supposed to be together—it's fated, and so it shall be. There is something about her that gives me chills. I wish you would stay away from her."

I let out my breath in a small gasp. They were talking about *me*. How could I possibly give someone like *her* the chills?

"You know I can't do that."

"Then I wish you would think carefully about the legend. There are so many things we don't yet know. About who she is. What she can do to us."

"You're scared."

"I don't have the capacity for fear." Her tone was simple, matter-of-fact. Like she was saying she wasn't very good at math.

"Because you've been sheltered by the Order. You don't understand how dangerous it is out here."

"I can understand the danger without being afraid of it. It's you I'm worried about. That's why I'm here."

"And you shouldn't be. You have no choice except to let me see this through to the end," he said flatly. "Neither of us does."

"But—"

"I was picked for this. It's an honor that I will not turn away from."

My heart was pounding, and I could hear Raven's voice shake as she spoke.

"Devin, come home," she said quietly.

"I have to finish this. We'll be together when I get back—"

"*If* you get back."

"*When.*" Devin's voice was firm. "When I get back. If I do what they ask me to, I'll have their respect. This will be a good thing for us."

"And if—when—you come back, we'll have the ceremony? We'll be bonded?"

"You know that we will."

There was a pause. Then Raven said in a low growl, "If you don't fix this, I'm going to."

I couldn't hear anything else. My hands, holding Devin's jacket, were shaking. Who was this girl? *You know what kind of mission this is.* I had no idea what that meant, but it sounded like she was the same thing as Devin: a Guardian. I couldn't shake how strange it was that they sounded as if they were supposed to be together, and yet . . . something about the exchange creeped me out.

Suddenly Raven walked by, so fast that her blond hair flapped sharply and I could feel a lingering breeze in her wake.

Steeling myself, I stepped out from behind the lockers. Devin was still standing over by his. His locker door was open, but he was just staring into it. One hand rested limply on one of his textbooks, as if he'd been about to take it out.

I approached him slowly. I wasn't sure if I should mention what I just overheard. But before I had a chance to open my mouth, Devin whirled around. Staring daggers at me, he slammed his locker door, grabbed his jacket from my hands, and stormed off.

"*Y*ou look distracted," Cassie said before taking a bite of a steamed carrot. The cafeteria bustled around us. "You've got, like"—she motioned under her eyes—"bags or something. Are you okay?"

"I didn't sleep well last night," I said, yawning.

"Maybe it's post-traumatic stress. You know, from being an avalanche survivor. Maybe you should talk to the counselor, see about getting into a support group. I shudder every time I think about what happened to you."

I seriously doubted that there were support groups for avalanche survivors, but it was pointless to argue. My problems were far greater than surviving the avalanche.

"No, I'm completely over that," I said. Involuntarily I

glanced across the cafeteria. Asher sat at his usual table, surrounded by another crowd of girls. But today there was something different about him. When he looked up and caught me staring, the sly façade dropped, and his eyes went soft, serious. *"Hi,"* he mouthed. He waved slightly.

Instinctively I looked away. Why did he make me so nervous? Why couldn't I just say hi back?

"Skye," Cassie said. "Soooo, aren't you going to ask me about *my* day?"

"Huh?"

"Well, you know, we have been talking an awful lot about you lately. Not that it wasn't deserved, what with everything you've gone through, but . . ." She was chewing her bottom lip. I knew what that meant.

"Oh god," I said. "I'm so sorry. Don't be mad."

"I'm not mad, I'm just saying." She fiddled with a carrot. I looked at her.

"You're kind of mad."

"Okay. *Kind* of."

I put the sandwich down and put my elbows on the table, chin in hands.

"Cassie," I said. "How was your day?"

"Great! The Mysterious Ellipses have a gig next week at the Bean."

"The what?" I asked.

"The Mysterious Ellipses. It's the new name of our band. You like?"

"Yeah," I said. "It's very . . ."

"Trey thinks it's funny." She looked bored, though, as she said it, and I knew her interest in him was already half forgotten. "I think it has a catchier ring to it. No one knew what The Somnambulists meant."

"But why are the Ellipses mysterious?"

"Because when you put ellipses at the end of a sentence, they automatically make whatever you are saying sound mysterious."

I couldn't argue. How many times had Cassie and I stayed up all night composing the perfect text message? Probably seven out of ten had ellipses at the end to cultivate an air of mystique.

"So when are the Ellipses playing?" I asked.

"The *Mysterious* Ellipses," Cassie corrected.

"Do I have to say the full name every time?"

"Yes," Cassie said. "Otherwise it makes no sense. Anyway, you have to come. It's going to be awesome."

"Of course," I said. "How could I miss the Mysterious Ellipses' first show?"

"See?" Cassie beamed. "You're catching on."

I nodded, an awkward silence settling between us. It was hopeless. I couldn't make conversation with my thoughts so far away. And Cassie looked distracted, too. She kept looking over my shoulder every time someone walked past, but I was too tired to think about what was bothering her. I yawned again.

"Where's Dan?"

"What?" Cassie's head snapped back to me. "Why?"

"Um, no reason. Just wondering where he is."

"Who knows what that boy does with his free time," she grumbled.

I wished I could tell Cassie about the conversation I'd overheard between Raven and Devin. Things kept getting stranger, more confusing, harder to believe. I had to talk to Asher. I knew that he would tell me the truth.

Just as I was loading my backpack with books to take home at the end of the day, they cornered me: Asher at my left elbow and Devin at my right.

"Come on," Asher said. "Let's walk down the hall while we have a secret conversation."

"Another one?" I smirked, trying to maintain some semblance of cool. But inside my stomach was sinking. I wasn't sure how much more secret information I could take.

"There's more you need to know," Devin said. "It will help you in all this."

"All *what*, exactly?" My voice was getting louder. "What do you mean by 'all this'?"

"Calm down." Asher was cocky as ever. "There's more to the story than we told you yesterday. Maybe if you didn't have such a weak stomach, we wouldn't have had to schedule a Part Two. But you were all, 'nooo, to be continued' . . ."

"You're a real pain, Asher," I pointed out.

"And don't I know it." He raised an eyebrow at me. "Anyway, don't look so panicked. We're here to help you."

"It sure doesn't—"

"I know, I know, it sure doesn't seem like it. But trust me. We don't want to hurt you. And you're going to want to hear what we have to say."

We were at the front doors to the school at that point, and the sharp sunlight hurt my exhausted eyes. I lifted a hand to shield them.

"Where are we going?" I asked.

"To practice," Devin said gruffly.

"Practice? Practice what?"

"Your po—" Asher started to say, but Devin's head whipped around, and he gave Asher a stern glare. Asher looked sheepish. "Stuff," he said.

"Great," I mumbled under my breath. "My 'stuff' was getting rusty, anyway."

"Come on," Devin said, putting on sunglasses. "You're driving." He headed toward the parking lot.

"Skye." Asher turned to me when Devin was a few feet ahead of us. The after-school crowd swarmed around us, and he leaned in close so that he didn't have to raise his voice. "I know this is all a shock to you, and you have every right to be wary and freaked out. But I want you to do me a favor. Trust me. Can you do that?"

"I don't know," I said, instantly thinking about Ellie— and Jordan. I didn't know if I could trust Asher, not yet. What did I really know about him?

He looked a little offended. "I'm not going to hurt you," he said, and walked down the steps.

After a pause, I followed.

We drove a few miles outside of town, to a field where Devin was convinced no one would see us. He led the way as we crunched across the icy grass. I walked behind him, and Asher held up the rear. None of us said much. I didn't know about the two of them, but I was too nervous to string words together coherently.

The light was bleak, the field colorless and anemic. As we approached the start of a path where it forged ahead into the woods, a winter bird perched on a nearby tree alighted in a flap of wings. The noise echoed across the empty field.

Devin stopped and faced me.

"Seems as deserted a spot as any," Asher said under his breath as he scanned the empty clearing.

"Before we explain anything else, let's get some things straight. Your parents are the nomads in the story Asher told you. On that we're clear?" Devin asked.

I nodded, my heart pounding. "And me?"

"Yes, you know what I'm going to say. You are their child. And—" He glanced at Asher, who nodded in some kind of agreement.

"Skye, for this to make sense, we need to tell you the truth," Asher said.

"Meaning what? You've been lying to me up until now?"

"You're being difficult."

"You're tearing apart everything I've ever known to be true. Did you think I wouldn't rebel a little?"

He gave me a warm grin. "Actually, I do appreciate the rebellion."

"You would," Devin said cuttingly.

"Okay. Enlighten me."

"The Order," Asher began. "They oversee Earth . . . but they're not exactly, uh, *from* Earth."

"Obviously." I didn't bother to hide my impatience. I was ready for straight-up honesty between all of us.

"We're unearthly beings," Devin cut in. "We're—"

I closed my eyes. I already knew what was coming. "You're angels, right?"

"Yes, in a manner of speaking," he said. "It's complicated. I suppose if it's easier for you to classify us that way, you can, though I barely know what that word means anymore. We are also known as *Malakh*, messengers. We believe we are the ones who keep Earth running."

"But yeah," Asher chimed in. "The wings are the same in any language."

"A lot written about us is pure fiction," Devin continued, ignoring Asher. "There is so much that's glossed over or interpreted in various ways for the sake of convenience."

Remembering all of Devin's complaints about Asher's aversion to following rules, I turned to Asher. "You're a Rebel?" He nodded. "You broke off from the Order and left Paradise? So what is that, like a *fallen* angel?"

"We're not exactly 'fallen,'" Asher said huffily. "I guess you could say we jumped."

"So my father, he was one of you?"

"Yup. Right up until the day he—"

"Met my mother, yeah, I know." It was beginning to come together. "Are you a messenger, too?"

"I often am," he said. "I'm often sent out on what you could call, like, counterintelligence missions. You know one of the basic laws of nature: for every action there is an equal and opposite *re*action?"

"Uh, yeah?"

"Well . . . if you think of the Guardians as messengers of fate, keeping order, balance, manipulating destinies—then we're dispatched to, you know, *stop* that from happening. We're like our own system of checks and balances."

"*Manipulate* is a strong word, Rebel," Devin argued. "Are you sure you want to start this now?"

"I'll start it up any time you want, but I think we'd better keep our focus on Skye at the moment," Asher spat.

"Uh, guys?" I shouted. "Enough? I have another question. A big one."

They looked at me.

"Ask it," Devin said.

"Well, if my mother was a Guardian, and my dad was a Rebel, and they were both angels but they were both mortal when I was born . . . what does that make *me*?"

"That," Devin said, "is exactly what we're here to find out. You are different. Special. The daughter caught between the Order of the Natural World and the chaos that tries to unravel it. Your destiny and your powers are completely unknown."

"My powers?"

"Oh yes," Devin said, smiling for the first time all afternoon. "Your powers."

A cold wind blew through the trees and swept across the field. Asher looked dubiously at the sky.

I shivered. "What kind of powers?"

"We're not human," Asher reminded me. "Of course we have powers. Some we were born with, some we developed out of what I'd call necessity."

"That's skipping ahead a bit," Devin said, placing a tense hand on Asher's shoulder. "But the gist of it is true. The Gifted are born with the Sight, as we've told you. And the Guardians in turn have other gifts. Nothing like foreseeing destinies but a few cognitive and precognitive abilities. A subtle influence on people's minds. One of the most useful ways this manifests is in our ability to intuit—to connect with—pain. And heal it."

"So you did heal my ankle?" I cried. "I knew it wasn't crazy!"

"Far from it. Though I shouldn't have revealed myself to you so soon, before you knew and understood the true extent of your heritage. I'm sorry for—"

"Freaking her out?" Asher cut in with a wry smile.

Devin bristled. "Precisely."

"You're one to talk," I said to Asher. "You freaked me out when you did the fire thing in the cave. Remember?"

Devin wheeled on him. "You showed her your ability to bring forth fire?"

"She was freezing. What was I supposed to do? Let hypothermia kick in?"

"You're incredible," Devin said, his tone indicating the opposite.

"Says the guy who healed her broken ankle."

"I've been ordered to protect her."

"So have I."

"Hey, guys, could we take the chest beating down a notch and get back to explaining to me how all this stuff works?"

They both averted their gazes.

"What about the Rebellion's powers?" I prodded Asher.

"Did anything change when you left the Order, or are yours the same as Devin's?"

"Skye, watching out for you is about the only thing Devin and I have in common," he said. "When the Rebellion formed and broke away, their original powers were lost. I don't know if the Order reclaimed them or if they simply faded when the Rebellion made their home on Earth. Over time, Rebels developed their own unique set of powers. Powers that they took from the earth itself and use to give back to it. Elemental forces. Water, fire, rain. We can create storms. The ultimate physical arsenal, to combat the Order's mental manipulation."

"Whoa," I breathed.

"Yeah. I say 'they,' because this was long before my time. Our new powers came over hundreds of thousands of years," he explained.

"Are you guys immortal?" I asked.

"No," Devin said. "Though our aging process works in an entirely different way from yours."

"Angels aren't gods," added Asher. "We're born, we grow old, and we die. We just do it all kind of . . ." He paused, searching. "Differently. Like Devin said."

"So you're not really my age? Or is it some weird trick of the light that you look seventeen?"

"I haven't been seventeen for a long time," Asher said, almost, if I interpreted right, a little wistfully. It made me want to rush over and hold him. What would it be like to live so long, to see so many changes occur?

"We do share many of the same properties as humans, it's true. We look like you, for one. We understand and speak your many languages." Devin was ticking things off on his fingers as though he was going through a memorized list. "But it's important to remember that we're not human, Skye."

"But . . . okay," I said. "Here's the thing. If I have—what you said—if I have, like, powers. What kind will I have? Will I become one of you, completely? Will I be an angel?" I paused, not sure I wanted to know the answer to the question that came next. "Will I no longer be human?"

Asher shook his head. "Well, you're already different from other people in ways you may or may not have noticed. Think about it. You're a little bit faster. A little bit stronger. Haven't you won every single one of your races this season?"

"Because I practice my ass off," I said defiantly. The sportswoman in me couldn't accept that I'd had an unfair advantage. My conscience would compel me to return all my trophies and medals. And how would I explain it? I had performance-enhancing angel genes?

"It's more than that, Skye. And didn't you just survive an avalanche—with your worst injury a broken ankle?"

"But I couldn't heal it myself," I protested. "Devin did."

"Doesn't matter," Asher said. "Just the fact that you survived is amazing. Devin, he's sort of influenced everyone into thinking that your fall wasn't that big a deal, but it was."

"If you weren't at least a little bit like us, you might not have made it," Devin added. His hands were in his pockets, and he looked almost sad.

Asher continued. "Your powers haven't completely formed yet. We don't know whether you'll develop the Guardians' abilities or the Rebels'. We don't know what forms the powers brewing inside of you will take. But when they do manifest, you'll be your own thing. Not all human but not all angel."

He took a step forward, and I could see the passion and fire in his eyes. He was trying to convey how important all of this was. "This is what you were born for, Skye. To be part of our world, to embrace your destiny," Asher quietly insisted. "Whatever your powers, being with us is what you were always meant to do."

"You don't have to be afraid of the path, Skye," Devin added. "Because it will lead you to us and to a calm you've never known."

"Okay," I said hesitantly. "Show me what I can do."

·21·

"Okay now, pay attention," Devin said. "I'm going to demonstrate—"

Plumes of fire exploded against the dark sky.

Spinning around, he glared at Asher. "We had agreed that I would give the first lesson."

"Sorry. I couldn't resist." But Asher didn't look sorry at all. He looked rather amused.

Devin turned his attention back to me. "What he just did, ignoring the rules, is not tolerated."

"By the Order. The Rebellion refers to it as independent thinking. Initiative," Asher said.

"It creates chaos—as you've just proven. Here we are wasting time with your games instead of teaching Skye what she needs to know."

Bowing deeply, Asher extended his hand. "Continue."

As much as I hated to admit it, the bickering helped me to relax just a little.

Devin straightened his wings and focused on me again. "You should be able to feel a well deep inside you and just reach in——" He flung his arms out toward the sky, and branches of the trees surrounding the clearing began dancing wildly. The strong wind hadn't even been a hint of breeze a few minutes earlier.

"Wow," I said. "Was that a cognitive ability?"

"It's more than that," Asher said. "Air is ethereal, of the clouds. Like the Rebellion controls the dark and stormy, earthy elements." He waved his hand out, and the ground rumbled beneath my feet, causing me to stumble and almost lose my balance.

Suddenly I was so cold that I was surprised I didn't freeze completely. I whipped around and Devin stood behind me, arms outstretched, smiling.

Asher sent fire rushing past me and my skin prickled with heat, but when the two elements clashed, they erupted with a loud crack—like ice being hit with heat—and died out.

"I'm supposed to be able to do all of that?" I asked.

"We don't know what you're capable of," Devin said.

"Just try and see what you can do. Start small."

"Okay." I searched for that well that Devin talked about, but all I found was emptiness. "I'm sorry. I'm just not feeling it."

"Like this," Asher said. "Watch."

For the next few hours, the two angels showed me the vast, terrifying extent of what they were able to do—what they thought I might be capable of doing, too. Thunder clapped. Bursts of fire flew toward the gathering dark clouds. Asher broke the ground apart; Devin caused it to reform, erasing all evidence of the destruction. The wind circled around us, but our hair stayed in place. Rain pummeled the earth, but somehow the three of us stayed bone dry. Their powers were so controlled. They could help or hurt. Heal or destroy.

As I watched the fire and wind swirl together, the pieces were finally coming together for me. My destiny. Though I reminded myself as I watched them that I might be able to do all or none of those things, I couldn't discount that there *were* strange things happening around me lately. The boiler. The thermostat. The bus heater. The avalanche. I could explain all of them rationally. And yet, I couldn't deny that what Devin and Asher demonstrated could also explain the weirdness a lot better than I wanted to acknowledge.

As they wreaked havoc around us, sometimes I couldn't tell who was responsible for what. Dark powers, light powers. I imagined if these two groups ever went to war against each other, it would be the end of the world.

Every now and then, they would stop and wait. Wait for me to follow their lead and cause a single spark or tremor. But all I caused was disappointment. The irony wasn't lost on me that the weird things that had been occurring all around me always seemed to happen when I wasn't prepared for them. Now that I was actively *trying* to make my powers manifest—they failed me.

"Skye!" Devin shouted. He was hidden by the shadows of the night that had descended around us. "Are you paying attention?"

"Yes!" I shouted back. "It's freezing and my fingers are numb!" I waved my hands around in front of my face. "No fire. No wind. No healing. *Nada*."

"I don't think you get how serious this is," he said, his white wings growing brighter as he emerged from the dark, bringing with him his own light.

"Look, maybe I don't have any powers at all. You said I might not."

Devin sighed. "I thought what happened on the bus . . .

with the heater . . . that maybe you caused that."

"Could have been bad wiring," Asher said. He blended in so well with inky blackness at the edge of the clearing.

"You don't believe that," Devin challenged.

"Doesn't matter what I believe."

"Let's pack it in for the night. We'll resume tomorrow at three fifteen sharp. On the school roof."

School. I had school tomorrow. After everything I'd learned that day, I almost laughed. How could I go back there and pretend to be normal when that was anything but how I felt?

"Skye?"

"Yeah," I said. "Okay."

Devin's wings closed in a rush of movement so fast I felt the wind on my face. Seconds later, he had vanished. Whether he had simply flown away or dissolved into thin air, I couldn't tell.

I looked down at my hands. Could I create fire? Wind? Would I be able to heal someone else's pain as Devin could? Did I truly have these powers churning inside?

A few feet away from where I stood, a branch hung from a nearby tree, broken and hanging at an awkward angle. I brought my hands up and pushed the air in front of me, hard. I focused all of my energy through my fingers, trying to channel what Devin had told me about healing. *Visualize the wound. Gather it to you. Feel the life force flow. Correct the balance.*

The branch swayed slightly in the wind.

That was it.

"Hey," came a voice from the darkness.

It was Asher. I hadn't even noticed he was standing there; his wings bled into the darkness as if they weren't solid.

"You have to rest."

"I want to keep trying," I said as I began to walk toward the tree.

Asher walked behind me, keeping pace. "You have to stop for the night," he persisted. "This is your first day. You don't want to burn out."

I ignored him.

"Did you get that? Just trying some Rebellion humor. . . ."

Instead of answering him, I wrapped my hands around the split in the branch, where it hung like an arm from a broken shoulder. That was how Devin had healed my ankle. He'd wrapped his hands around the swelling, his grip intense, and seconds later, the pain was gone. *What if I could make pain disappear? What a useful power that would be. Could I heal more than physical pain?* I wondered if I could cure emotional pain, too.

The branch broke off in my hand. I cursed under my breath.

I felt hands fall gently on my shoulders.

"Come on," Asher said. "Let's go."

My car was still on the road where we'd left it.

We'd walked back across the field in silence; Asher held a small flame in his hand to help us find our way. I took my keys from my pocket, and before I could even press the unlock button, Asher snatched them from my grasp.

"I'm driving," he said.

"I can do it," I told him testily.

"You're tense and exhausted," he countered. "Just get in."

I stared at him, trying to wear him down. He didn't budge.

"Fine," I said. "But if you wreck my car, you're dead."

I walked around and climbed into the passenger seat. When he settled behind the wheel, I asked, "Do you even know how to drive?"

"I know how to do everything."

I laughed and settled back against the seat. As my mind worked to process everything I'd learned the past couple of days, Asher's hand came to rest on mine. How was it that he always seemed to know exactly what I needed right when I needed it?

We pulled into my driveway, and he cut the engine. Without the hum of the motor, the quiet was vast.

"Thanks for driving me home," I said.

"No problem. You think I'd let you come home alone after a day like this?"

"Devin did."

"Devin is his own rare species of weird," Asher muttered. "Don't let him play mind games with you."

It was obvious the topic upset him so I let it go. I didn't stop thinking about it, though.

Are you *playing mind games with me?* I wondered. It was suddenly so hard to comprehend what was real and what wasn't. This hidden world, these magical powers—the unbelievable truth about my parents. How could they have never told me? Couldn't they have left me a journal or something? But then they hadn't expected to be ripped from my life so soon, either.

"Asher," I said in the dark. "Do you want to see something?"

He nodded without saying a word. I opened my car door and got out. Seconds later, he did the same. I took his hand and pulled him with me around to the side of the house, looking upward. The ladder crawled up the deep brown shingles, disappearing where the roof ledge dropped off into the velvety black sky. It was tangled in vines that had grown over the years, mistaking it for a trellis.

"Come on," I said, starting to climb. It was a route I could travel in my sleep.

Asher put his hand on the bottom rung. "I get the feeling I should have asked where we were going." In the shadows, I couldn't see his face. *I can trust him*, I thought. *Right?*

"Come on," I challenged. "What are you, afraid of heights?" I kept climbing. My shoulders worked and my legs stepped carefully and it felt good just to move, upward, and think. Or not think.

Soon I crested the roof ledge and crawled several feet across the sloping surface. Asher was right behind me. I pulled my knees to my chest and stared out at the stars. He sat down next to me. Our breath made clouds of steam in the freezing night air.

"Is that where angels are from?" I nodded at the stars.

He chuckled. "Nah. It's really more of an alternate realm than a city in the sky. I've never even been there." He looked up. "Anyway, the Rebellion camp is somewhere else."

"Where?"

He looked pensive. "On Earth, actually."

"Where?" I asked again.

"Far, far away."

It was so quiet on the roof. I couldn't even hear any passing cars from the road. The only sound, for miles, was the distant howl of a coyote.

"Maybe you'll see it, one day," Asher said.

"So we're not so different," I said quietly, almost more to myself than to him. Asher glanced at me sideways, shifting uncomfortably.

"In that way, no."

"Do you ever regret leaving the Order?"

"I was never in it. Most of us weren't. Only the very first Rebel Elders were a part of it. And we're not allowed back there now." He paused. "So I live here. But based on how bound Devin is to his commands . . . I have to say that I'm very glad not to be part of the Order."

"Why does he think they're so important?"

"He's brainwashed."

Or was Asher? How could I know which side was the right side—if either was right? How did I know which was where I truly belonged? Maybe I belonged here, exactly where I was. It had been a very long time since I'd missed my parents so desperately. I wished they could be here to guide me.

"I came up here every day over the summer," I said.

He was silent.

"It's a good place to think. When I'm not skiing, this is where I feel the most at peace."

We just sat there. After a second or two, I rested my head against his shoulder and breathed deep. He smelled like grass and pine needles. Our breath intertwined in the cold air.

"I know," Asher said quietly.

It took me a moment to figure out what he was saying.

"You know what?" When he didn't respond, my heart beat faster. "You know this is where I feel the most at peace?"

He nodded slowly.

"How do you know that?" I asked, sitting up.

Asher sighed, as if he'd been avoiding this. "When we met? That wasn't the first time I'd seen you."

"Then what *was*?" I stared at him. "Enough with the cloak and dagger—just tell me."

"Before that."

"Like how far before that?"

"Pretty far."

"Like what, a year?"

He was silent.

"What, two years?" Nothing. "Three?"

"Long enough to know you pretty well." He coughed and cleared his throat awkwardly. "It was, um, part of the assignment. That's how we knew when to make ourselves known to you. When your eyes flashed that first time, things were about to start."

When my eyes flashed. I tried to remember something my father used to tell me when I was little. Holding me up to the bathroom mirror each night before I went to bed. Something I couldn't quite retrieve, some memory I couldn't reach . . . we were staring at my eyes. . . .

"Wow," I whispered. I didn't know whether to feel scared or protected . . . or a little of both. "Have you . . . seen things? I mean, what do you know about me?"

"Everything, Skye."

"I seriously doubt that," I said, getting ruffled.

"Try me."

"Fine." I shoved him. "Okay. What's my favorite lunch?"

"Turkey sandwich and an apple," he said, buffing his nails on his shirt and mock-yawning.

"Too easy," I said. "You could have seen that this month. What about favorite color?"

"Obvious." He snorted. "Sky blue. Has been since kindergarten."

"Lucky guess. You just said that because of my name. Favorite book?"

"*Persuasion*, by Jane Austen—though you'd never admit it to anyone. You secretly think it's romantic that they have all these feelings for each other that they can't express."

I looked out at the constellations. "You lie," I said.

"No way, it's true. You did your seventh grade end-of-year presentation on how it was bullshit, but anyone really watching you knew you loved that book." He shifted his position and added, "It's why you stayed with Jordan for so long, even though you knew he cheated on you. You were hoping he still loved you."

I hadn't told Asher about my evil ex-boyfriend.

Slowly I turned to face him. He was still looking off into the distance, squinting like the light from the moon hurt his eyes. In that moment, I almost let myself think he was kind of beautiful.

"What else do you know?"

"I know you haven't dated anybody since him."

"Yeah," I said. "So?"

"I know you haven't let yourself *like* anybody since him."

I fiddled at a stray yarn on one of my gloves.

"You don't know a thing about me," I said, looking away. "Not really."

"I know a lot more about you than you know." He looked out past the moon again. "During the day, you get this look. It's like no matter how much fun you're having or who you're talking to, there's still something haunting you. Ever since the day I first saw you. But when you sleep, *this*"—he touched his index finger to the little worry crease between my eyebrows—"goes away."

He let his hand fall away, the back of his fingers trailing down my cheek. Goose bumps pricked along my neck and arms.

I swallowed, trying to keep it together.

"You watch me when I sleep?"

"Once or twice." He smiled. "I don't exactly make a habit of it. It's a weird feeling, being in someone's room when they don't know you're there."

"No kidding! How would you like it if I spied on you?"

"You'd have to find me first."

I punched his arm—hard. He didn't even flinch. "Don't ever come into my room uninvited again."

"I was watching over you."

"Yeah, well, do it from somewhere else." And I thought of something else. "Does Devin come into my room?"

"I don't know. I've never seen him there."

"Does he know that you've been watching me? It seems

like you have an unfair advantage."

He looked away. "I'm sure Devin has other things he should be more concerned about."

"Yeah." I nodded. "Like Raven."

He whipped around. In a second, his eyes had grown cold, sharp.

"How do you know about her?" he asked.

Was he not supposed to know?

"Is she *here*?" he said.

"What? No, no. I just heard, I mean, from Devin—"

"Don't lie to me, Skye, I swear to god—"

"Isn't that a little blasphemous?"

"Dammit, Skye, can you be serious for like two seconds?"

"Oh, *you're* one to talk! You're going to tell *me* to be serious? I don't think you've stopped cracking jokes at my expense since you've been here! Oh, wait, no, I'm sorry, since I *knew* you were here!"

"I'm only doing it to protect you! Do you think this is easy for me? To lurk in the shadows and watch like some poor creep and not be able to do a damn thing about it? To not help you? Warn you?"

"Well, you're sure making up for lost time with your party tricks and your snow caves and your fire. God, you're infuriating. You come here with this insane news and then you let me go on a *ski trip*? You let me eat lunch in the—in the *cafeteria*? While you flirt with other girls as if you hadn't just shattered my entire life?"

"Do you know why I joke all the time?" He stood up as if he'd been wound up and sprung. His eyes glinted in the moonlight. "Do you know why I've been keeping things all light and devil-may-care? Because if you knew—if you *really* knew what was happening—inside of you, within the Order, within the Rebellion, if you knew what the angels are saying, what's *waiting* for you, you would be sobbing, Skye. You would be paralyzed with fear. *That's* why I tease you. I'm doing it for you. Because if I didn't, you wouldn't make it. You wouldn't last another week."

I stood up, too, brushing snow off my jeans and pulling my hat down tighter over my ears. "Well, how lucky for you," I said. "I'm about two seconds away from crying anyway."

Asher shoved his hands in his pockets. "Shit," I heard him mutter.

I folded my arms across my chest and glared at him.

"I have to go," he said. "Raven is dangerous. If she's here, something bad is up."

"Go," I said. "I'm going to bed."

Asher turned and started walking toward the ladder. When he got there, he turned around. A small smile tugged at the corners of his mouth.

"You were mad that I was flirting with other girls?"

"Go!" I yelled.

Wednesday morning, I walked into homeroom with blinders on, determined not to
meet anyone's gaze. After last night, the
last thing I wanted was to be confronted by Devin or
Asher. Actually, I didn't want to be confronted by either
of them at all that day.

Busy scribbling in her notebook, Cassie barely glanced
up as I took my seat. I was kind of grateful, because I knew
she'd notice the dark circles beneath my eyes. I felt terrible. Bleary-eyed. I'd barely slept.

I kept replaying my fight with Asher over in my head.
What did Raven being here mean? I couldn't shake the
feeling that there was something he wasn't telling me.
Something they both weren't telling me.

Throughout the morning I managed to outmaneuver them. If one of them was walking down the hall, I ducked into the bathroom. If I saw either of them approaching me, I whipped around and pretended to be deep in conversation with whoever was nearest. Instead of going to the cafeteria for lunch, I went to the library and settled at a table in a back corner.

I had intended to catch up on some studying. Instead I grabbed a book on angels from the shelves and flipped through the pages. The past two nights, I'd done extensive research on the internet, but it hadn't proved very helpful. As Devin had said, a lot of myths and stories were associated with angels. How could I even begin to identify what was truth and fiction?

I knew I could go to the source—Devin or Asher—but I couldn't help but feel that they each had an agenda. They were on opposite sides and I was caught in the middle.

I jerked back as Devin dropped into the chair across from me.

"You're avoiding us again," he said, his voice low. Not because he was respectful of library rules but because he didn't want anyone to hear us, I figured. Although with his hang-up about rules—who knew?

"You're paranoid," I whispered, turning another page.

"You won't find what you need to know in there."

"You don't know what I need."

"I know you need to concentrate on accepting and controlling your powers."

"Right now, the only power I'm interested in is the one that will make you leave me alone. By the way, our appointment at three fifteen? Forget it. I have ski practice."

"Your destiny is more important."

Folding my arms on the table, I leaned forward. "Do the Gifted see me on that roof today?"

His cheeks turned red, and he looked uncomfortable.

"They don't, do they?"

He glanced around as though everyone around us was eavesdropping. His voice was even lower, more secretive when he spoke. "There's a lot about you they don't know. You're an enigma. It's . . . troubling."

Taking pity on him, I reached across and placed my hand on his. He laced our fingers together and then stared at them as though he'd never before seen intertwined fingers.

"I'm sorry, Devin. I just need some time. A couple of days."

He lifted his gaze to mine, and I could see the earnestness

in the deep blue. "You'd be happy with the Order."

"Are you happy?"

"Not when I'm here. There's too much . . ."

"Chaos," I filled in for him, my mouth twitching.

His eyes sparkled. "Yes."

His fingers tightened around mine. "You know, you *are* special, Skye."

"Because of who my parents are."

"No, because of who you are. You're smart and funny and determined. You're like no one I've ever met before."

I smiled. "Back at you."

"Meet us today on the roof."

"I can't. Not today."

I almost caved in when I saw the look of disappointment on his face. "I made a commitment to the team," I tried to explain. "It's a responsibility. Just like yours to the Order."

"But all this"—he threw his hand out in a gesture that encompassed everything—"is pointless if you come back to the Order with me."

"Even if I have the powers, I don't know that I can leave this behind. It's my world."

"You can't stay here."

The bell rang then, saving me from having to answer him. "Gotta get to class," I said as I gathered up my things.

"Tell Asher that you're both off the hook. No angel training this afternoon."

Before he could protest—because I knew he would—I was heading for the door.

I didn't go to ski practice. I just went home. After my experience with the avalanche, I was afraid of what might happen once my competitive edge took over. I thought I should probably quit the ski team. I didn't want anyone getting hurt because I couldn't control whatever it was I was supposed to control.

Friday night, I slept fitfully. I'd had a tense dinner with Aunt Jo, trying to put off telling her my decision, and another internet search turned up nothing.

I woke with a start. The room was pitch-black, and the house was silent; it was the middle of the night. I turned over beneath my warm comforter, about to fall back asleep—when I realized that my nose and cheeks were cold.

My eyes flew open. I caught a sharp, earthy fragrance. A shadow fell across a patch of moonlight coming through the window, and I scrambled back until I hit the headboard.

"Damn it, Asher, I told you not to come into my room anymore."

"I'm sorry, but I don't think you'll be angry when you find out why I came by."

"Yeah, and why's that?" I demanded.

"Freedom. Get dressed and bundle up. Meet me outside."

He went out the window. I closed and locked it behind him, not that it would do any good if he wanted in. I guessed his powers included the ability to manipulate locks. I was tempted just to go back to bed. Instead I changed into jeans and a soft sweater, wool socks, and snowboots.

I crept down the stairs and through the dark house. The last thing I wanted to do was wake Aunt Jo. I threw on my parka and slipped outside. Asher was waiting at the edge of the trees. He was straddling a snowmobile.

"Thought you might enjoy feeling the wind rushing around you," he said as I approached.

"If I wanted that, I could ski."

"Yeah, but you can't hold on to me when you're skiing."

True. And I missed skiing so much. "I don't know."

"Come on, Skye. I know the past few days have been overwhelming. I also know that you didn't go to ski practice today."

I felt a spark of anger surge through me. "Ellie told you."

"No. I went to watch you practice."

I stuffed my hands in the pockets of my parka and studied the moonlight glistening over the snow. "I wanted to go. I really, really did. But I was afraid." I lifted my gaze to his, and knew he understood. "What if I cause another avalanche? What if someone is hurt or killed?" I couldn't risk it. Not unless I figured out how to control myself, or discovered I had the ability to heal. But even then . . . It was too scary to think of the damage I could cause.

"So you need this," he said. "For tonight—let's just pretend that neither of us has any powers and no one is watching to see what we do. We won't even talk about the Order or the Rebellion. Let's just have fun."

It was probably a very bad idea. Still, I threw my leg over the back of the vehicle, settled onto the seat, and wound my arms around his waist. "I'm ready."

He revved the engine, and we were soon flying over the snow, zigzagging around trees, racing down slopes, speeding toward peaks of snow. The moonlight illuminated everything in a whitish-blue glow. I inhaled deeply, breathing in the scent of the woods and earth and Asher— so warm and solid in front of me. I tightened my arms around his waist.

And I knew that he was generating heat to keep me from freezing as the wind whipped around us. I was content for the first time in days. The worry that I would create some catastrophe vanished.

Asher brought the snowmobile to a halt at the top of a rise and we both got off. He unfolded a thermal blanket and I sat, wrapping my arms around my legs. Then he created tiny balls of fire that floated around us, creating a cocoon of warmth.

"How do you keep those going without touching them?" I asked.

"Practice."

"Did you do that in the snow cave? After I fell asleep?"

"I did what I had to do to keep you alive."

"Because the Rebellion wants me alive?"

"Because I do." He dropped down beside me. "And we agreed not to talk about any of this."

"What will we talk about, then?"

"Why do we have to talk at all?"

Good question. I rested my chin on my knees and studied the vast expanse of stars, noticing as one streaked across the sky.

"What did you wish for?" Asher asked.

"I forgot to make one again," I said. I turned to look at

him. "What did you wish for?"

"That you would be happy." He dusted off some snow from his jeans as though it was suddenly important that it not be there.

"Are you happy?" I asked.

"Pretty much. I'm alone with a pretty girl on a mountain at night." His grin flashed in the moonlight. "What's not to be happy about?"

"Are you ever serious?"

His grin disappeared. "More than you know."

"Shouldn't it be Ellie who's here with you now?"

"There's nothing going on between me and Ellie. Nothing real, anyway. She's just a girl who's there. Not someone you have to work for." He met my gaze.

"You give the impression that you like her," I said.

"I give the impression that I like Ms. Manning. It doesn't mean I do. And I guess, if I'm honest, I sorta like that she makes you jealous."

"I'm not jealous!"

"Really?" he needled. "Not even a little bit? That's not what you implied last night."

I opened my mouth to argue but had nothing to say. He was right.

"So there's nothing going on between you and Ellie?"

"Nothing like this." He glanced at me, but I looked away. I knew my eyes would reveal too much.

"You were right," I said after several minutes of the silence easing between us. "I needed this."

As the fireballs faded away, I was afraid that maybe I needed him, too.

A cold rain fell Monday, smattering against the windows and creating icy puddles of slush in the parking lot at school. After Asher had dropped me off at dawn on Saturday, I'd been left alone—and hated to admit that I'd missed the angels. But when I got in the car this morning, I'd found a note sitting on the steering wheel.

Vacation is over.
Today, 3:15.
No excuses.
—D

I'd almost torn it up, but Devin was right. I needed to stop avoiding them and face whatever was waiting for me.

Neither Asher nor Devin was in class. It struck me as odd, but I had to remember that they weren't normal students. They weren't even human. They didn't need to be here. Did *I* need to be here? I was still thinking about it in history, third period. I hadn't paid attention to a single lesson all morning.

Ms. Manning clacked down the rows between our desks in her heels, handing back our Battle of the Somme papers—the one that counted for 40 percent of our final grade. Her calculating eye scanned our faces from behind her wire-rimmed glasses. She stopped in front of me, and a paper fell from her hands to my desk—a big scarlet D scrawled across the top of my report.

My stomach dropped clear to the floor. Never before had I seen that grade on any of my papers. It made me ill.

I knew I'd messed up, big-time. My mind had been so preoccupied lately that even when I was studying, I might as well not have been.

"Skye," Ms. Manning said as I walked past her desk at the end of class. I hung back.

"I know," I said. "I'm so sorry. I don't know what happened."

"You're my best student, Skye," she said. "What's going on? I've never seen you get a grade like this. I don't know what to think."

"I've been really . . . busy," I said lamely. "Preoccupied. I've been struggling with some decisions since the ski trip."

"I heard you quit the team."

"Yeah, I . . . the avalanche . . . it just kind of spooked me, I guess. I decided I needed a break." I'd spoken with Coach Samuelson on Friday before I went home. I hadn't had a chance to tell Aunt Jo before she'd left.

Ms. Manning eyed me with a mix of severity and worry. "Should I be worried? Do you need to talk with a counselor?"

"God no," I said too quickly. "No. Please let me do some extra credit. I'll make it up."

She sighed heavily.

"I'll give you an additional paper to write after school today. You'll have an hour, from three fifteen to four fifteen. But, Skye"—she looked at me over the top of her glasses—"you'll have to get an A on this paper or your grade for the semester will be seriously affected. Don't blow this."

My throat went dry, and I had to swallow before I could say, "I won't."

I was supposed to meet Devin and Asher on the roof at three fifteen. How could I be in two places at once? I'd have to choose. I felt the color drain from my cheeks.

"Skye." Ms. Manning took her glasses off in concern and came around to my side of the desk. "Are you sure it's not more than just leaving the ski team? Something I should know about? Family? Boy problems?"

"Everything's fine—I'll be there," I said. "I promise."

"I'm glad," she said, a smile returning to her face. "You have so much potential, Skye. I see such great things for you one day."

"Thanks, Ms. Manning," I said. Tears pricked my eyes. I wish I knew what I saw for myself. Right now, when I looked to the future, all I saw was a huge question mark.

"Three fifteen, room four-oh-eight."

"Yep!"

I turned to the door in a rush so she wouldn't see the hint of tears glazing my eyes. Ms. Manning's reflection in the glass window of the door stared after me in concern.

If only she knew.

At three ten, I stood at my locker, putting the last of my heavy textbooks away for the night. I looked down the hall as it began to empty out, closed my locker, and sighed.

Ms. Manning was waiting for me when I got to room 408.

"Skye," she said, "I placed the assignment on that desk by the window. You'll have one hour from the time you start. I'll be here if you have any questions." She took her seat behind the desk at the front of the room.

I walked across the classroom to the desk she'd motioned to. An essay assignment was typed neatly at the top of the page. I sat down, took out a pencil, and began.

Knowing that I was supposed to be up on the roof, I felt strange sitting there in the silent classroom as my pencil scratched across the paper in front of me.

It almost felt as if school shouldn't count anymore. And yet here I was, working on an extra-credit assignment.

My mind wandered to all the strange things I'd caused seemingly by accident. The thermostat. The school bus heater. The boiler exploding at Love the Bean. The avalanche.

Of course, none of these incidents had been confirmed as initiated by me, but I couldn't help but believe they were. And if they were, could I do it on purpose? Could I harness my powers, whatever they were, and *make* these things happen? Now that there was quiet, and Devin and Asher weren't breathing down my neck urging me to try harder, I wondered if it might not be so hard after all.

I focused on the radiator under the window. Ms. Manning was absorbed in grading papers at the front of the classroom, tapping her pen absently against the wire frame of her glasses.

I stared at the radiator, letting every single emotion from the past few weeks flow through me. My mind flashed to Devin trying to instruct me. Sitting next to Asher on the roof, our breath rising in clouds toward the stars, our shoulders barely touching. My cheek against his rough jacket. Then the liberating snowmobile ride, the way he always seemed to know what I was feeling. I had the vague feeling that thinking about Asher in this way was verging on dangerous territory. He wasn't *human*. He wasn't even from this world. Was falling in love with a Rebel against the sanctions they'd just been teaching me? Would it be as punishable as what my parents had done? I knew nothing about who Asher really was, even though he seemed to know lots about me. Did he think about me as often as I thought about him? My palms got sweaty, and I could feel myself burning up. But I kept focusing, channeling everything through me and at the radiator. And then, all of a sudden, I smelled something.

Smoke.

A small trickle of smoke roped through the vents of the radiator. My heart pounded.

I couldn't see any fire, but I knew it must be there somewhere. I stared harder. The wisp bloomed from the slats of the radiator into a beautiful flower of smoke. I stared, a smile forming on my lips.

I did this.

"What's that smell?" Ms. Manning asked, looking up from her papers, and then said, "Jesus," as she saw the smoke, jumped up from the desk, and spilled the stack of tests to the ground. The sprinkler system in the ceiling turned on, and water began to spray everywhere.

"Oh, damn!" she cried, bending to gather the papers to her. I looked up—just in time to catch Asher's wicked grin hanging upside down on the other side of the window. He winked at me. Then he was gone.

My heart skipped a beat.

I hadn't caused the fire after all. It had been Asher the whole time.

"Skye, I'm sorry," Ms. Manning said as she straightened back up with the stack of papers in disarray. "We'll try this again later in the week. I have to go see someone about that radiator." She smoothed her skirt and readjusted her glasses. The smoke had vanished.

My footsteps echoed on the stairs as I pounded up three flights to the roof. I hadn't done it. I hadn't done *anything*.

Asher and Devin were in the exact same positions they had been in the last time I'd pushed through the fire door to the school roof. Asher stood on the ledge of the roof, arms outstretched. The only difference was that this time, his huge inky wings were outstretched, too. Devin leaned against the water tower, his wings tucked away. Not a hint of emotion played on his face.

"You're late," he said flatly, and I wondered if he knew I'd been with Asher alone. Twice now. Devin would most definitely disapprove.

"I was trying to get some extra credit," I shot back. "I haven't exactly been focusing my attention on the right things, lately. You know, before you guys showed up I was actually a straight-A student."

"You've been focusing on *exactly* the right things," said Asher, jumping from the ledge. "You just have to do some re-prioritizing. Maybe A's shouldn't matter so much anymore."

"Thanks for the advice."

Asher's eyes crinkled in the corners, but he didn't smile. It was weird seeing him here with Devin, not able to talk the way we had lately.

"Asher's right," Devin said gravely, stepping away from the water tower. "Your powers should be emerging, and you should be able to control them at will."

Asher was suddenly behind me, which was strange because I hadn't seen him move. He whispered in my ear, "Don't let him freak you out. You can do it."

"What are you saying?" Devin's voice was hard. He looked at Asher, deep unease written all over his face. "Do you know something I don't?"

"Hmm, I don't know." Asher's eyes grew hot as flames. "Should we ask Raven?"

"You leave her out of this."

"So she *did* stop by for a chat?" Asher continued. "What, do you need reinforcements? Can't do it all on your own?"

"I said leave her out!"

"If it involves *Skye's* safety"—Asher's voice was so low it came out as a growl—"you'd better not be hiding anything."

The air was getting colder as the sun slipped farther below the mountains, and the edges of the sky tinged with unfathomable darkness. A burst of white light nearly blinded me, and Devin's mammoth white wings rose from behind him, a gust of wind billowing beneath them. His eyes glazed over, his golden brows furrowed darkly, and his mouth set in a straight, tight line.

"I dare you," he said so quietly, evenly, it sent chills trickling down my spine. "I just dare you."

Asher stepped forward, his own wings rising behind him as if he was bringing the night with him. "Do you really want to challenge me?" The menace in his voice was terrifying. And then, from beneath his wings, a gust of wind raged forward with such unexpected force that I stumbled backward. It hit Devin square in the chest, and he was knocked against the concrete wall of the roof entrance so hard that he fell to the ground.

"Stop!" I heard myself yell, but before I could take a step toward him, Devin was on his feet. Asher raised his hands and shoved something invisible in front of him; a ball of fire rocketed from his outstretched hands. In a blur of white, Devin was at Asher's back, pinning Asher's arms behind him with one arm, the other wrapped tightly around his neck. Asher choked as the fire hit the side of the concrete building and fizzled out, leaving a wide charred circle the size of a window.

"Get off of him!" I yelled at Devin, tempted to rush at

him and pull his hands away myself. But I knew how stupid it would be to get in the middle of a fight like this. "If you hurt him, I'll hurt you so badly you won't be able to *find* your other realm!" He glanced up at me, faltering. He loosened his grip.

It was the moment Asher needed. He twisted in Devin's grasp, spinning him around and gripping his neck in the same choke hold Devin had him in moments before. "You're going to wish you hadn't done that!" Asher yelled.

"I don't believe in wishing!" Devin shouted gruffly, throwing all his weight against Asher's chest.

None of us had noticed that heavy clouds had rolled in, and the sky had grown black and grim. Lightning flashed, and the very atmosphere around us seemed to reverberate. "I've had enough of you," Asher spat as Devin struggled against him. Freezing rain began to pelt against the cold concrete.

"If you kill each other, you'll deserve it!" My whole body sang with anger. My heart was pounding and my nerves were raging—I could feel the heat rising in my cheeks and up the back of my neck. As Asher and Devin struggled, I could feel something brewing inside of me. It felt like I should be able to control it, but instead it was controlling me. And before I had a chance to do a single thing, to figure out the slightest way to control whatever surged within me, there was a thunderous crack as the side of the water tower split open like the simplest seam and water burst onto the roof.

The two rogue angels stopped in mid-fight and stared. I couldn't tell what either of them was thinking, but I didn't care. I was overcome with a sudden wave of exhaustion and fell like a rock to the flooding ground.

The last light of day seeped in under the cracks of my eyelids. The rain had stopped, and the light was a normal, late-afternoon kind of color. My head pounded with an unforgiving rhythm.

Slowly sounds and voices began to crystallize around me.

I could make out Asher cursing. "Hold the water back!" he shouted as his strong arms scooped me up, and I was lifted off the ground, someplace—

My eyes shot open. *Off the ground?*

I looked up and found myself staring into Asher's face. His massive black wings flapped once, twice, and my vision was a rush of inky feathers. As we soared above the school, my stomach dropped, and I threw my arms around his neck. I closed my eyes tight, burying my face against his chest. When my body had gotten used to the swooping, jerky motion of flying, I opened them again, tentatively.

Asher glanced down at me, and I could see in his eyes a glimmer of worry. His grip tightened around me, and he leveled his gaze to see where he was going. The wind whipped past us, and the cold air felt crisp against my face. I strained my neck to catch a glimpse of Devin—who had stayed behind us on the roof—just in time to see a roiling wave of water flow back into the open seam in the water tower, and the seam seal itself back up like the petals of a flower closing in on itself.

Then it was too dark to see anything.

"That's enough for today." Asher's voice sounded far above the wind rushing past us. "I'm taking you home."

"Stop protecting me," I demanded weakly. "I'm fine." But I didn't have the strength left to argue.

We flew in silence. Below us, the valleys and fields stretched and yawned as little lights sprinkled on in the houses below and cars snaked like toys along winding mountain roads. I tucked my head under Asher's chin and felt him swallow. Being this close to him made me feel dizzy, like the closeness was a drug and I had to be careful or I might do something reckless. I'd never felt that way before.

Through the fuzziness in my brain, I tried to process what had happened on the roof. I didn't know who had been responsible for causing what, but for the first time, it really felt like what Asher said was true. Something was inside of me, waiting, just waiting, for the chance to get out. And when it did . . .

We stood outside of my front door. The windows were dark, not a surprise since Aunt Jo had left that morning to take another group out. I was grateful she was away. How would I explain all this to her tonight?

Asher had placed me down gently on the ground just moments before, and the memory of feathers against my skin made me flush. With the slightest of self-conscious looks, he folded them behind his back, and they vanished. The sky instantly looked lighter.

"Are you okay?"

I nodded tentatively

"What happened up there—what stopped us—was that you?" A trace of a mischievous smile flashed across his face.

I realized that I'd been taking it for granted that I'd see

Asher and Devin every day—but I had no idea where the two of them were living. Maybe they lost their corporeal, human form at night. Maybe Devin crossed over into the Order's realm, and Asher flashed to the Rebellion's camp. The night was freezing and my teeth were chattering, my hair still damp from earlier. After everything we'd been through that day—the past few weeks—I didn't have the energy to keep talking outside. I was numb.

"Do you want to come in?" I asked.

Asher looked uneasy. "Um. Sure." As I fumbled in my jacket pocket for my keys, he looked distracted, his eyes darting everywhere except at me.

The heat flared up almost immediately when we walked in.

"Whoa," Asher said quietly. "What was that?"

I took a deep breath. I wasn't afraid of sounding crazy anymore. "I *think* it was me. I don't know for sure. It could have just been static electricity—"

"You know it wasn't," he said.

I deflated even more. Yeah, I knew it wasn't. "So okay, I short-circuited the thermostat a couple of weeks ago and it's been wonky ever since."

"You're getting stronger." It wasn't a question. Asher looked too grave.

"But obviously not more controlled," I joked, trying to keep the mood light. My voice hung in the air of the empty hallway. "Come on, this way."

The full moon cast a white beam of light through the windows of the living room, and even though the lights in the house were off, we could see where we were going.

We walked up the stairs to my room. It was cozy in there, with the rest of the house so quiet and empty. I went into the bathroom, grabbed a couple of towels, tossed him one, and began to rub the other briskly over my hair to get it dry enough that I was no longer shivering.

Sitting on the edge of my bed, I clutched the towel in my lap.

Asher took off his jacket and draped it over my desk chair. "Jeez, Skye, you wanna turn down the heat a little? It's roasting in here."

"Um," I said, "I don't exactly know how to, uh, reverse it yet."

What I didn't want to say was that I was pretty sure that my accidental powers tended to flare up when I was feeling emotional—especially this weird thing I had with heat. I figured that the reason the heat had blasted when we walked in the front door had more than a little bit to do with my being alone with Asher.

I wondered if he knew this.

Could he somehow tell? Were my eyes flashing silver?

"Here." He came over to me, took the towel, tossed it aside, and brought me back to my feet. "I'll help you. Close your eyes." I did, and I felt him take my hands in his. I could sense the room growing even warmer. Something passed between our hands. A spark. I knew he felt it, too, because his hands twitched in mine. But he didn't take them away. "Just pretend that everything inside you is lots of unfiltered electricity. Imagine what you want to do with it. And then imagine flipping a switch—and turning it on." He paused, and I opened my eyes and looked at him. His eyes were searching mine, impossibly deep. I had to control myself. "The Gifted," he said, "start small. They focus on nuances. A whisper of a breath. A hair out of place. They manipulate each and every small thing on this earth. And every little thing has an effect on something else. Just think of what a big change can do: It could sway the path of someone's life, the outcome of battles, the course of history."

I swallowed, hard, mesmerized by the look in his eyes.

"It's our job, as the Rebellion, to stop them from controlling what they have no right to control. You could help us do that."

A warning bell went off in my mind. I broke away from Asher, and he didn't try to stop me. *Was he just using me?* The room was too warm. I took off my jacket and then pulled my sweater over my head. Suddenly I felt self-conscious, standing there in my tank top in front of Asher, when I was so used to piling on the layers of sweater and fleece and Gore-Tex. I glanced over at him. He was staring.

"What?" I asked.

"Nothing," he shot back. His eyes darted again, this time focusing above my head on the bookshelves behind me. "Oh, hey. Let's play checkers."

"Are you serious?" It was one in a stack of games left over from when I was a kid. I hadn't played in years.

"Sure, it's a game of strategy." He went to my shelf and pulled down the red-and-black cardboard box. "It'll help."

He spread the game out on the rug, and we sat down, facing each other. I crossed my legs.

"Well," he said, reaching for a black piece, "see if you can handle this." He made his first move and for a little while we were neck and neck, anticipating each other's strategy, moving and then counter-moving. Neither of us could pull ahead. I knew the game would end in stalemate.

"You'll never win this," I bluffed.

"I'll go down trying," he replied.

I looked up and caught his eyes. They flashed for a second before darting back down to the board.

"Nice move," he said.

"It's not my first time playing."

I don't know what it was. Maybe the fact that I was sitting there in my tank top and jeans across from an angel with black hair and incredible eyes or the overwhelming heat in the room, but I realized I was flirting with Asher. And then I realized something else.

For the first time in a year and a half, I thought I might actually be falling for someone.

And it had to stop. As if I needed my life to be any more complicated.

I stood up. "I'm tired," I said. "I slept like crap this weekend, thanks to you."

Asher stood up slowly, too.

"Yeah," he said. "Listen, I'm sorry about that. And about today, the fighting. It all got out of hand. I . . . this mission is . . . hard, the hardest, and. . . " He paused, running his hands through his hair. "It's been stressful for all of us."

"Gosh, has it been stressful for you, too? I'm so sorry. Maybe try spending half a minute in *my* shoes. In case you haven't noticed, I have no idea what I'm doing!" My temper flared.

"Skye, come on, I'm sorry."

We stood there staring at each other. After several seconds, I could make out a tapping noise growing louder and more impatient. I looked down and realized it was Asher's foot.

"Stop it," I said. "What's with you tonight? You're being weird."

"Nothing," he said. "I mean no, I'm not." I challenged him with a hard stare. The light from my lamp cast a soft glow on his face, and I felt so much for him right then that it hurt. It would never work between us. He was a player, like Jordan. He'd try to use me. He wasn't even human. But in the heat and the dim light of my room, it was nice to just *feel* something. Asher took a step toward me and stopped.

"Look, I'm not going to kiss you, okay?" he said, beginning to pace. "So you can stop trying to get me to."

"What are you talking about?" I panicked. Maybe he *could* tell after all.

"You—you're doing that, that *thing*. With the tank top. And the checkers. And inviting me up here—"

"Ex*cuse* me? You're the one who wanted to play checkers." I tried to regain my control.

"—well, forget it. I'm not doing it."

"Good!" I shouted, my face red. "Who says I want you to?"

"Oh, you want me to, you *definitely* want me to."

"I *so* do not!" I yelled. "Especially not when you're *driving me crazy!*"

He paused. And looked at me.

"You don't?" he asked. "I am?"

Then all of a sudden he'd taken two giant steps toward me, and before I knew it, had taken my face into his hands and the rest of me into the darkness of his wings, and he was kissing me and I was kissing him and we were kissing each other in my little bedroom, in my little house, in my little town, while the mountains soared into the sky.

I could sense the earth rumbling quietly beneath us. Something was moving, but all I knew right then was that it wasn't dangerous.

For now, there was only Asher.

After he left, the house was silent. I was too excited to sleep, even though fatigue pulled at my body like gravity—threatening to topple me at any second. I wandered around absently, ducking into empty rooms, peeking out the windows at the full moon. I felt like if I stood still for more than a second, I would drown in its light.

My cell phone rang, nearly giving me a heart attack. I looked at the number and was flooded with relief. How had Aunt Jo known that I needed her?

"Hey," I said as I curled up in a chair.

"Hey, yourself. I just wanted to check in since I had cell reception tonight. You doing okay?"

"Yeah, I'm fine."

"I'm sorry I have to spend so much time away lately."

"I'm a big girl," I said.

"I guess it's good for us," she mused. "Gives us a preview of what to expect when you go off to college."

"Yeah." If I went off to college. I was having so much trouble lately concentrating on my schoolwork, and I still had that stupid paper I needed to do for Ms. Manning.

"I'll be with this group until Wednesday afternoon," she told me. "Best behavior till I get back."

"Promise."

After several I-love-you's, she hung up. The house echoed in the silence.

I wondered if my mom had ever told Aunt Jo about her life as an angel. Probably not. I hadn't told Cassie about all the strange things going on in my life. Some things were impossible to explain.

I wound up in the kitchen, rummaging in the refrigerator for something that wasn't prepackaged food. The yellow light spilled out across the room, and the refrigerator hum made me feel less alone. On the top shelf, I spotted a plate of cookies left over from the batch Aunt Jo had made a while ago. They were probably beyond stale by this point, but they'd have to do. I took the plate out and put it on the counter. I turned on the overhead lights, pulled up a stool, and grabbed a magazine from the growing pile of mail.

I snatched a cookie and was just about to take a bite when something clattered outside. When I looked up, my heart froze in my chest.

There was a face at the window. Shocking blue eyes. Porcelain skin. Straight blond hair. Though I'd only seen her twice before, I'd know her anywhere.

Raven.

I started to panic. What did she want? I knew so little about her, but Asher's uneasy reaction to the news that she was here in River Springs made me nervous. I got off my stool, unsure of my next step. But when I turned around, it looked like the choice had been made for me.

Raven stood in my kitchen, her blinding white wings unfurled from her small frame. It shocked me how such enormous, menacing wings could come tumbling forth from such a small being. The feathers glinted sharply in the moonlight—and for a moment, I had a horrifying vision that they could slit my neck with one quick swoop, open my arteries, and cause my blood to come spilling to the floor.

I backed away.

"That's right, back away," she said, and the calm of her voice gave me chills. "You don't know how dangerous I am."

"What do you want?" I tried to hide my fear, but it was like she could sense it.

Her hair flashed in the moonlight.

"Poor little Skye. Two sides to choose from. Two sets of powers *vying* for your attention. What will you do?"

"I—I don't know. I didn't know about any of this until the other day."

Raven circled me like a cat eyeing the mouse it plans to pounce on. "Of course, how could you know? *The human child whose future the Order cannot see and the Rebellion cannot claim.* Isn't that how it goes? The old foretelling that brought the Rebel and the Guardian to watch you in the first place? The whole reason this mission came to be. How could you know if the Order doesn't?"

"What? I thought the Order sees everything?"

"Funny, isn't it? The one girl who has the power to destroy everything, and they can't even see how their own mission will end."

"What are you talking about? Asher and Devin haven't told me anything like that."

"Oh, the boys don't know. They are just little pawns in the game. And isn't it always the girls who run the show, anyway? You'll be stronger than them before they know it, and they won't care about you, then. They'll leave you if they think you're better. And you will be." She took a small step toward me, then another.

"Why are you telling me this? What do you want?" I was somehow able to push down my fear, and my voice sounded clear and confident. I almost fooled myself.

Suddenly she was behind me. The sharp edge of her wing pricked my neck.

"Leave Devin alone," she said. "Let him come back to the Order. He is mine. The Gifted have foretold it and so it shall be."

"It's not like I sought him out," I said defensively, trying to keep still so the feathery blade wouldn't slice me. "I didn't ask for this."

"*You're* the reason he's changing." I broke away and stared. "You didn't know that, did you? But he is. Don't you understand what you're doing to Devin?" Her voice softened. "How you're tempting him? He likes you. He's not supposed to feel *anything* for you. You are a mission. He can't see you as more. He'll fail if he does. And if he fails . . ." Her voice faltered, and when she spoke again, it was with renewed strength. "It must come to an end."

"Huh?" I thought about Devin: tranquil, peaceful, confusing as ever. "You must be kidding."

"The forecasts are shifting. The Sight is changing. And

all they know, little Skye, is that it has something to do with you."

"I don't know how to stop it." My next words surprised me. "I won't stop it. I have to see it through."

"Then make everyone's job easier. The Order is waiting for you. They will find you. There will be no place on Earth where you can hide."

When I didn't answer her, she hissed, "I will always be watching you, Skye."

Her wings beat wildly, the cacophony of feathers deafening.

I shut my eyes tight, wishing that would block out the noise, block out everything.

When I opened them moments later, I was alone.

I lay in bed, wide awake, willing sleep to come. Raven had accused me of changing Devin, but my hair smelled of Asher: spicy, earthy, dark. It made my heart pound to remember our kiss, his hands warm against my neck, fingers entwined in the strands of my hair.

"*I've wanted you,*" he'd murmured, his lips barely touching mine, "*for so long.*"

Energy rose off my skin in waves. Euphoric.

I couldn't get comfortable. I rolled over onto my stomach, buried my face in my pillow, and laughed and laughed until I didn't know if I was laughing or screaming.

If I did what Raven said and joined the Order, I'd never see Asher again.

As I drifted off, Raven's words echoed in my head: *They're just little pawns in the game.* The last thing I consciously remember thinking of was the wounded look in Devin's eyes as Asher scooped me up in his arms and we left him standing there on the school roof to repair the damage.

And then the morning breeze rustled my curtains, sweeping a feather along the floorboards. It must have fallen when Asher had been in my room earlier. I watched as the wind blew it here and there, leaping, lightly touching down. Dark, like the night, like Asher's eyes.

26

As I pulled into the parking lot Tuesday morning, I was surprised to see Cassie's green Volvo come to a jerking stop a few spaces over from mine. I got out and walked over to see her slam the driver's-side door and kick her wheels in frustration.

"Cass!" I called, waving as I approached. "Are you okay?"

She gave me a cold look but didn't refuse my help as I bent to inspect the tire. "It's not the tire," she said. "It's something with the engine. It's been giving me trouble the past few days." She looked away. "Not that you'd know."

Instantly I felt bad that we hadn't talked much lately, but I was now too tired and preoccupied to engage her in an argument. Time had been flowing really weirdly, in stop-start patterns, lurching forward and then dragging on for millennia. Besides, we didn't have a rule that we had to spend every waking minute together, did we?

She locked the car, and we walked to homeroom together. We kept talking, even though it was clear that there was some tension between us that we weren't mentioning. The fact that she was mad at me annoyed me. The world *always* revolved around her, and the minute I had some major drama in my life, she couldn't deal with the fact that I wasn't focused on her.

"It's so frustrating," Cassie said as we found our seats. "I just got a tune-up at the beginning of the year. My dad makes me get them, otherwise there's no way I'd remember. I don't know what could already be wrong with the engine. It just keeps stalling for no reason."

"I don't know, Cass," I said, aware that Devin was watching us as we sat down, and that Asher caught my eye before glancing away. "Can you take it in again?"

"No way. I totally don't have the money right now. Ugh, I hate my life."

"Don't worry," I said, determined now to make up for any lost points in the best-friend book so that Cassie would stop being mad at me. "We'll figure something out."

The rest of homeroom seemed to last forever. Asher sat behind me, and his nearness sent tiny shivers down my neck, made my heart beat too fast. Devin sat next to him, and I couldn't stop trying to figure out what was really going on. Could I trust either of them? My mind kept replaying my encounter with Raven the night before.

You're the reason he's changing.

I couldn't understand it.

In the hall after class, Asher caught up with me. "Hey," he said. We stood there, facing each other.

"What's up?" I asked, smiling up at him.

"How are you?"

"Good," I said, though it was an effort to think of the right words to say when he was looking at me. "Last night was . . ."

"Yeah." He looked like he was either searching for the right words or contemplating kissing me again. I was thrumming, every single fiber of my being alive and happy. "It was intense. A little too intense, actually."

I jerked away from him as if I'd been slapped.

"What?"

"I just think, you know, we should be careful. Maybe

cool it for a little while. I don't want either of us to lose our focus. This is so important, Skye. It's bigger than we both know."

"That's not what this is about," I said, my hands beginning to shake. "You're just scared."

"That's not true, Skye. I——"

"No, you're right," I said, cutting him off before he could say anything else. "This whole thing was just a giant mistake. We shouldn't have kissed in the first place." I could feel tears pricking my eyes, and I tried not to let them spill over.

Whatever I had been feeling for him, whatever I wanted to keep feeling, shriveled within me into a cold, hard pit. And I walked away. As I turned the corner to the staircase, I caught Devin's eye from where he'd been standing, watching the whole thing.

After school, Devin was waiting by my locker. I was relieved to see Asher was nowhere to be found.

"Hey," I said as I approached. "Where's your other half?"

"Indisposed." He sized me up. "You seemed stressed today. Do you want to go for a walk or something?"

"With you?"

"Yes, of course with me."

"Um, okay," I said, wondering if I was walking right into a trap. Raven's warning echoed in my ears, but she didn't control me. Devin was sent here to protect me and help figure out what kind of strange powers I might be developing. I couldn't just stay away from him. Besides, it was nice that he'd noticed I was upset. I needed a friend who understood what I was going through, and at that moment, I felt so far away from Cassie, Dan, Ian, and my normal life.

We ditched my car by the entrance to one of the trails that Aunt Jo always took people out on. It was one of my favorites—well maintained but not too heavily trafficked. It was a nice afternoon. Devin listened as I told him how freaked out I was about everything.

"I don't get it," I said, dejectedly kicking a tree branch that had fallen under the weight of a pile of snow. "This isn't working." I knew I was being petulant, saying things just to be difficult. "Maybe I'm not as special as you think—maybe I'm really just a normal person after all."

"Do you really believe that?" Devin asked. "Because I don't."

"Yes. No. Probably not." I bit my lip. "It's just not going well. None of this." I paused and snuck a glance at him out of the corner of my eye. "And I don't know why."

"He's impulsive." I looked up, surprised at his words. "He says and does things without thinking." Was Devin trying to give me advice? About Asher? "It's . . . stupid."

I did something kind of inappropriate. I couldn't help it. I laughed.

"What's so funny?" He looked confused, and then slowly the firm, unwavering line of his mouth broke into a shy smile. "Are you laughing at me?" His smile widened, and then I was smiling and laughing harder.

"Sorry." I gasped. "Sorry! It's just, you, trying to give advice . . ."

"Hey," he said. "I give good advice. That was good, right?"

"Well, it was okay. But you didn't really tell me what to do."

"What do you mean?"

"You just commented on something. You didn't offer any constructive feedback."

Devin looked thoughtful.

"How can I tell someone what to do?" he asked.

I looked at him. He really was from another planet or something.

"You just say, 'Skye, suck it up,' or 'Skye, stop falling for idiots.' It won't work, but hopefully I'll have learned something for next time."

"I can't do that," Devin said. A note of sadness crept in there somewhere.

"Why not?"

"I can't tell anyone what to do. I can't give orders." It dawned on me what he was saying, and my smile faded. "That's the Gifteds' job, not mine."

"Oh," I said. "Sorry."

"It's certainly not your fault," he said stiffly. I sighed. How could I get him to laugh again?

I looked at him sideways, thinking.

"So, unlike Asher, you'd never do anything impulsive," I said.

"Absolutely not. I follow my orders. I never stray from them."

"What do you do when something unexpected happens?"

"The Gifted can see our destinies so we always know what is going to happen."

"Soooo . . . you know that I'm going to do this?" I scooped up a mound of snow, quickly packed it into a ball, and hurled it at him.

It broke apart, leaving a burst of snowflakes on his jacket.

He stared at me as though I'd lobbed a fireball at him.

"What did you do that for?"

Now it was my turn to stare. "You've never been in a snowball fight?"

"Why would I?"

"Uh, because it's fun?" I gathered up more snow and tossed it at him.

He sidestepped.

"Now you're getting it." I attacked again. "Throw some snow at me. Or can you not—if you haven't been ordered to?" I taunted.

"We can defend ourselves," he said, slowly breaking into a grin.

"Oh yeah? Show me."

As he bent down, I took cover behind a tree—which apparently confused him, based on the deep furrow of his brow when he looked up. "Why did you hide?"

"Because we're at war and my strategy is to hide."

He dropped the snow he'd been gathering, threw his hands up, and all the snow that had been on the branches above my head cascaded over me. With a shriek, I back-pedaled away from the tree.

"Not fair!"

He was laughing. Deeply and richly. He didn't stop even when my next snowball hit him square in the face.

Snow was suddenly swirling around me, a whirlpool of white. I was at a disadvantage. My fledgling powers couldn't compete with his. So I lowered my shoulder and charged toward him.

It was something else the Gifted apparently hadn't foreseen—because I smacked into him and we both tumbled into the snow. His laughter abruptly stopped. Everything stopped.

As I straddled him, I was acutely aware of the stillness: his, mine, the woods. His arms were around me, holding me to him. Our faces mere inches away. His eyes were that incredible blue beneath a layer of ice. I wanted to fall into them. Find the peace and tranquility they offered. Leave schoolwork and bruised hearts and insecurities behind.

"What's your world like?" I asked.

"Beautiful," he said, tucking a strand of my hair behind my ear. "We know our destinies so we don't have to worry about the future. We all follow the rules, so no one is hurt and there are no unexpected consequences. It's an eternal state of bliss. Nothing is unplanned or unexpected."

"And you're happy there?"

"I love it there. We have no jealousies, no pettiness. When I walk through the school here, I'm bombarded with anger and envy. I overhear people saying unkind things about one another. Here people are mean, cruel. Selfish. With the order, there is a beautiful lightness to our being."

"Your zen state," I said, smiling.

"Something like that. Yes." Tentatively, he reached up and cradled my cheek in his hand. His palm was warm, his fingers gentle. His thumb neared the corner of my mouth and I had a feeling that he wanted to trail it over my lips. The blue in his eyes deepened. "My descriptions don't do it justice. I want to be able to share it with you. I want to share so much with you."

He blinked as though he'd been in a trance. The intense moment between us faded. He shook his head. "I guess this means you won."

"Yeah, of course," I said, forcing myself to disguise the shaking in my voice. My body quivered.

I thought I'd felt confused before, but now it was even worse. I thought I'd been falling for Asher—but now, here with Devin, I wasn't sure what I felt.

They were so different. Light and dark. Peace and chaos. If I had a choice, I didn't know which I would choose. Would my powers choose for me?

Gathering my wandering thoughts, I smiled brightly. "I knew I'd kick your butt."

I rolled off him and shoved myself to my feet, avoiding

eye contact as he got up. I wondered if he'd been able to read my thoughts. How embarrassing that would be. I glanced around.

The sunlight peeked through the cracks in the trees as it sank lower in the sky. It was nearing sunset.

"Hey, do you want to try something?" he asked hesitantly, and I wondered if he was grappling with the same emotions that were overwhelming me.

Slowly I turned around. "Sure. Okay."

"Over here."

He took my hand as though it was the most natural thing in the world to do. We walked toward one of the largest trees and stopped at a tangle of wild alpine flowers. Devin bent down. At first I just stood there, but he looked up at me, nodding his head for me to bend down next to him on the trail.

He pointed to a small lavender winter flower. The edges of its petals were browned and faded, the green of its stem blackened and sickly.

"It's dead," I said.

Devin nodded. A vague, subtle light emanated from his hands. He cupped them around the flower, and the light grew momentarily brighter.

When he pulled both hands away, the flower was an

intense, thriving purple, its stem long and tangled and green.

It was beautiful.

"I wanted to wait until we were alone to share this with you," he said.

"Can I . . . do that?" I heard my voice waver.

"That is one path for your powers to take."

"Can I try?" He nodded for me to proceed. I reached over to find another dying flower amid the branches and stems. My hand brushed against his, and I felt him shiver. But I wouldn't look up. Not yet. Devin brought his hands close to mine, cupping my own around the faded flower. Light still shone from his outstretched hands, illuminating the area so I could see what I was doing.

Slowly, holding the flower in my right hand, I brought my left hand over to cover it. I wasn't sure if I was supposed to feel anything, but nothing stirred within my cupped hands. I waited. I could feel Devin beside me, holding his breath.

"Open them," he whispered finally.

I pulled my left hand away, revealing the tiny blossom within.

It was still dead.

Silently, we headed back before the sun dipped too far behind the mountains for us to see where we were going. To my surprise, Devin walked me to my car.

"How are you getting home?" I asked. "Wait, where *is* home?"

"I'm renting an apartment. There's a little complex over by Evergreen Street." I looked at him, and for some reason, the thought of Devin in a small empty apartment made me sad.

"I'll drive you," I offered. "Come on, get in."

"You're sure it's not too far out of your way?"

"I'll be fine." I smiled at him. He grinned back. We got into the car.

"Today was—" He cut himself off, instead busying himself with buckling his seat belt.

"What?" I prodded. "Fun?"

He smiled sheepishly. I opened my eyes wide in mock surprise, and he nodded.

"I haven't laughed so hard in a long while," he said. "It was nice."

"Me neither," I said. "It was."

My car hugged a tight curve, hurtling along the winding mountain roads in the dusk. The sun had set, and the sky was a deep, mood-ring blue, the kind of blue the ring gets before it turns really, fantastically black.

Devin was quiet in the passenger seat, every now and then letting me know when to turn, how far we had left to go. I wasn't very familiar with that part of town, but it wasn't a long drive at all. The complex consisted of a few rows of drab, brick homes. Devin directed me to his.

I pulled in to the driveway and cut the engine.

"This is . . . interesting," I said. "How did you find this place?"

"There aren't too many places to rent an apartment in this town," he said. "It was sort of this or sleeping out in that field back there." He was trying to make a joke, but it wasn't especially funny.

"Devin?" I said. "Thanks again. For today. It was a big help."

He smiled again, and a kind of happiness filled the car.

"You're welcome, Skye. I'm glad." He got out, unlocked his apartment door, and disappeared inside. A second or two later, I saw a light appear in an upstairs window.

Suddenly in the car, in the quiet, I was gripped by loneliness. I couldn't call my friends—they wouldn't understand. I thought about calling Asher, but I didn't even know if he *had* a phone or if he'd want to talk to me.

I was miserable and exhausted. I just wanted to feel something different from what I was feeling. I didn't want to go home to my empty house. I didn't want to be alone.

I got out of the car, walked up the short, concrete driveway, and rang the doorbell. A few seconds later, Devin opened it.

"Skye?" he asked, confused.

"Can I stay here tonight?" I didn't explain. I knew if I did, I would start crying, and I didn't want Devin to see me like that. I needed a friend, and right now, he was the only one who understood what I was going through.

Without a word, he opened the door wider, allowing me to pass.

27

The dawn light crept in through the blinds. I'd slept so soundly, hardly waking up in the night. It was the most rested I'd felt since turning seventeen. Then I noticed Devin's arm slipped around my waist, and became aware of his body pressed against mine, moving softly in time with his breathing.

I was afraid to move for a minute or two. I didn't want to wake him. Instead I tried to relax, getting used to the feel of his arm around me. Getting used to being held. I closed my eyes again and tried to fall back asleep. It was all I wanted—all I needed, right then. But still something didn't feel right.

Carefully I turned to face him. He was fast asleep, and it was funny to see him that way, so unaware of my presence.

It made me feel closer to him, somehow. I almost didn't want to wake him. But I knew I had to.

I nudged him gently and watched as he groggily opened his eyes. "Hi," I said.

"Hi. . . ." He blinked then recognized me. Immediately he pulled his arm away, like I'd burned him. "What are you doing here?"

"I slept here, remember? Except when we fell asleep, I was over here, and you were waaay over there." I nodded toward the other side of the bed.

"Oh." He laughed, still confused, still half asleep. "Sorry."

"S'okay." I closed my eyes again sleepily, and when I opened them, he was looking at me. Our faces were so close together. Despite everything, I could feel my heart pounding.

Then Raven's words echoed sharply in my ears.

I will always be watching you, Skye.

Fear suddenly gripped me. Did she know I was here right now? My body spasmed, and I sat up abruptly.

"Raven . . . what is she to you?" I asked.

He pushed himself up. "What exactly do you know about Raven?"

I decided to go with the CliffsNotes version. "She introduced herself to me."

He buried his face in his hands and shook his head. "Raven, what are you doing?"

Crossing my legs beneath me, I turned and faced him squarely. "She's your girlfriend."

"No." He lifted his gaze. "It's hard to explain. She is . . . the one for me."

"So you love her?"

"No. I"—he combed his fingers through his hair—"I don't know what I feel for her. We're destined to be together, but it's gotten . . . complicated lately."

"Because of me?"

"Partly."

My heart hammered against my chest. I wanted to stay here all day. I wanted to run. I chose to run.

"I have to go," I said, flinging myself out of bed. He didn't protest. I got my boots on and grabbed my jacket from a chair by the door. Before I ran down the stairs, I turned to look at him. He was propped against a pillow. Watching me without the slightest hint of emotion. He wasn't wearing a shirt, and the sheets were crinkling around his smooth, chiseled body. My stomach jerked involuntarily. *"Bye,"* I mouthed, my voice caught somewhere in my throat.

He didn't follow me, but when I got outside and was able to breathe again, I heard the lock click into place behind me.

28

The thought of sitting through homeroom with
Asher and Devin one row behind me sent my
body into convulsions, so I wandered the halls
surreptitiously for a while, figuring if a teacher saw me,
she'd probably think I was on my way to the nurse with
an advanced case of the flu. It probably looked like it. I
felt nauseous and dizzy, my mind caught between too
many different things. Finally my legs felt as if they were
going to give out from under me, and I found my way to
the seldom-used bathroom in the basement by the music
rehearsal rooms. Sometimes Cassie and I hung out in there
before she went to band practice and I had skiing. Someone who spent a *lot* of time in those rehearsal rooms had
dragged an old armchair into the bathroom by the sinks.

The thing had seen better days; its mustard yellow velvet upholstery was threadbare, and stuffing burst forth in several places.

I loved that chair. I always sat in it while Cassie propped herself up on the sink to do her makeup. Now I opened the bathroom door, threw my bag on the floor, and sank into the chair. It was as if the world-weariness of the old chair opened the floodgates. I started to cry.

Vaguely I was aware of the door opening and a familiar voice saying, "Lady, you have got some serious explaining to do."

I shook my head, hard. Cassie crouched on the floor beside the chair. "I only do this for my most special and loyal people," she said, resting her chin on the arm of the chair, "but I think today calls for a cut day."

I looked up, and through my tears, I could barely manage a grateful smile. "Finally someone around here who makes *sense*."

Cassie lived in a small ranch-style, powder blue house with white trim that she shared with her parents and younger brothers, and everywhere, *everywhere*, there was evidence that a family lived there. It was the exact opposite of my house. Cassie kicked aside a yellow plastic dump truck with the gray suede toe of her bootie as we got out of the car. Instinctively I headed for the front door, but she intercepted me.

"Hey," she said. "Remember what used to always cheer you up?" She headed toward the side of the house, flipped the lock on the ancient wooden fence, and we walked into the backyard. I smiled when I saw the swing set.

"Tire swing!" I called, claiming it. Cassie took the bucket swing, which she hated. After a few rounds of musical swings, we finally ended up side by side on the hard-seated bench swings, kicking our feet off the frosty ground for momentum.

"You're torn between the two of them," Cassie said. "Aren't you? I know my best friend. I knew you weren't telling me something." She giggled. "Ellie's full of shit, isn't she?"

I laughed. "Yeah, something like that." On one level, that was totally true. I was torn, trying to choose between two things: Asher or Devin. The Order or the Rebellion. Self-preservation or heartbreak. Control—or finally letting go. And so far, I was just as undecided as my powers were. "So perceptive, Holmes."

Cassie smiled. "Well, I've had years of practice. So what are you going to do?"

"Flip a coin?"

"Seriously, Skye." She eyed me. "You already sort of know what you want to do, don't you?"

I thought for a moment. Did I? Cassie seemed so sure; how was it possible that I wasn't?

"I don't know."

Cassie kicked off the ground, flying forward in a graceful arc. "Well, if I know my best friend, I'm sure you'll make the right decision. I have no doubts about that."

"Yeah," I said. "I hope so."

We swung back and forth, both of us ignoring the cold.

"Cassie?"

"Mmm?"

I stopped my swing, digging my heels into the ground, hard. "Sorry I haven't been, you know, all there lately."

She stopped her swing, too. "Mmm, I don't know if I can let you off that easily," she said. "How about a little groveling first?"

"Shut up."

"'Kay."

We kept swinging.

"Skye?"

"Yeah."

"I forgive you."

"Thanks."

She smiled at me sideways, the way she smiles when she's getting an idea. "Remember that time in third grade, we got into the huge fight over who would be the first one to wear the floral leggings we both got, and I accused you of copying me, and you gave me back your half of our friendship necklace?"

"Of course," I said. "And then we both wore them on the same day, and everyone called us the Olsen Twins. And that's when we founded the copycat club, where we had to wear the same thing once a week for the rest of the year."

"Yeah. Well, I kept the necklaces. I knew you'd want yours back someday."

"Are you serious?"

"Totally. Come on."

In her room, she opened her jewelry box and held up two gold chains with half of a tiny gold heart dangling from each. One said *Best*. One said *Friend*.

"I think you need this back now," Cassie said. "You're my best friend. Don't disappear on me like that again, okay? I missed you." I gulped, trying not to feel too guilty. Whatever had happened in the past few weeks, I knew it was only going to get more intense from here as my powers—whatever they were—really took shape. And I knew there was no way I could let Cassie in on that part of my life. Not really. No matter how much I wanted to.

I put the necklace on, feeling the ridges with my thumb. If I was going to listen to anyone, if I was going to trust anyone in this world, it was Cassie.

We fit the halves together, the jagged edges interlocking exactly the way they used to, and it struck me as weird that the tiny heart hadn't grown or changed in the years since we'd neglected them, even though *we* had.

I knew that she was telling the truth.

I would make the right decision.

29

The house was gaping with emptiness when I got home. I deleted the voicemail from school informing Aunt Jo that I had missed classes. I felt guilty about it, but I would make up for everything starting tomorrow. I couldn't focus on homework, obviously. So I decided to go out back to the field and see if I could make anything strange happen. On purpose, for a change.

I was already hard at work by the time Devin showed up, with Asher walking slowly behind him. When our eyes met, my stomach dropped. He looked just as bad as I did. Maybe worse.

If Devin noticed, he didn't say anything. In fact, he didn't look much better. "Oh, good," he said. "You've been trying on your own. That's great."

I could have been imagining it, but he seemed tenser than he usually did. The laughing Devin from yesterday was gone. I wondered if he was thinking about last night. I tried not to—especially with Asher there—but I couldn't shake the memory of him sitting up, watching as I scrambled to put on my shoes and jacket. The sound of the door locking behind me.

We spent the rest of the afternoon out in the field, working on teasing out my powers. They tried all kinds of things, but often they just showed me something that one of them could do and then tried to get me to do it. But as evening approached and I couldn't really imitate either of them, it began to affect everyone's mood.

The weather had slid down the awful slope from cold and clammy to a mix of sleet and rain, and my hands turned numb from the cold as Devin tried relentlessly to get me to fasten an icicle that had fallen to the ground back to its branch.

"You're not trying hard enough!" he yelled into the wet, driving wind. "Use your *mind*, Skye. Focus your energy."

Asher stood behind me, blasting icicles on various branches near Devin's head. "Fasten *those* back," I heard him mutter.

"I *am* trying!" I yelled. I had been practicing using Asher's trick of flipping the switch but to no avail. Nothing was happening—nothing at all. Though Cassie's encouragement had strengthened my resolve, it had also made me realize how much I missed my life the way it used to be. I would have given anything at that moment to be curled up in her room watching a movie or hanging out at the Bean and playing pool with her and the boys.

My wet hair clung to my face and neck as I tried again and again. My eyes felt wild. I didn't have to think too hard to figure out what color they were.

"Hey, it's okay," Asher said. He walked over, tentatively reaching out both hands to me, and with no effort at all, a flame sprang up between them. I wanted to lean in toward the heat. But I looked away.

"It doesn't help if you do everything for her," Devin said, and I couldn't quite identify the emotion in his voice. Envy, maybe—but Guardians didn't feel envy. Wasn't that what he'd told me?

"I think we can all agree that your approach is a dismal failure," Asher said.

"Do you guys have to constantly bicker?" I asked.

In Asher's hands, the fire disappeared, and the cold began to weave its way back into me.

"I'm calling it a day," I said.

Devin left in a huff. I noticed that he avoided looking at me as he soared off through the trees with his massive wings, several of his pure white feathers spiraling down below him. They fell to the ground, where they soon turned the color of mud, just like everything else.

Asher and I just stood in the empty field facing each other.

"Skye—" he said.

I stared back at him. There was so much that I wanted to say. Instead, I turned sharply on the heels of my snow boots and trudged back to the house. I kicked my boots off when I walked into the kitchen, padding the rest of the way upstairs as the freezing wet hems of my jeans soaked through my socks, leaving little wet half-moons on the carpet. I shed my clothes in a heap just outside the bathroom door and, zombielike, stood in the shower for a second or two before realizing that I hadn't turned it on. I let the steam fog up the mirrors and fill my lungs, and the hot water washed away my anger and sadness. Soon feeling had returned to most parts of me.

As soon as I could feel my toes again, I began to cry. Great, heaving sobs that shook my body and made it hard for me to stand. I was so tired, anyway. My legs gave way and I fell to the shower floor, where I kept crying, hugging my knees to my chest, watching the sudsy water swirl around me on its way to the drain.

I didn't know what I wanted anymore. Was I really trying as hard as I could to manifest and control my powers? I just felt like a time bomb, ticking down the seconds until I was ready to explode. And it didn't help that the only people who really understood, who knew what I was going through, weren't people at all.

Stepping out of the shower, I wrapped a plush towel around me and wiped my hand across the mirror above the sink. This girl stared back at me. She had wet black hair, a swollen pink mouth twisted in confusion, a splotchy red face, and silver eyes. Not gray. Silver.

I put on my flannel boxers and T-shirt and got into bed, letting myself slip under the covers. I curled into as small a ball as possible, trying with all of my might to disappear into the soft folds. What I wanted, more than anything in the world right then, was my mother.

Early the next morning, I became aware of Aunt Jo hovering in the doorway, stepping one foot past the doorframe and then edging back into the hall, afraid to commit one way or the other. I had no idea when she'd gotten home, though it must have been sometime last night after I'd already fallen asleep. I eyed her warily through a little gap in the cave I'd made under my comforter.

"Skye?" she finally called. "Are you awake?"

I mumbled something unintelligible.

"I'll take that as a yes. I have to head back out to the Collegiate Peaks this afternoon. I'll be gone for ten days. How about I fix breakfast to make it up to you?" she asked brightly, as if pancakes with syrup would solve all of the world's problems.

Ten minutes later, I was shuffling into the kitchen in sweatpants, snow boots, about four different long-sleeved shirts layered on top of one another, as well as a huge knit scarf that I'd wrapped around my neck three times. I couldn't decide if going to school was worth it.

Aunt Jo took one look at me and her eyebrows crinkled. "Oh dear," she said. "Are you auditioning for a horror movie after school?"

"I plead the fifth," I muttered as I parked myself at the kitchen table and smothered a short stack in syrup.

She sat down across from me. "My late hours and all the time I'm away are getting to you, aren't they?"

"No."

"Guy troubles?"

I sighed. "Sorta. There are two. . . . I don't want to talk about them."

"Do I know them?"

I shook my head. "New guys at school."

"The ones you mentioned before."

I nodded

She raised a questioning eyebrow but didn't press the issue further.

"Listen, uh, did Mom ever tell you about . . . her family?"

"Only that she didn't have one. She was an orphan. I've told you that."

Aunt Jo was an orphan, too. It was one of the reasons they'd bonded when they'd met. A common thread.

"Are you feeling a need to connect with your roots?" she asked.

Was I? I hadn't even stopped to consider that I might have a set of grandparents on each side: one in the Order, one in the Rebellion. I wondered if they were rooting for me. Why hadn't they made contact now that Asher and Devin had? They must have known about me.

"I don't know. I'm just . . . thinking about a lot of things lately."

"I wish I had some answers for you, hon."

I wondered how she'd feel if she knew some of my questions. I poured more syrup on the pancakes. "I think a lot of the answers are right here."

I popped more pancake into my mouth.

She laughed. "They can cure just about anything."

"Definitely," I said.

After finishing my pancakes and giving her a big hug, I walked out the door. No one was more important in my life. As long as I had Aunt Jo, I could make it through anything.

I was taking some books out of my locker that morning when a folded-up piece of paper fluttered to the floor. I bent to pick it up, thinking, reflexively, that it might be from Asher or Devin. But when I saw my name scrawled across the front in familiar, loopy script, I knew it was from Cassie. She never just texted me like any of my other friends did. She didn't believe in texting. She believed in calling and ceremonious note writing. Say what you would about Cassie, but she did everything with major flair.

The note read:

Cassie and the Mysterious Ellipses request the pleasure of your company at our very first GIG!

Tonight! 8:30 p.m.

Love the Bean

75 Main Street

River Springs, Colorado

Kindly RSVP by returning this note to my locker by

3 p.m. SHARP so we can give Ian a head count.

*Accepts with Pleasure*_____

*Declines with Regret*_____

I laughed, writing my name into the "Accepts with Pleasure" slot and slipping the invite into the front pocket of my backpack. Going down the hall to swing by her locker on the way to my next class, I saw Asher leaning against the locker door. My heart jolted. He was the last person I wanted to see at that moment. I whirled around and took the long way to class, the RSVP still in my pocket.

I got to lunch before Dan but after Cassie, who was already sitting at our table with her guitar out, scribbling something in her music notebook. As I sat down across from her, I waved my RSVP note in front of her face.

"Not to interrupt," I sang, "but I have a present for you. . . ."

"Ooh!" she squealed. "Yay! So many people are coming, I hope we have room for everyone at the Bean! What are you going to wear? Promise me you'll dress up? I'm *so* excited!"

I dropped the folded-up paper on the table in front of her and unwrapped my sandwich. I tried to push the memory of Asher guessing my favorite lunch out of my head. "I don't know what I'm wearing," I said. "I hate dressing up."

"Oh my god, if you lame out on me tonight I'll kill you. You're definitely coming, right? Right?"

"Of course! Yes, I'm definitely coming."

"Good. Because there's something I need to ask you."

"What?"

She paused, letting the drama of the moment build between us. "How do you feel about taking risks?"

"What?" I asked again. "What kind of risk?"

"There's something I'm thinking about doing tonight. And it's kind of scary."

"Cass! Seriously? What is it?"

She played with a long twisted curl that had come loose from her side braid. "I've never done anything like this before. It's a big risk."

"Riskier than singing on stage in front of a hundred people?"

"Are you kidding? I'm a performer. That doesn't scare

me one bit. If I did this, it would be, like, *epic*."

"Well, I think you should do it," I said before I even knew the words were coming out of my mouth. "Will you at least tell me what it is?"

"I guess you'll find out tonight," she said with a wink. When Dan and Ian walked up to our table seconds later debating the health benefits of spray cheese versus Kraft Singles, I noticed that she blushed, and the conversation was over.

I was getting books out of my locker for the last few classes of the day when Devin came up behind me. "Put those back," he said with a small smile, taking the books from me and shoving them back in the locker. "We're leaving."

"Oh, *really*?" I said. "Where are we going?"

"We're cutting school for the rest of the day."

The hall was emptying out; the bell was about to ring. I looked around for anyone who might care.

"Oh, great," I said. "Don't worry about my education. I'm sure I can get a job as a short-order cook somewhere."

"Skye," he said testily, the look in his eyes not one to mess with. "Don't think we haven't noticed how you're avoiding us again. But it's time to get back to work."

"Okay," I said slowly, shutting the locker door behind

me. The day before I'd stayed after school to take that essay test for Ms. Manning, so we hadn't practiced. As we walked down the hall, I noticed that only *my* footsteps echoed behind us.

Outside by my car, Asher was waiting. He had sunglasses on, and I could feel my knees weaken even as we walked across the parking lot. I got in behind the wheel, Devin sat next to me, and Asher hopped in the back. When I turned the key in the ignition, the car roared to life.

We were up in the mountains.

It was unseasonably warm considering how cold and miserable it had been since New Year's. The previous day's rain had left the snow melting in patches along the path, revealing spots of brown dead grass. It seemed like every step I took higher and higher up the mountain path revealed more and more of the dirt underneath. As I left a trail in my wake, I wondered how much of this was the weather and how much of it was me melting the snow with all my cosmic energy.

Finally we reached a clearing. The snow was packed hard on the ground and dripping icicles hung precariously from the branches of the evergreen trees that surrounded us. Devin stopped walking and turned to face me and Asher.

"Skye," he said gravely. "I know the last week or so has been hard for you, but I want to see you make a breakthrough today. I want you to impress me. *Show me what you can do.*"

"Come on," Asher said, spreading his enormous wings and shaking off a dusting of snow. "Enough with the speeches. You know what you have to do, Skye. Remember what I told you. Close your eyes. Find the switch. Flip it."

"Why do you guys care so much? If I fail to ever demonstrate any control, is someone going to shout, 'Off with her head!'"

They both shuffled their feet, looking uncomfortable.

I planted my hands on my hips. "Seriously? Is that what's going to happen?"

"No," Devin assured me. "It's just important that your powers emerge. What they are will decide your destiny."

"You mean my powers will decide who I get to fly off into the sunset with? What if I don't want to go with either one of you?"

"You have a choice only if you have powers associated with *both* the light and the dark," Devin said, his voice losing some of its cool detachment.

I flung my hand at Asher. "The Rebellion originally had powers of the light and they chose to jump into the darkness. So if I have only one power why can't I jump into whichever path I want?"

"You can," Asher said. "But if you jump to the opposite side, you'll lose that power."

"But I have a choice."

"Yes," he said.

"No," Devin said at the same time.

He glared at both of us. "If you exhibit the power of the Gifted, you belong with the Order."

"It doesn't matter at this point," Asher said, clearly frustrated. "The Elders are wise. They know things. Things they haven't told Devin or me. Our mission is to help you find your powers. So please, try to call forth your powers."

So I did.

I closed my eyes and searched the darkness behind my lids for what I hoped was there. I had no idea what I was looking for.

When I opened them, Asher and Devin were staring at me.

"Did I do anything?"

I thought I could actually hear crickets chirping in the woods surrounding us.

"No," Devin said with a sigh, his brow furrowing. "Try it again."

I stared at him in anger, my frustration pulsing just beneath my skin. If only I could focus *that* energy, I could get rid of Devin and my problems would go away. If I could just flip the switch and with one swift motion . . .

At that precise second, a boulder resting on the edge of an overhang above us rolled over the edge, tumbling right toward Devin. And everything happened so fast, it felt as if time were overlapping back on itself, everything occurring all at *once*.

My hand shot out instinctively in front of me.

Something was surging out of my palm.

Asher shouted something in a blur of winged blackness.

Devin suddenly wasn't where he'd been.

And the boulder stopped in midair. Stopped. Just like that.

Stopped in midair and *reversed direction*. It lofted on the wind and was borne back to its perch on the overhang, where it sat calmly, as if nothing had happened.

Asher and Devin stood with their mouths agape, staring at me.

"What did you do?" Devin demanded. "How did you do that?"

"Not bad," Asher said, smirking. "Maybe next time, you could forget to reverse the rock, though, save us all from Devin."

"Do it again," said Devin, ignoring Asher. "Whatever you just did, I want you to do it again."

I tried over and over again to recreate the moment, but I couldn't—what ran through my head was the fear that if I did, I wouldn't be able to stop myself from letting the boulder run Devin over this time.

"Try harder!" Devin yelled, and several small icicles fell from the branches as his voice echoed across the clearing. "You have to try *harder*!"

"I am!" I cried. "I don't know what else you want from me! I am doing the *best I can*!"

"I won't accept that," Devin said, his eyes shifting behind me, unfocused. "You have something in you. . . ." He paused, and I suddenly realized what a struggle this was for him. He looked like he was barely in control. Across the clearing, Asher was watching us. "I know it's there, Skye. Why don't you?" Devin's eyes glittered, and I was reminded of how different he was when it was just the two of us. The night I slept on the far side of the bed and woke up in his arms. "You must"—he paused between each word—"keep *trying*. Or else I don't know—"

"Are we done?" Asher sauntered up. He fixed Devin with a stare that would set Antarctica ablaze.

Devin looked at me again, and I could tell there was

something he was holding back, something more he wasn't telling me. Were there choices he was being forced to make that had nothing to do with what he wanted? For the first time, I truly understood how resentful he must have felt toward Asher.

Why had Devin never joined the Rebellion? Was it a question of duty versus self-sacrifice? If he could give up what he wanted so easily for the sake of the war between the Order and the Rebellion, what else was he capable of doing for the Gifted?

"Come on." Asher put his arm around my shoulder and drew me away from the icy blond angel. "You've done all you can for today."

"No." Devin's voice was almost pleading. "No, don't leave. Please."

My stomach twisted. I wanted to do something for Devin, but I was so tired of the pressure.

"Don't stand in our way," said Asher stonily. "I won't let you push her any harder. You know as well as I do that whatever is to come will come. Whatever is inside of Skye will manifest when the time is right."

"You don't know what you're doing, Rebel," Devin spat, and Asher flinched at the surprisingly hateful tone of Devin's voice.

"I'm not so sure you do, either," he said softly.

"Both of you, enough!" I yelled. My voice echoed off the rocks and boulders and trees and sky. "Stop fighting! Both of you. I can't stand it! I'm my own person, and I can take care of myself!"

The clearing, for the first time all day, was silent.

"I'm ready to leave," I said into the utter quiet, and it shocked me how loud my voice sounded, how sure of itself.

With a last glance at the two of them, I turned and walked back through the trees, back toward the path that would take me down the mountain. Soon, I would have to make a choice. It would be Devin on one side, Asher on the other.

And me, as always, in the middle, struggling for the right way out.

That night, I decided to follow Cassie's advice and get dressed up. I rooted around in my closet for the dress she had made me buy the last time we went shopping, and I tried to remember where Aunt Jo kept her good boots. Ten minutes later, I was back in front of the mirror, this time wearing the off-the-shoulder black sweaterdress, black tights, and brown motorcycle boots. My hair was loose and wild, and I'd put on a little makeup. A thrill went through me. I looked *good*. Who was this person?

And who, I wondered, did I want to impress?

When I finally pulled into town, the streets were already lined with cars. I parked in a spot a few blocks down and cut the engine. I sat in the solitary chill of the car, not quite ready to go in. Would Asher and Devin be in there? Tonight all I wanted was a break from everything, a chance to hang out with my friends without Devin breathing down my neck about my so-called powers or feeling heartsick over Asher. With a breath to steel myself, I got out of the car and walked down the street.

Love the Bean was warm and someone had put the twinkle lights back up. It wasn't hard to guess who.

Everything looked soft and lovely and magical. Lately I didn't even recognize my own life, but standing here, I thought everything felt perfect.

Cassie was stomping around on the stage in studded black ankle boots, decked out in a totally-inappropriate-for-the-weather sequined minidress, a tiara of tiny violet flowers perched on a messy upsweep of red hair. When she saw me, she gave me the thumbs-up, wiggling her eyebrows seemingly to indicate that she was ready for whatever big risk she had been thinking about taking ear-

lier. I waved and blew her a kiss. I wondered what she was
going to do.

Behind her, the rest of the band was warming up, adjusting the levels of the amps and tuning their instruments.
Dan caught my eye from the front row and waved me over.

"Hey, you made it," he said, giving me a hug. I noticed
his eyes flicking behind me, and I grimaced inwardly.

"They're not here," I said. Dan just looked at me, and I
wasn't sure exactly what more to say.

"Haven't seen you a whole lot lately."

"Yeah."

"I mean, like, other than lunch sometimes."

"Yeah . . ."

He raised his eyebrows.

"Which is great and all—I cherish our time eating
French fries together—but remember when we used to *do*
stuff? And, like, talk?"

"Dan, I know. I'm . . ."

"Everything okay? No situations I need to jump in and
take care of?"

I bit my lip. I was starting to realize, no matter how much
I wished it wasn't true, that we were growing up. There
were some things that your best friends just couldn't fix
simply by being there for you. "Thanks," I said, knocking

him on the arm and giving him a smile. "I'm *fine*."

"If you say so," he said, looking a little disappointed. "I was hoping for a fight or something. It's been a while since I roughed someone up."

"Kindergarten?" I said.

"Man, Tommy Evans didn't know what hit him."

"Well, sorry to get in the way of your big plans."

"Listen, S," he said, throwing his arm around me. "You're like my sister. I just want to make sure you're being careful. And if I need to whup some new-guy ass . . ."

"Dan, you don't have to—"

"I'm just saying. I don't like the way they look at you. Like you're something to win or whatever."

"Dan, if I need someone to step in, you'll be the first person I'll call, okay?"

He smiled, his shoulders relaxing. "I'll hold you to it."

"I promise," I said.

A mic shrieked loudly, and we turned abruptly to the stage.

Cassie finished tuning and looked out at us, smiling. She gripped the mic with both hands, her red hair blurring into the soft twinkle-lit room. Dan smiled, too, the corners of his eyes crinkling, as she started singing.

She was amazing. The Mysterious Ellipses jammed behind her, and the crowd was totally into it.

After a bit, she said, "This song is for my friends." Cassie looked determined, like she was psyching herself up for something big. Behind her, Trey and Jonah put their instruments down and watched as Cassie picked up her acoustic guitar and took center stage.

But then she started to play. And everything around us began to fade away.

The strumming of the guitar filled the room, and Cassie's voice rang out like a bell.

I suddenly got the distinct impression that she wasn't singing to her friends anymore—she was singing to one friend in particular. Dan stood next to me, nodding his head to the music.

He was staring at Cassie, looking at her like he'd never really seen her before at all. Looking at her like he finally understood. His eyes widened, and I saw the corners of his mouth turn up slowly.

As she sang, Cassie opened her eyes and looked out at the crowd. She found us. She found Dan.

The way she looked at him just then made something in my heart sink. Cassie had liked Dan this entire time, and I hadn't even realized it. I was a terrible friend.

Ian sauntered over and punched Dan on the arm. "She's amazing, dude."

Dan smiled. "She so is."

"She should make a CD or something."

"I'm sure she's already thought of that." Dan was grinning like I'd never seen before.

Ian turned to us and motioned to the coffee bar. "You guys want anything? My treat."

"Ian, seriously, how are you not fired?"

"I dunno, Skye, some people love me." It felt like a deliberate jab, and suddenly I felt a little guilty. Cassie and Dan hadn't been the only ones I'd been neglecting.

"I'll take a chai latte," was all I said in response.

Trey banged his drumsticks over his head as he counted out, "One, two, three, four," and struck up another song, a faster one. Dan and I started dancing to it, jumping up and down and waving at Cassie, who beamed as she belted out the lyrics.

Out of the corner of my eye, I spotted Asher come in from outside, shaking off a light dusting of snow and looking around. I pretended not to see him and shook my head wildly, letting my hair fan out. Dan laughed. When I glanced up at Asher, he was watching us, looking moodier than I'd ever seen him. Ian came back with our drinks, and as I sipped my latte, I carefully turned back around. Asher was gone.

Cassie began singing another song, this one a bit slower and softer than the others. Dan and Ian were watching the performance, paying little attention to me.

"Want to dance?"

I spun around so fast that my latte nearly spilled over the side of the mug. Devin was standing there, looking both unsure of himself and hopeful.

"Uh . . ."

"I'm sorry for being so impatient. I thought a dance might be a better way to say it."

"Sure. Okay." I put my mug down on a low table and took his hand.

Devin held me close, his hands on my waist while I placed mine on his shoulders. There were a few other couples dancing around us. I didn't usually slow dance at the Bean, and something about the whole thing felt awkwardly formal.

Even so, as I let his cheek brush against mine, I remembered how nice it felt to wake up in bed next to him. To let him hold me.

"Not bad, Devin," I said, grinning.

"Years of practice." I couldn't see his face.

Decades? Centuries? Millennia? I wasn't sure I wanted to know exactly how long he'd been around.

He paused, slowing us down mid-turn so that we were barely moving. "I know I've been difficult. I'm not—I can't do things as easily as Asher can. But I only want—" He pulled away from me, and the look in his eyes was intense. "I care about you, Skye. I don't want you to make a bad decision."

"One that might lead me to the dark side?" I teased.

But Devin didn't laugh.

"Just know that you're important, and I'd do anything for you."

His gaze never strayed from mine. In his, I read honesty and something much more.

When the music shifted into something with a faster beat, Devin let go of my hands. He walked away then. And like Asher, he didn't look back.

During the set break, Cassie jumped off the stage and ran to us. Her hair had fallen out of its bun, and her cheeks were red. "Guys!" she crowed. "What did you think?"

"Um, Cassie, you guys are *good*!" Ian said.

She did a little bow. "You like?"

Dan was suddenly quiet, as if he wasn't sure what he was supposed to say. He just kept pushing his floppy hair back and then smoothing it down, and then pushing it out of his face again. So I jumped in. "Yes! Amazing.

You know we need to celebrate."

Cassie smiled brilliantly. "I know. I was hoping you'd say that. With your Aunt Jo away, I was thinking . . ." She glanced at Dan and then back to me.

"Oh, no," I said. "No way. She'll kill me."

"Come onnn, Skye! We haven't had a party since your birthday, and your house is totally *empty*! Didn't you even say yourself that it was too quiet?"

Why was I hesitating? I'd been stressed out and anxious since my birthday, and Aunt Jo was away all the time, which was basically like *asking* for her kid to have a party. Didn't she know that's what would happen if she went away for weeks at a time?

"Okay," I said. "Let's do it."

"Really? Yay!" Cassie squealed. She ran back to the stage and jumped onto the platform, grabbing the mic with a little shriek. "Hey!" She called out, raising one arm to get everyone's attention. "Party at Skye's after the show!"

I turned to Dan. "This is either going to be the best idea ever or a very, very bad one."

It turned out that my house was the perfect party spot. The big windows let the moonlight in, creating a romantic ambiance, and the lack of partition between any of the rooms kept the party traffic flowing. I made a mental note to invite everyone back in the summer when we could spill out onto the big deck that looked out over the mountains, ignoring the nagging voice that wasn't sure where—or what—I'd be by the time summer rolled around.

Maggie Meltzer's older brother brought over a keg, and we stashed it in the kitchen, under the window where Raven's face had appeared not too long ago. I hated that everywhere I looked now, my old life was peppered with reminders of my new one. No matter how much I tried to push them away.

I stood by the keg, sipping from a red plastic cup and talking to some of the girls from the ski team. Things with Ellie had been a little tense for me since the ski trip, but she didn't bother me quite so much anymore. Of course, the memory of walking in on her and Asher by the ice machine still made me feel nauseous. But so did the thought of Asher going back to the Rebel camp when this was all over and leaving me forever.

Cassie came bounding up to me, sloshing beer over the side of her cup and pulling me away into a corner of the kitchen.

"Okay," she said. "So are you okay with everything?"

"Mm-hmm." I smiled.

"I haven't said anything all year because, well, we're all such good friends, and I didn't want to, you know, upset the balance."

"Cassie, I promise, you don't have to worry about that."

"So you're okay with it? I mean, I guess if he feels the same way, too?"

"Are you kidding? I'm more than okay with it! And trust me, he feels the same way. You should have seen his face when he realized you were singing to him."

Cassie beamed, and I knew it was the right thing to say. If

Cassie and Dan got together, it would change the dynamic of our group, but I couldn't help thinking about Asher and how much I wished there was nothing standing in *our* way. I needed to start getting used to things changing.

I wanted to tell Cassie about my parents—about the truth behind Asher and Devin's sudden appearance at our school and my own role in all this. The kitchen was loud, but we were standing off in a corner where it was quieter and with the way our heads were tilted together, I knew no one would be able to hear us.

"Cass," I started, my voice shaking a little in the way that it did when I got nervous. "I have to tell you something."

She eyed me carefully. "I knew you weren't telling me everything."

"It's . . . um . . . it's hard to talk about. But I want you to know. You're my best friend, and I've been keeping these things from you, and I just . . . I'm so sorry. I've wanted to tell you this entire time."

"Whoa, Skye. Shh, it's okay." She put her hand on my back. "I'm not mad. You can tell me anything, and I promise it will stay between us."

"Okay." I took a deep breath. "Remember the story that Asher told at the campfire?"

Cassie's eyes were growing wide and excited. "Yeah? Is this about Asher? Are you guys—"

"No," I said. "Well, kind of. I mean—there's more to the story than that. It turns out—" That sensation of being watched had suddenly pricked at the back of my neck, and as casually as I could, I looked behind me.

Devin was standing on the other side of the marble island. He wasn't looking at us, but from the look on his face, I knew he'd heard every word. I had to think fast. I had to play this off like I'd meant to tell her something completely harmless. Cassie looked a little bewildered, waiting for me to finish the story.

"It turns out," I continued, "that he never even liked Ellie. We kissed. He liked me the whole time." It was still the truth, after all. Just a very, very big omission. I hated that Devin had to hear it, but better that than he hear me spill all of his secrets to Cassie.

Cassie's eyes were huge. "Oh, Skye!" she exclaimed, throwing her arms around me. "That's incredible! You have to fill me in on *everything*!"

"I will, definitely. But I think you should go look for Dan now. I bet you two have a lot to talk about." I gave her a pointed look. "Besides, I should go check on the party. I am the hostess, after all."

"Okay!" She started to back away toward the open living room. "This is so romantic!" She squealed again, clapping her hands together before she took off.

My heart still pounding at the near miss, I turned around and found myself face-to-face with Asher. Devin was nowhere to be seen. It was a little creepy the way he could disappear like that.

"What's so romantic?" he asked, his head tilted to one side and studying me as though he could read my mind. He looked so good, in a soft, chocolate-colored sweater and jeans. I wanted to bury my face in his chest and feel him breathing beneath my cheek.

"Nothing to do with you, obviously," I said, turning away again.

"That's not what it sounded like," he said, catching up to me and leaning down, his voice low in my ear. "It sounded like the opposite, actually. Were you telling Cassie about me?"

"No!" I sputtered, spinning back around. "And what are you even doing here? I don't remember inviting you."

"You didn't. But if you'll recall, your friend Cassie invited everyone at the show. And that included me. So don't be rude. Are you going to offer me a drink or not?"

"Not," I said. "Why did you come?"

Asher looked taken aback, even a little hurt, but he kept up the light tone.

"I wanted to see you."

"But—"

"In case you've forgotten," he said under his breath, taking me gently but firmly by the elbow and turning to face me, "I have a job to do, remember? And that's to look out for you."

"Well, you haven't been doing so hot the past few days, have you?"

"Hey, will you stop being difficult with me for like five minutes, or is that too hard for you?"

"I'm complicated, remember?" I said. "I've got *dual* natures."

"Oh my god!" he said, running a hand through his hair in frustration. "You are impossible! Look, I haven't heard anything from the Rebellion camp in a while. And it makes me nervous that Raven's still lurking down here. Someone must have sent her. There's no way she could come on her own. She has to follow orders. She's a Guardian, that's what she *does*."

My heart beat more rapidly. I hadn't heard Asher admit to being nervous before.

"So?" I jutted out my chin.

"So something else has to be going on. I just wish I knew what."

We stood there facing each other for a second or two.

"Hey, you look really nice," he said suddenly.

"Really?" I said, pleased with my new favorite outfit and forgetting that I should pretend not to care what he thought.

He leaned in as if he meant to kiss me but straightened up at the last second.

"Sorry. Look, I'll just stay out of your way. But I'm not leaving." He backed away. "This is me lurking. Okay?"

"Fine," I said, sighing heavily. "I don't care. Do whatever you want."

Eric Walsh, who sometimes deejayed on underage nights at the only club in town, hooked his iPod up to the speakers in the living room, and the keg, miraculously, didn't run out. At one point, I couldn't find Cassie or Dan, and Ian was busy talking to Elizabeth Seifert. I was glad for him. He deserved someone who could appreciate him. I grabbed my jacket from a hook by the door and made my way to the sliding door that led onto the deck. But I never made it outside. Asher's frame was silhouetted by the moon as he leaned against the railing. He didn't see me through the glass doors behind him. He was looking up at the stars, watching the sky.

Instead of joining him like I had done on my birthday, I took off my coat and headed back to the kitchen for another beer. I wasn't going to hide from my party this time.

Red plastic cups rolled across the kitchen floor like tumbleweed. Instead of cleaning, Cassie and I were sitting on the counter in the kitchen, finishing what was left of the food. The last stragglers had just left, and it was something like two in the morning.

"I have to go home," she declared, jumping off the counter. "Brunch tomorrow? Someplace greasy?"

"Are you sure you're okay to drive?" I asked. "Are you done sobering up yet?"

"I haven't had anything to drink for like two hours. I've been busy," she added with a cryptic smile.

"You're really going to make me wait until tomorrow

morning for this story, aren't you?" I asked, following her out to her car.

"Mm-hmm!" She hummed as she got in.

"Fine!" I slapped the roof and backed up. "Call me for brunch."

Cassie turned the key in the ignition, but nothing happened. She tried again, but all we heard was a sick-sounding hum coming from under the hood. "Uh-oh," she said, getting out again. "Well, eff my life."

"Hooray!" I breathed a sigh of relief. "Now come inside like a smart person, sleep over, and in the morning, I'll drive you to the gas station to get a tow truck, okay?"

"Greasy eggs before the tow truck, though?" Cassie asked hopefully.

"Of course," I said. "It will be just like old times."

"That's what we *should* have done after your birthday," she said as we walked back toward the house. "Stupid boiler."

In my room, we pulled pillows and blankets down to the floor, just like we used to.

"Skye?"

"Mmm?"

"Dan and I kissed."

"I *knew* it!" I cried.

"I'm really happy," Cassie said sleepily. "Promise it won't change anything?"

I didn't say anything for a while, hoping that Cassie would think it was a rhetorical question. Eventually I heard the soft sound of her snoring, and I let out the breath I'd been holding. I wasn't upset. In fact, it was completely the opposite. It's just that I knew that things change really quickly. And you're not always prepared for them.

We woke at noon to the sunlight streaming through my window. A cold wind blew through my room, seeping into the spaces in our blankets.

"What the hell is that?" Cassie groaned from under a pile of pillows.

"I think my room became the Arctic overnight." I yanked the blankets tighter over my head.

"Seriously, that has to stop."

I shoved the blankets down a bit and peeked out. My window was wide open.

"Close it! Close it!" Cassie shrieked. "Oh my god, why did you open it?"

I hadn't. But I knew who had.

"I must have opened the window in my sleep. I've been

getting up in the middle of the night and forgetting. It's bad. Sorry."

I scrambled out from under the blankets, shut the window, and dove back under again.

"The cold air is making me crave an omelet, though," Cassie said, hopefully. "With hash browns."

Clad in soft sweatpants and hoodies, we drove to Big Mouth's for brunch. In the car, Cassie called her mom.

"Yeah, I slept at Skye's after the gig. I'm sorry I didn't call last night. Yeah, it went great! Yeah, we're going into town for breakfast. Oh, my car died, so I have to get it towed. I don't know, Mom. Hopefully it won't be that much. How should I know? I've never had my car towed before! Look, fine. Whatever. I'll call you later. Bye." She hit the End button violently and huffed. "Jeez, parents are such a waste of space." Then a look of horror washed over her. "Oh my god, Skye. I'm so sorry. I didn't mean that!"

"Don't worry about it," I said lightly. "Your parents are definitely annoying." It did sting a little, though, not to have anyone to call and let know I was okay or that I was driving into town to Big Mouth's and the gas station. Not for the first time since she'd been away, I hoped Aunt Jo would get back soon.

Brunch was greasy and delicious. Afterward I drove us

to the gas station so Cassie could get a tow truck back to my house. When she went over to the attendant behind the counter, I went outside.

"Skye?"

I spun around and came face-to-face with Devin.

"Oh my god, you scared me!"

"I'm sorry," he said, and in that second he looked like the fun Devin I'd hung out with the other night. The night I slept over at his place. It seemed like forever ago. "What are you doing here?"

I nodded toward the front of the store. "Cassie's car is at my place. It won't start. We need a tow truck."

Up front we heard Cassie yell, "*How* much?"

I laughed.

"You know," Devin said, "I've always been fascinated with cars, even though I don't need them to get around. That's probably why they intrigue me. Anyway, they're kind of a hobby. I've done enough tinkering on them over the years so I have a pretty good grasp of engine repair. I could come over and take a look."

"Really?" I asked incredulously. "You'd really do that? It would be a huge help. Cassie can't afford much right now and her parents are pretty strict when it comes to money."

"It would be my pleasure. Why don't I go there right

now and have a look? You two go off and do something fun for the afternoon. I'll be done before you know it."

"Wow, Devin, that is so nice of you. Thank you." I smiled. He smiled back, the same smile that had been so endearing the other night.

"Don't mention it, please."

"Okay, see you later! Cassie!" I called, bounding up to the front counter.

As we turned to leave the store, Devin smiled at us and waved. I thought it was weird that he hadn't said a single thing about working on my powers that day but decided not to overthink it. Instead, Cassie and I drove to the mall.

It was the best twenty-four hours I'd had in a long time. The gig at the Bean, the party, the sleepover, brunch, and then a full afternoon at the mall. Cassie made me buy this amazing winter white sweaterdress that was clingy in all the right places. She instructed me to wear it with tights and boots like I'd done the night before. I couldn't wait to see Asher's face when he saw me in it at school.

Maybe it was thinking about him that caused him to appear while Cassie was in the changing room with no fewer than a dozen outfits. I was wandering nearby, trying to find something else that might interest me when suddenly he was standing in front of me.

"Don't look so surprised," he said. "You gave me permission to lurk."

"At the party. Not when I'm shopping."

"I don't think you specified."

"What are you doing here?" I asked impatiently.

"Lurking."

"Seriously."

He lifted a shoulder, sighed. "I thought maybe we could do something together, something that has nothing at all to do with your powers. Maybe go to the Bean. Shoot some pool."

"You mean, like a date?"

"Sure, why not?"

"Asher, I don't like these games."

"It's not a game, Skye. I know I should avoid you, but all I can think about is being with you. I know the Elders won't be pleased—"

"But they should expect it, right? You're a Rebel."

He flashed a dazzling smile. "They might expect it, but they will definitely not like it. Anyway, I don't care. Not anymore. I want to be with you. We can go skiing. Or just sit outside. I don't care. Let's just go do something."

It sounded so appealing, but . . .

"I can't. Not right now. Cassie is with me. At least until Devin is finished working on her car."

"Devin is working on her car?" he repeated, his smile vanishing.

"Yeah, the engine died. She doesn't have the money for the repairs, and he offered to fix it for her."

He furrowed his brow. "Why would he do that?"

"Because he's being nice?"

He shook his head. "No. It doesn't work that way. He has no free will. He can do only what the Order tells him to."

Not true! I'd wanted to shout. He'd let me sleep in his bed. That was him, not the Order, who wanted me there.

"You can't trust him, Skye. If he's messing with her car—"

"He's not messing with it. He's fixing it."

"Not unless the Order told him to. And why would they do that?"

"Maybe they want him on my good side. To influence me to choose them? I don't know. He's doing us a favor."

"You just don't get it. Something's not right about this. I need to find out what's going on."

"I think you're overreacting. You're just trying to make him out to be the bad guy."

"I hope you're right."

With a final look at me, he walked away. My heart sank. Why couldn't things just be normal between us, for once?

"Okay," Cassie said, coming up behind me. "Since I don't have to pay for car repairs, I'm buying two new tops and springing for frozen yogurt."

As we sat at a small table in the food court, I could almost pretend that we were back in the pre-angel days, when everything was so much simpler.

On our way to the car, swinging our bags, that's when it happened to me for the first time.

The clouds swept in so suddenly, covering the parking lot in darkness even though it was still early evening. I wavered and then pitched forward, falling hard against the concrete. "Skye?" I heard Cassie calling as if from far, far away. "Skye!"

And then I couldn't hear her anymore. It was so black that I couldn't see a thing. The wind howled and the ground moved underneath me as if it was liquid. And then it all stopped.

I wasn't in the parking lot. I was on the ground still, but nowhere near where I'd been only minutes before. The clouds had dissolved into a cold blue sky, and I lay on my back, staring at the lush, green leaves on the soaring trees above and the verdant forest surrounding me. I wasn't in Colorado anymore. That was the first thing I noticed.

The second thing I became aware of was a voice, calling my name from somewhere above me. "Cassie?" I tried to say, but it was like when you try to talk in a dream and you can't make any sound come out. But it wasn't Cassie's voice, I soon learned. No.

It was Asher's.

"Skye?" He was shouting. "Skye? Stay with me. . . ."

"Asher?" I tried to say, but the same thing happened to my voice again. "Asher? I want to. I want to stay with you. Please. Help me." Nothing came out. "Help me!"

His face swam in and out of focus, and I noticed cuts and bruises that I'd never seen before. "Are you okay?" I tried to ask.

"We're going to find help. We'll be okay, now that we're here. They'll help us. They want you to live."

Then the sun grew bright, too bright, washing out everything around me. "Asher!" I yelled. "Don't go!" But I knew he couldn't hear me.

And before I knew it, I was back on the blacktop of the parking lot at the mall, heaving forward as if I might be sick.

"Skye!" Cassie was kneeling beside me. "Are you okay?

You just passed out, like, in the middle of the parking lot! Are you still hung over? Do you need something else to eat?"

"No," I said, trying to move. Cassie gave me her arm, and I leaned against her as I stood. "I'm fine." Was I fine, though? What had I just seen? What had happened to me?

"Come on," she said soothingly. "Let's get you home."

As Cassie drove, I leaned back against the leather seat and closed my eyes. I knew the past twenty-four hours had been too good to be true, too easy to forget about what was really happening to me. Had the vision been one of my powers trying to emerge? The only thing was I didn't know what sort of power it could possibly be.

When we got to my house, we saw Cassie's car sitting in the drive but no sign of Devin.

"Think he's finished with it?" Cassie asked.

Either that or Asher had chased him off.

"Try it and see."

She climbed in and turned the key, which was in the ignition. The car responded by purring to life. We cheered as she pulled it out of the driveway a little ways. She leaned her head out the open window. "Devin is a *saint*. This is amazing! I don't think the engine has ever been this quiet."

"Who knew he had it in him?" I had to admit, I was impressed. Sometimes he could really surprise me. Asher had painted him as a villain, but Devin had a good heart. He'd shared it with me during small moments. I made a promise to myself to find him at school on Monday and thank him.

"Are you sure you'll be okay?" Cassie asked. "Want me to come in with you?"

"No, really, thanks," I said. "I just need water and sleep. I'm probably just dehydrated."

"Okay, well, call if you need anything?"

I nodded. "Sure."

But I knew I wasn't as fine as I pretended. Something was happening to me, something scary.

Cassie took off, and I headed back into the house. I felt more alone than ever. A draft was blowing in from the sliding door, and I grabbed a heavy wool throw from a chair in the living room and, wrapping it around myself, walked through the sliding door onto the deck.

The sun had dropped behind the mountains, and the

sky was just fading from a velvety blue to a darker, inky smudge. The moon was rising, but it wasn't yet dark enough for it to shine as brightly as it would later. It was the in-between time.

I recognized the silhouette sitting in the Adirondack chair as soon as I stepped outside. He didn't see me at first—he had his back to me, looking up at the first stars of the night. Watching, as he had been the night before.

I knew, suddenly, what I wanted to do. I walked over to him and climbed into his lap, wrapping the blanket around the two of us. He seemed surprised, but he smoothed my hair back with one hand as he let me tuck my head under his chin.

"Did you chase Devin off and fix Cassie's car?"

"No. He was gone when I got here, but I did check out the engine. Appears he fixed it."

"You sound baffled. He healed me. Why couldn't he want to fix a car?"

"The Order just doesn't work that way."

We sat in silence for several long moments. I simply absorbed his nearness.

"Asher?"

"Yeah?"

"I'm scared."

"I know. You'd be stupid not to be."

"But what am I *becoming*?" His arms tightened around me. Protecting me from what he was about to say next.

"Your powers are sporadic and choppy so far—and none of us know how they'll develop—if they continue to at all. Not for nothing, Skye, but I think they will." He leaned in and whispered in my ear, "I think you're strong." I shivered. "All of this has been to prepare you. And if I can do anything to help prepare you for what's to come, then I promise that I will. The Order is ruthless. They don't care about you. They only care about the power they stand to gain—or prevent us from gaining—and that they are able to keep manipulating destiny at will." He shifted my weight so that he looked into my eyes, and for a moment, I felt a longing so sharp, I thought I would stop breathing. "And I think the one thing both sides agree on is that you're going to be different from anything we've seen before. And that we haven't even seen half of what's to come."

I wanted to tell him about what had just happened in the parking lot of the mall. But something about it scared me too much. I wasn't ready to say it out loud yet.

"So I was thinking," he said, playing with a strand of my hair.

"Again?" I asked.

"Do you want to hear it or not?" He looked up at me.

"Amaze me."

I could tell he was fighting not to laugh.

"Well," Asher said slowly. "Have you ever been so close to something you've wanted for as long as you can remember, something you never thought you could have, and been afraid to reach out and just . . . take it?"

"Yes," I said, my heart racing.

"The whole point of the Rebellion is so that we can live by our own rules. That's the entire reason we jumped," he said. "Right?"

"If my history lessons have served me correctly," I said, trying to keep my voice from shaking, "then yes. I do believe you're right."

"I know that Devin doesn't have any choice," he said, "and I see how much that hurts him. And I know you're stuck between two choices, and you don't exactly have a conscious say in the matter. Your powers will take over when it really counts.

"But *I* have a choice, Skye. I have the power to choose whatever I want. And there is nothing that I've ever wanted more." He gulped. I could feel it beneath me.

We were quiet for a few minutes. I leaned my head on his

chest and listened to the sound of his breathing.

"You don't have a heartbeat," I realized.

"Does that bother you?" he asked.

"No." I thought for a minute. "As long as you can feel things and care about things."

"It's a misconception that you need a heart to love," Asher whispered into my hair.

I looked at him, the way his eyes crinkled at the corners even though his mouth stayed so serious. He had a little dimple near the left side of his chin.

I kissed him, and he wrapped the heavy wool blanket tighter around us as the moon rose brighter in the sky.

34

I usually slept late on Sundays, but something woke me up that morning. I was out of bed and halfway to the bathroom to get ready for school before I realized that what woke me wasn't my alarm clock at all. It was sirens passing on the road. I got back into bed.

The sunlight filtered through my curtains and sliced its way across my face, making it hard to fall back asleep. I couldn't make my eyes stay closed even for a second. I lay in bed, staring at the ceiling. The glow-in-the-dark stars I'd stuck up there as a kid looked so different in the light than they did in the dark. Now they just looked like stickers.

I felt like a different person from the one who'd stuck them up there all those years ago. I'd changed so much, even in just a few weeks.

Turning over in bed, I wondered if maybe Asher was right, that whatever was in me had always been there in some form. I had obviously awakened it. I now needed to learn to control it, to figure out if it was the powers of the light or the dark. I hoped that was something I could do.

I got up and wandered down to the kitchen to make coffee, reveling in the little things that I had always loved but taken for granted: the smell of the wooden staircase, the smooth banister as my fingers glided over it, the geometric pattern that the light made as it filtered through the big plate glass windows in the open living room behind me, the feel of tile under my bare feet, the crunch of coffee grinds as I scooped them from the pouch, the earthy smell as the steam plumed from the pot, and water through the filter sounding like soda being sucked through a straw. The quiet as I poured coffee into a mug. The light clink of spoon against ceramic as I stirred in milk.

I brought my mug back up to my room and sat in the big overstuffed armchair by the bay window, pulling my legs up underneath me.

The light filtered in the window at a certain slant just at that moment, catching something metallic that glittered at me from my bookshelf. I stood up and walked over to it.

It was my birthday present from Cassie and Dan—the one I'd never opened. I reached up to the top shelf and took it down. *Happy Birthday, Skye!* was still scrawled across the top in goopy-looking glitter glue. For some reason, looking at it now made me inexplicably sad. I took a letter opener from the mug of pens on my desk and carefully slid it through the tape that was keeping the tinfoil in place. I smiled, picturing Dan wrapping this thing, not having a clue as to what to do.

The tinfoil fell away, and I finally saw what was inside. It was an iPod plug for my car. It was such a thoughtful present—I was the only person we knew who still listened to the radio. My heart fluttered in my chest. I knew my life would never be that simple again.

Restless from the coffee, I went back down to the kitchen to make myself some breakfast and try to clean the house a little bit. How long had it been since Aunt Jo had left? I had completely lost track of time.

I'd managed to pick up all the empty red cups and mop the kitchen and hallway before taking a break to make myself a bowl of cereal. I was reading the back of the box when the phone rang.

The drive to River Springs County Hospital wasn't one I'd ever made on my own. In fact, the last time I'd been there was when I was six, and that time, I was in the back of an ambulance. A memory flooded through me as I passed road sign after road sign.

"Stay with me, Skye. Come on, stay with me, girl." I was lying on a stretcher, and I couldn't move any part of me. I was crying, but my tears kept running in between my cheeks and this plastic thing that was covering my mouth and helping me breathe. I was breathing very fast. I kept trying to ask where my parents were, but my words got trapped in the plastic thing, too. The nurse held my hand next to me and told me I had to calm down. I had to stop crying. She said, "Stay with me, Skye. Come on." I wondered how she knew my name.

"Skye!" Dan was waiting for me in the lobby. He jumped up when he saw me run through the automatic doors. He looked devastated, his eyes bloodshot with the hint of tears. "I'm so glad you're here. Hospitals freak me out."

"Is she okay?" I asked hoarsely, feeling tears begin to swell in my own eyes.

Dan looked crestfallen. "She's unconscious. The doctors say they think she'll be okay, but she hasn't woken up yet."

We walked to the reception desk, where I signed in.

"I hate hospitals, too," I said, shivering.

There were gurneys everywhere. "Where's my mom?" I asked frantically when I figured out that all I had to do to be heard was pull the plastic thing off my mouth. "Where's my dad?" I was sobbing and sobbing. All I knew was what the nurse had told me: they were in a different ambulance right in front of ours. They were on stretchers, too. The nurse reached for me and held the plastic thing in place. I tried to breathe normal like she told me, but it was hard. "Where are they?" I wanted to scream. "Which stretcher is them?" But no one could hear me. My words got trapped in my breathing, which stayed in the plastic thing and traveled away down many tubes.

Cassie was in room 512. All down the hall, there were people in wheelchairs, people hooked up to oxygen tanks, people with IVs stuck in their arms. There were gurneys everywhere. My breath caught in my chest, shallow and quick. I knew I was sweating, and I was starting to see black spots in front of me. I pushed open the door. I'd had a room just like that one. Eleven years ago, almost exactly.

Cassie's mother, Evelyn, looked as though she'd aged a hundred years. I hugged her tightly.

"I'm so sorry," I said.

When we separated, she explained that Cassie's two brothers, Charlie and Matty, were upset and rowdy, so

Cassie's dad had taken them down to get Jell-O in the cafeteria.

As I moved toward the bed, I cringed, trying not to let it show. Cassie had a black eye and bandages all over her arms. One leg was covered by a thin white blanket while the other hung suspended from the ceiling in a cast. She was asleep.

"Cassie," I whispered. "What happened to you?"

Evelyn placed a comforting hand on my shoulder.

"Her brakes weren't working," she whispered. "She spun out and hit a lamppost. That damn gas station did a hell of a job fixing her car!"

"The gas station didn't fix it," I said, something dawning on me. "I'll be right back."

I knew they were somewhere in the hospital. If I was there, they couldn't be too far behind. I scoured the halls. I took the elevator to each floor, searching for any hint of feathers, dark or light hair. Anything.

Devin was a Guardian. Devin had the power to heal. Devin could heal Cassie. He could make her better. I would make him do it.

I found them in the lobby, hovering by the reception desk. Asher looked worried. Devin's expression was harder to read. Did he already know her destiny? No, I wouldn't believe that. I wouldn't allow her to die.

When Asher saw me, he ran to me and let me throw myself against his chest. "Is she okay?" he asked. "Is she badly hurt?"

"She's in a coma," I said. "Or asleep, or unconscious. I don't know. She hasn't woken up yet. Devin! You have to heal her! You have to fix her, okay? Come on!"

Devin looked confused. "What?"

"She's in room five twelve. Come on! Why are you being so slow? Let's go!"

A strange look crossed his face. "I can't," he said awkwardly. "I can't heal her. I haven't been given the order to do so."

"The order?" I repeated.

I haven't been given the order to do so.

The Order.

"Yes," Devin said warily as if I might hurt him. "I can't heal her unless the Gifted command me to."

His words reminded me just how much of a puppet he really was. I could never align myself with the Order. Never. Not if that's what it meant. I'd choose to become a Rebel right now, whether or not my powers agreed.

"There's nothing you can do?" I asked slowly, pointedly.

"You got her car to start, after all. Did the Gifted command you to do that?"

"The Gifted have circuitous ways of working sometimes, Skye," he said emphatically. "It's not always immediately clear what their intentions are. We have to trust them. It will all come to light soon."

"But what if Cassie doesn't wake up?" I asked, horrified. "What if she . . . ?" I couldn't finish the sentence. What if she died, just like my parents had? What if Cassie left me, too?

"Then it will all be part of the master plan," Devin finished. I couldn't speak.

"I told you, Skye." Asher was getting worked up. "I told you the Order works in frightening ways. They don't care about anyone."

"We work for the greater good of the world," Devin retaliated. "We keep life in balance."

"You don't care about life!" I shouted. "You don't care about anyone's lives! I bet you don't even care about mine."

"There isn't anything I wouldn't do for you."

"That's not true. Not if you'll do only what the Order gives you permission to do."

"Skye, how can you say that? I—" A curious expression replaced the mask of complacency he'd been wearing. Even

Asher stopped to look. "I have to go," he said suddenly. "I'm sorry that I can't cure your friend. I hope you can find another way to help her." And with that, he turned and walked out through the automatic front doors.

Asher turned to me. "I don't know what that's about," he said helplessly.

Why had he walked out like that? The facts were suddenly arranging and rearranging themselves in my brain. Devin had to follow the direct commands of the Gifted in order to keep the course of fate running according to the Order's master plan. That meant that someone had to have given him the command to fix Cassie's car. But why would they do that unless . . . unless they didn't want to fix Cassie's car at all. Unless they wanted to cut the brakes. Unless they wanted to hurt Cassie.

"Asher, do you think it's possible Devin cut the brakes on Cassie's car?"

"I don't know. I didn't check them. I only checked the engine."

"But why would the Order want him to hurt Cassie?"

"I don't know," he said again. "I wouldn't rule anything out at this point. I'm going to go try to get some truth out of him, and check in with my camp. Stay here, Skye, okay? You'll be safe here. The Order is changing the rules, and we have to act accordingly."

"You're leaving me?" I gasped. "Asher?"

He looked down at me, tracing his thumb across the freckles on the bridge of my nose.

"I'll be back really soon. Don't worry."

And then he was gone.

I tried to think back over the last few days to what could have possibly made the Order want to hurt Cassie. I worked backward. We went to the mall while Devin worked on her car. We saw him at the Shell station. Cassie and I went to Big Mouth's for brunch. We woke up the morning after the party, with the window open. The party . . . talking to Cassie about the campfire story . . .

Suddenly I stopped cold. Devin had been there when I'd almost told Cassie everything. His creepy stare had been the reason I'd stopped. He'd heard everything. He'd heard me almost spill all of my darkest secrets—and his. He knew Cassie was the only one I'd ever dream of telling. And if he needed me alive but the secrets to remain secrets, the surest way to keep me from telling her would be to kill her.

Could the Devin I'd come to know really be capable of something like that?

Or was Asher trying to turn me away from Devin by

making me suspicious? He did have a choice. He could do whatever he wanted. And they'd certainly always been competitive. Especially when it came to me.

I was back to not knowing if I could trust either of them.

I returned to Cassie's room. Her mother had gone to get some coffee, according to Dan, who was there holding Cassie's hand and whispering to her.

He looked up at me as I moved to the other side of the bed and wrapped my fingers around hers. "I should have told her I liked her a long time ago. I think I've loved her forever," he said.

"She's going to be okay."

"How do you know?"

"I just . . ." I wondered if I could make a deal with the Order. Let Devin heal her, and I'll come to your side—willingly and enthusiastically. Or maybe I could heal her myself if I concentrated hard enough.

I closed my eyes and searched for the well of power that Devin had told me about, tried to find the switch that Asher visualized when he brought forth the elements. This was important. So important. My emotions were ratcheted on high. I had to make this work. I couldn't lose Cassie. I'd lost my mom and dad. I'd been powerless to do anything for them.

I. Could. Not. Lose. Cassie.

Grief slammed into me at the thought of my life without her. And with it came anger. Why would I go to the Order when they were the kind who would refuse to help someone simply because they hadn't been given permission? Why wasn't blanket permission given? See someone who needs to be helped. Help them.

Why were they stingy with their gifts?

I couldn't, wouldn't, believe that of Devin. He had to be there now, begging for permission. For me. He would do that for me. I knew he would.

I remembered how worried Asher had been in the snow cave when he'd discovered I was hurt. He'd said that he couldn't help. I hadn't thought anything of it at the time, but now I knew he'd regretted that he didn't have the same powers that Devin did. Yes, fire had kept us warm until we were rescued, but it couldn't heal. It wasn't the greater power.

The rebellious angels of long ago had paid a high price for their desire to leave Paradise.

And Paradise was what the Order provided. At least according to Devin. He wanted to go back there, desperately. He wanted to take me with him.

Could I go if Cassie died?

If Cassie died . . . if Cassie died . . . if Cassie died . . .

The refrain echoed through my head. My anger built. My frustration reached new limits. My grief threatened to consume—

A loud bang erupted from the corner of the room. I jerked my eyes open. The machine monitoring Cassie's vitals was smoking, the readings going berserk.

"Crap!" Dan shouted, reaching for the buzzer to signal for a nurse.

I released my hold on Cassie and backed into a corner. I wanted to slide down to the floor and weep. I couldn't help her. I couldn't help anyone. All I could do was destroy things.

The boiler, the thermostat, the bus heater so hot it burned my fingers. The avalanche. Now the machine that monitored her vitals. What if I'd sent this negative energy through Cassie and killed her?

Two nurses came rushing through the door. "I need you

to leave," one ordered.

"Is she going to be okay?" I asked.

One nurse was messing with the machine, unhooking Cassie, as the other pressed a stethoscope to her chest, listening to her heart. Dan just stood there, looking as lost as I felt.

"She's going to be okay, right?" I said. "She has a heartbeat, doesn't she?"

"I really need you to leave," the nurse taking care of the machine repeated.

When Dan and I both just stood there like statues, she grabbed our arms and ushered us out into the hallway.

"What the hell happened in there?" Dan asked when the nurse disappeared back inside Cassie's room and the door closed behind her.

"I don't know," I lied.

We sat in a couple of chairs in the hallway. Eventually the nurses emerged. They confirmed there was no change in Cassie, but the monitoring machine was destroyed. They'd wheeled the broken one out and brought in another.

I wanted to tell myself that the machine was old, faulty. But who was I kidding? I'd ruined it. Because I couldn't control my powers.

When everything was properly set up again, the nurses

gave us permission to go back in. Dan was pushing open the door when he looked back to see that I was lingering in the hallway. "You coming?"

I couldn't risk doing something that would inadvertently hurt Cassie. "No, I think I'm going to head on home. I'm really tired."

It was a stupid, lame thing to say. But there were no words I could utter that would make my leaving seem all right.

"If—" I shook my head. "*When* she wakes up, call me."

I could tell from the confusion in his eyes that my leaving was the very last thing he expected.

"Yeah, sure, okay," he said. As if I wasn't leaving only Cassie, but him as well.

I watched as he pushed open the door and went inside. I desperately wanted to go with him. But I couldn't. I knew I couldn't. I didn't belong here any longer. The problem was, I didn't know where I belonged.

Adjusting my bag on my shoulder, I headed toward the elevator, then changed my mind. The way my emotions were rioting, I had no idea what would happen when I pushed the button for the first floor. I could knock the elevator out of commission or send it plummeting to the concrete below. So I located the stairs and hurried down them, flight by flight, grateful that none of the lights exploded as I passed beneath them.

When I reached the bottom of the stairwell, I went through the door marked EXIT and emerged in the parking lot. It was dark, the cars illuminated with halogen lights. I'd lost track of the time since I'd entered the hospital. I was surprised to find that night had fallen.

As I neared my car, I dug my car keys out of my purse and pressed the Unlock button. I reached for the door—

"Devin is losing his resolve." Raven's voice sent a piercing fear down my spine. I looked over. She was standing beside me, and I didn't know where she'd come from.

"I knew he wasn't cut out for this mission," she continued. "I told him he should ask to be taken off it—for his own sake—but he wouldn't listen. Something about pride and integrity, blah blah blah." She brought her hands out from behind her back. In them was a twisted metal object. "Oh, don't look so confused, little innocent Skye. You know exactly what this is. It's the brakes to your friend's car. And do you know how I got it?" Raven smiled slightly. "You're worried it was Devin, aren't you?"

"You bitch," I said in a gravelly voice.

"Skye, I'm only looking out for you! If *they* won't tell you what's really going on, I will. And who knows? Maybe in the process we'll trigger those elusive powers of yours." She came toward me, and I found myself backing up against the side of my car.

"Here's how it works, princess. I know you'd love to think that Cassie's accident is the first time the Order has become, let's say, *involved* in your life. The Order is involved in everyone's lives, at some point or another. But yours above all, because you're *special*." She spat the word, like she couldn't wait to get it out of her mouth.

"Let's have a little history lesson. Let's see, where to start? Your favorite color is blue, isn't it, Skye? Because you liked the tune of "The Blue Song" on *Sesame Street*? How cute. Then you learned about the color sky blue, and you thought it was named after you. I mean, it's so precious I could scream. In another house, on another street, too far away for you to have met him yet, another little boy loves the same lyrics, even so much as to ask his parents to buy him only blue clothing. On the first day of kindergarten, you walk into your shiny new classroom. There are empty seats next to a little blond girl with pink ribbons in her hair, a girl wearing a yellow dress, and a boy wearing a sky blue sweatshirt. And who does little Skye sit next to?"

"How do you know that?" I whispered.

"His name is Daniel Rosenberg, and he's your best friend

until you miss the bus one morning a few days later. . . ."

"Who told you all this?" My hands were shaking.

"Don't interrupt, Skye. Didn't your Aunt Jo teach you that it's rude? Where was I? Right, you miss the school bus a few days later, and while you're walking down the street you find a notebook with the name Cassie Saunders inside. And when you find Cassie and give her back her notebook, you realize she has peanut butter on her fingers. You discover you both love to put peanut butter in chocolate pudding cups. This is the basis of an eleven-year friendship."

"How do you . . . ?" We still ate those sometimes.

"Skye, the Gifted see everything. They make things happen. They know. And should I bring up the reason why you're oh-so-terrified of birthdays? Your own, in particular?"

"No," I whispered.

"Could it be that your parents died on your sixth birthday, Skye? In a—oh, what a coincidence—car accident?"

"How dare you bring that up," I said. "That day changed my life. That day changed everything, forever. It was my fault." I was screaming, crying. "Mine! I lived and they didn't! I did this to them! And you have no right—"

And then it all came crashing down on me. *Coincidence?*

What had Devin said—the Order works in circuitous ways? They caused Cassie's car accident. Was it possible that . . .

"The Order killed my parents," I said numbly. "They orchestrated that car crash. Just like they did Cassie's."

"Bravo." Raven burst into applause. "You deserve a big gold star."

"They wanted me dead, too, didn't they? They saw something about me, and they wanted to prevent my powers from ever emerging."

"Oh, they were right about you!" Raven cooed. "So very smart."

"But I didn't die."

"No, you *didn't* die."

"How come?"

For the first time, Raven looked slightly uncomfortable. "No one knows. The Gifted saw that you would die alongside your parents. But then . . . you didn't. It was the first and only time this has ever happened. It's why they wanted to watch you so closely. To see what would develop. Until . . ."

"Until what?"

"Now they can't read your future at all anymore."

"I already know that."

"Good for you. But did you *already know*," she said this mockingly, "that they can't read the future of those around you, either? You're blurring the destinies of others."

I inhaled sharply. "I am?"

"You've certainly changed Devin's destiny," said Raven, leveling me with an even gaze. "The Gifted can no longer see it. And it's only since he's been around you."

I swallowed hard.

"He used to be mine," she snarled. "And you *took* him from me."

"I didn't take him!" I protested. "He isn't mine."

"You'd be surprised," she said, "how much he is."

Silence echoed between us.

"What?" I whispered.

"Devin is a Guardian, like me. We do not act on our own whims. The choices we make are not our own." She paused, and I thought I detected a sadness creeping into her voice as she said, "Everything is decided for us. And whatever feelings are growing inside of him are going to destroy him. I know him well enough to know that." Her eyes grew hard again.

"Feelings?" My heart hammered at my rib cage. What was she talking about?

"Yes. You're causing him to do things, things he's not

supposed to do. They ordered him to sabotage the brakes. Luckily I checked. If they found out he disobeyed a direct order . . . I don't even want to think about what they'd do to him. It would not be pleasant. I can tell you that."

"If they can't see his destiny, then how do they know that what he's feeling for me isn't what he's supposed to feel?"

"Because they could see it at one time. They lost sight of it only right before your seventeenth birthday. It's got something to do with your eyes."

Flashing silver. Little silver bells. When they ring, we'll know.

"That's why they're watching you so closely. Because you are a dangerous girl, Skye Parker. Very, very dangerous to them."

"Why would they wait until my sixth birthday to try to kill me?"

"Oh, Skye, silly Skye. They tried to kill you lots before then. That one just had the most . . . collateral damage. The Gifteds' sight is perfect, but sometimes sloppy Guardians come and mess. It. Up." She held up the brakes to the car.

"And they haven't tried to kill me since."

"Well, after that day, they knew you were more special than they'd ever realized. They wanted to see what happened."

"Why are you doing this?" I asked.

"Because," she said. "Someone has to. And they told me to."

"I thought Devin was the Guardian they sent to watch me."

"*I* thought you were catching on, Skye. They sent Devin for an entirely different reason. Think about it. Haven't you gotten all of your information from me—not him?"

Could she be right? My heart hammered away. *What if Devin wasn't sent here to protect me after all?*

"He was supposed to lure you—make you want him enough that you would willingly come over to our side."

Could he have been playing me all along? But if so, why hadn't he followed the order about Cassie's brakes?

"Anyway," she said. "Hope your Aunt Jo's okay. Pity about that trip leader of hers breaking her leg in that nasty fall. What was it? A faulty carabiner? And now Jo is out in the woods with no way to reach you? I do hope nothing happens to her."

Anger unlike anything I had ever felt was blooming in the pit of my stomach.

"If you touch her, I'll kill you," I said, my voice rising. "You can't take her from me! Not after you took my parents and Cassie!"

The ground beneath us began to shake, and car alarms began going off. Raven's eyes went wide. "It's true," she said in awe.

"Leave me alone!" I cried. "Leave all of us alone!"

Then the parking lot lights went out, and I was someplace else.

36

It was a vast white landscape, like the Antarctic during a snowstorm. I couldn't tell if we were indoors or out. It wasn't cold. It wasn't warm. No breezes or gusts of wind blew through my hair. It didn't feel like much of anything.

Slowly, through a white mist, shapes began to materialize. The curve of an arch here, the angular edge of a step there. Figures were moving slowly. But I couldn't make out anything other than the vaguest of shapes. I couldn't even tell if they were human.

The mist swirled around me. Whitening out everything else.

And just as suddenly as I'd appeared in this place, I was back in the hospital parking lot, grasping the car door handle with both hands for balance. Facing Raven.

"Oh my god," she said. "This changes everything!" And then she was gone.

Panic surged through me. *Aunt Jo!* I had to find her! What if Raven was on her way there now? What if that's where the Order had set their sights next? Aunt Jo was in danger, and I had to find her, wherever she was.

I felt around in my purse and dug out my phone. I pressed the number for Aunt Jo and the call went immediately to voice mail. "Dammit!"

She was probably out of cell phone range. I called the office, and no one answered. They always had someone at the office to field calls in case of an emergency. They could always get in touch with Aunt Jo via satellite phone. So why was no one there?

I jerked open the car door, slid in, and revved the engine, peeling out of the parking lot as I simultaneously riffled through my glove compartment for any maps Aunt Jo might have left in there. Where did she say she was? The Collegiate Peaks? I hadn't been there in years, but I knew it was west, toward Denver. I gunned it toward the highway. What was I going to do when I got there? She was out in the backcountry. How could I find her?

As I drove, my mind turned over everything I knew now. What people had told me over the years—and even as recently as today.

The day I turned six years old, my father had been driving me and my mother home from my birthday party at the county fair in the next town over. It was raining, but everyone at the party had had the best time. Cassie, Dan, and I got to ride ponies, and all three of us were as dirty as if we'd rolled in the mud with the farm animals. It was my best birthday ever. I was so happy.

On the drive home, Dad missed the exit on the freeway and ended up crashing into a Buick before he could reach the next turnoff. They found me in the backseat after they'd pulled my parents from the wreck. The car was totaled, but I didn't have a scratch on me.

Gurneys were everywhere. "Mom!" I called. "Dad!" My arms wanted to flail, but something was holding me down. I was okay, though. I wasn't bleeding, and I didn't even have scratches anywhere. No broken bones. The doctors and nurses were using words like miracle *and* amazing. *I just wanted to see my parents. I was in a bed in a hospital room, just sitting there, eating red Jell-O, when they told me. "You're alone now, Skye."*

They probably didn't say it exactly like that, but that's how I remembered it. "You're alone now." That was before Aunt Jo, my mother's best friend, adopted me. Before I moved into this house with her.

In the car, with the trees and primary-colored road signs flickering by, I started. *Alone.* What did that word make me think of? *You're alone now, Skye.*

I wanted to wait until we were alone to share this with you.

Devin. He'd said it just a few days ago, the night he tried to show me how to heal a flower. Raven was right. The Order did want to get me alone, didn't they? They'd arranged for Cassie's brakes to fail so she'd get into an accident—hoping to kill her and wipe out anything I might have told her. They'd fixed Jenn Spratt's fall so that Aunt Jo would be the one to go out on extended trips, leaving me alone in the house while my fate came crashing down around me. The Order wanted to isolate me, get me alone. So I could be that much easier to pull away from my old life—everything I once knew. So I would be weak. And Devin had been their pawn. Until he'd stopped following orders and Raven had taken over.

That's what I was thinking when my car hit an ice slick on the road and sped wildly out of control. I panicked and shoved the wheel to the right, narrowly missing a huge tree. I fought to turn the wheel to the left to avoid another one coming straight at me. But I couldn't spin it fast enough. I couldn't stop this from happening. It was going to, whether I was ready or not.

My car was smoking.

I flashed back to the last car accident I'd been in.

Skye, stay with me.

Miraculously I wasn't hurt again. The car wasn't even totaled—but it didn't look good. I grabbed my purse from where it had been flung to the floor of the passenger side and got out. It was freezing, an even more biting cold up here in the mountains than in town, where the buildings blocked some of the wind. I reached into the car for my parka, put it on, and zipped it up all the way.

Aunt Jo had made me program the number for AAA into my phone when I'd gotten a car, so I dug around in my purse for the phone. I pulled it out, went to punch in the programmed number, and froze. No reception. I slammed my palm on door.

"Do you have any idea how easy it is to block a signal so it doesn't reach a cell phone? Child's play," a sickly sweet voice taunted in front of me. I looked up to see Raven standing among the trees in a white puffy jacket with a furry white hood. "I think it's sweet that you want to protect your adoptive mother," she said with a smile.

"Because you couldn't save your real one."

"What do you want from me?" I screamed.

"Well, I think you know that," she said. "I want you to follow me."

"Why should I follow you?"

"Oh, Skye, when are you going to learn that running from your problems isn't going to do you any good? You can't run from your destiny. It follows you everywhere."

I swallowed. "Where are we going?"

Raven smirked. "You'll find out when we get there."

And so, with nowhere else to turn, I followed her.

37

We entered a clearing at the top of a mountain, not unlike the one I'd practiced in with Asher and Devin. The earth was hard and frosted over. The sky was a violently bright blue above us, and the clouds wisped out into a fog that covered everything. It felt like we were no longer on Earth. I guess, in a way, we weren't.

Raven stood just behind me. Before us were two angels I'd never seen before. One had huge ivory wings extending from his back, yellowing in the way that a polar bear's fur might. He looked strong, though advanced in years. Wrinkles fanned out from the corners of his eyes and mouth, and his hair was a salt-and-pepper gray. From what Asher and Devin had told me about how angels aged, he must have been thousands of years old for him to look like an old man. The other angel's wings matched Asher's. They were blackest black. He looked slightly younger than the man beside him, though white patches gave his temples a dignified appearance.

Devin and Asher stood next to who I assumed were their respective Elders. They avoided meeting my eyes and looked at the ground instead, hands behind their backs as if they were following orders.

"Well," said the angel with the white wings in a low, velvety voice. "She's come."

My two messengers looked up, each with a different expression flickering across his face. Asher radiated fury. Devin, fear. I sensed somehow that it wasn't fear for himself but for me. And they both looked like they were in pain.

"I am Astaroth, one of the Order's Gifted. And this"—he motioned with one long elegant hand to the angel beside him—"is Oriax. He is a Rebel Elder."

I gulped, and immediately thought everyone had heard. Astaroth raised one gray eyebrow.

"We seem to have a . . . situation." His eyes flicked behind me. I whipped my head around.

Raven. She stood smugly off to the side, her white wings

outstretched and her hands clasped behind her back, looking like a delinquent schoolgirl in her little white jacket. When our eyes met, something freezing shot through my veins.

If you don't fix this, I'm going to, she'd said to Devin.

I felt as if I was in one of those dreams where you're shoved onstage to be the lead in a play you've never even heard of. I balled my fists tightly behind my back. What was it that always made the strange things happen? When I was emotional, or exposed to the elements, or near electricity . . .

I closed my eyes and tried to focus what energy I had. The rush of wind in the sky around me. A bird chirping. Asher's spicy scent curling through me from across the clearing. How warm and safe he made me feel. Devin, who I would never understand.

"Your powers have emerged." Oriax's voice echoed from the other side of my closed eyes. "They're more than we'd ever imagined."

My eyes flew open in time to catch Asher and Devin exchanging uneasy glances.

"Light and Dark, in small ways and large," said Astaroth. "In many ways, combined even. But dangerous, yes." He picked up a rock off the ground and tossed it in the air.

When he caught it again, he looked me square in the eye. "So very dangerous to us all."

"To *some*," Oriax said with a look toward Astaroth, the excitement in his voice growing. He turned back toward me. "Your other ability, the whole reason we have our messengers watching you . . ."

What? What whole reason? Wasn't it to see what kind of powers I had? I looked wildly to Asher, to Devin, but they were avoiding eye contact. I knew they'd been hiding something, that they'd been vague about the parameters of their mission. *What was it?*

"Yes, your . . . ability," Astaroth said with preternatural calm. "Your ability to obstruct the one thing we hold above all else. But what to do with such a dangerous girl? What to do, indeed."

"What ability?" I cried, whipping around to look at Raven.

"Skye," Asher jumped in.

"Silence!" Astaroth commanded. "Have you no control over your Rebels, Oriax?"

Asher stepped back, his head down. It was the strangest thing, to see him so submissive.

Oriax seemed nervous. "You know what must come now, Skye, don't you?"

"I think," Astaroth said in a booming voice, "before

anything else, we must have you choose. You must give your power over to one side and one side alone."

Raven smirked from the side of the clearing.

She'd been the one to tell them to interfere. After my flash at the hospital parking lot. But what had that been? And how did that mean I was dangerous?

One side alone.

Alone.

Why did that word continue to bother me?

"You may return to the Order now, Raven," Astaroth commanded. "You have accomplished your mission here."

"But—"

He gave her a look that would have ignited her into flames if he'd possessed the earthly powers. Lucky for her, he didn't.

She bowed submissively. "Yes, sir."

As I watched her soar gracefully over the treetops, I couldn't help but think that sometimes beauty camouflaged the ugliest creatures.

"Well, Skye?" the Rebel Elder said, cutting into my thoughts. "What will you choose? Will you align yourself with those who believe in free will? Or"—he gestured to Astaroth and Devin—"with those to whom humans are mere puppets?"

"We keep the world in harmony," Astaroth said. "Without us, the Rebellion would destroy humanity with chaos. You know which you must choose, Skye. *Choose*."

The Order had been trying to manipulate the events in my life to get us to this point. But why hadn't the Rebellion prevented this moment from happening? My mind scrolled back through memories, through snippets of words, clips of my life, like a movie reel.

Not a scratch on you.

Gurneys, everywhere.

Stay with me, Skye. Come on. Stay with me, girl.

The Order had been capable of crashing Cassie's car.

She's blurring your destiny.

And they crashed my parents' car, too.

"Mom!" I screamed. "Dad!"

They were responsible for my parents' deaths.

"You're alone now, Skye."

And they had wanted me dead, too. But what about now? What did they want from me now? Could I trust them?

Raven is dangerous, Skye. If she's here, something bad is up.

Could I trust *either* side? Did the Rebellion want me for its own reasons? What was it that Raven had said at the hospital?

You are dangerous! They were right!

And the only reason I was still alive was because the Rebellion interfered to save me. Asher was on their side. But I knew somehow that it didn't mean what I'd thought it meant. They'd wanted to save me because they could *use* my powers. The ability they were talking about? It was my ability to blur destiny. It must be. But then what was it about my flash at the hospital parking lot that had made Raven call them, bring me here? What had that been?

It was clear to me why the Order wanted me. I had a power that they wanted to control and to keep safe. Because if they didn't, it could cause chaos for them. Chaos that the Rebellion, I was sure, would love to get their hands on.

The truth hit me so fast I never saw it coming.

Asher didn't care about saving me from the Order. He wanted to use me as a weapon against them. He'd said as much, but I hadn't fully understood it.

"No!" I shouted before I had a chance to think twice.

"No?" The collective murmur rose from the group.

"I choose neither!" I cried. "You killed my parents!" I pointed at Astaroth, letting my gaze fall in the process on Devin. He flinched. I turned to Asher. "And you don't care about me at all. You've been using me. You lied to me this whole time."

Asher looked like I'd smacked him across the face, but I didn't care. "I want nothing to do with either side. I want my life back!"

"I'm afraid that's impossible," the Gifted One said. "But if you refuse to choose—we will choose for you."

"Get her!" The Rebel Elder said frantically, turning to Asher with a rising fury.

"Don't touch me!" I flared at him.

"He has a mission," the Elder growled. "He must complete it."

Asher stepped forward, between us, one hand on my arm. I flung him away. A day ago, I couldn't let him go. But now I never wanted him to touch me again.

"What about your ability to choose? Or is that only when it's convenient?" I demanded.

"There's so much you don't understand, Skye."

I felt my temper rising.

"Oh, I understand. Much better than you think. So tell me. Is that all I am to you?" I cried. "A mission? Some way to earn cosmic brownie points for the Rebellion?"

"Skye, no!" Asher saw it just before I began to feel it. My temper. The rumbling of the earth underneath us. I felt something overwhelming rush through my body. "Control it! Flip the switch!"

Everything I'd been holding inside since this whole thing began finally burst out of me. I knew my eyes were flashing silver. I could feel the electricity surging through them just as the earth began to quake.

Astaroth was staring me down from the opposite end of the clearing. The earth shook beneath us, and outside the clearing, I could hear a tree or two cracking thunderously as it fell to the ground.

I couldn't have stopped it even if I'd wanted to. The power raged within me, and I felt everything pouring out of me all at once. Anger for disrupting my perfect world. For being forced to abandon my friends. My home. For not having an easy choice, and for caring about Devin and Asher when they only wanted me for the power each side stood to gain. For looking into the unknown and not having any idea how it would unfold. For not ever realizing what I would become.

Clouds rolled menacingly across the clear blue sky, shrouding us in darkness as rain began to pummel the ground. And I realized what it was I was capable of. The Order had mental control. The Rebellion had taught themselves to control the elements. And me? I could disrupt all of those things. Blur out the Order's control over destiny. Disrupt the Rebellion's power over the elements, draw power from the earth itself, heat from its core, shifting the weather. And what else? Because I knew somehow that this strange mix of powers didn't stop there. I was capable of much more. More I didn't even know about yet.

My life had been controlled by someone else since the very day I was born. Call it fate, call it manipulation, call it the choices of others. The Order and the Rebellion had always watched me. They'd molded and shaped my life to unfold exactly how they'd wanted. How it would best suit them. My birth, my parents' death, coming to live with Aunt Jo—my friendships with Cassie and Dan.

Even falling in love.

Everything I thought had been real—everything that made me *me*—had been a lie. Both sides wanted me. Both sides were at fault. The Order wanted to keep me under close watch to prevent the Rebellion from grabbing hold of me. And the Rebellion wanted to use me to fight the Order every step of the way.

That's what Raven had meant this whole time. That's why no one would tell me. It was all part of the plan. And both sides had one.

The wind howled, rising to a gale. The rain slanted sideways.

Trees were cracking more rapidly now, falling into the clearing as the earth shuddered violently. As one tree fell just feet from where I was standing, a flock of crows rose as one from the branches, flapping over us in a dark blanket. Their frantic caws echoed above us even after the birds had flown away.

"Skye?" Devin said uncertainly, moving toward me with arms outstretched, palms outward, like one might move toward a wild beast. He reached out his hand for me to take as another crack ripped through a nearby tree. As if in slow motion, it began to fall toward us. Devin stretched his hand out farther to me. "Skye!"

I stared into the bluest eyes I'd ever seen. I couldn't move, trying to figure out exactly what I saw in them. I was rooted to my spot. The tree fell faster, roaring through the air.

I saw everything flash before me. Devin yelling for me to take his hand. Oriax's huge black wings as he lifted himself into the air to avoid a tumbling rock. Astaroth's intense, unflappable gaze as he stared at me from the very edge of the clearing. The world tilted on its axis, turned dark.

But where was Asher?

Strong arms wrapped themselves around me tightly, knocking the breath out of my lungs. Black feathers grazed my hair and batted against my cheeks, and I was enveloped by the warm, earthy scent I knew so well. I was lifted up and up, above the clearing, into the air as the tree finally fell. The mountain echoed as the tree crashed right into where I'd been standing moments before. We touched down on the other side of the clearing, close to the Gifted One.

Asher held me close to him. "Shh," he whispered, squeezing me. The quaking earth subsided, and a sudden quiet blanketed the mountaintop once again. I looked up into his eyes, shaking. He brushed the hair off my face, let his fingers trace down my neck. "I told you I wouldn't let anything happen to you," he said. "I wasn't lying about that."

Several steps away from us, Devin was watching us with a look that I couldn't read.

Astaroth took a step forward, smoothing his robes from the storm. "So it's true," he said gravely. "Your powers are uncontrollable. Your refusal to join a side also makes them dangerous. Not just to us but to humankind as well."

"Yes." Oriax nodded once next to him.

I watched in awe, still wrapped tightly in Asher's arms. From beneath his robes, Astaroth drew out a long sharp blade. He held it in front of him, and the sun filtering through the cracks in the clouds above hit the polished silver at an angle, filling the clearing with a blinding light.

In the glow, it looked like no form of metal I'd seen on Earth. It was otherworldly.

The Gifted One showed no emotion. In a movement that was so fast and fluid I almost missed it, he whipped the sword high above his head, and drove it deep into the heart of the Rebel Elder by his side. Oriax's eyes filled with fear and confusion, before he vanished into the swirling rain.

Asher gasped. He let go of me suddenly, bounding to the place where his mentor had disappeared into the elements. He whipped around to face Astaroth. "What have you done?" he cried. "There is a truce in place! You've broken your bond!"

With unearthly calm, Astaroth turned to face Devin. "You know what your orders are."

"No," Devin whispered, his face growing pale. "I take it back. I've changed my mind!"

"If you don't, you know what will happen."

"I won't do it!"

Astaroth lifted himself to his full height, towering above us. "You have no choice." Every inch of him, from his cruel eyes to his long elegant fingers seemed to radiate a terrifying light.

Asher, still crouched on the cold ground, looked wildly

from one to the other. Devin's arm moved slowly to the hilt of the sword at his side, his jaw set in a grimace.

"Get her out of here!" Devin yelled to Asher. "Now!"

Before I knew what was happening, Asher sprang toward me. Devin dropped to his knees, shuddering in obvious pain. His shoulders shook uncontrollably. I ran to him.

"Devin!" I cried. "What's wrong with him?" I wasn't thinking; I couldn't for the life of me understand what was happening. All I knew was that Devin was on the ground, and he was in pain. And while I hated him, felt betrayed by him—I couldn't stand back and let him die. He looked up at me, not bothering to hide the struggle in his eyes. Asher reached me, pulling me back.

"Stay away from him, Skye. Don't you understand?"

"Let me go!" I screamed, but Asher held me tighter. I couldn't see anything but Devin before me, writhing on the ground as Asher pulled me away.

"Skye . . . stop . . . struggling!" Asher yelled, pulling me back with all his strength. I broke free from Asher's grasp.

In the flap of a wing, Astaroth had Asher in a hold around his neck.

"Skye," Devin whispered, his body wracked with pain.

He was beginning to shake. His face was obscured by the shadows cast by fallen trees, the branches creating intricate patterns on his face. "I—I can't. . . ." Suddenly he reached out for my hand.

Should I take it?

"Don't, Skye!" Asher called from behind me. "I don't care if you're mad at me, just don't believe him!"

I stood my ground in the middle of the clearing. Asher struggling in Astaroth's grip on one side and Devin on his knees across from me.

"Everyone, enough!" I cried, and the trees shook. Thunder boomed. I didn't know how my heart could take it all in and still survive, not burst. From across the clearing, I could see the muscles in Devin's jaw clench.

"Skye!" Devin called, mustering strength in his lungs. "I have to warn you!"

My limbs went numb.

"Warn me?" I stood there, immobile, rooted to the ground like a tree. "About what?" I called to him over the wind.

"About what happens next," he whispered, and suddenly he was gone.

"Devin!" I cried.

He reappeared inches from my face.

"You're—" I started, but I never got to finish my thought. A cold blade, icy and sharp, plunged through my stomach.

I couldn't feel the pain, though I was sure that would come momentarily. All I could feel was the same sense of falling that had gripped me every morning after my parents had died. The world before me lurched and tumbled forward. And I fell to the ground with an icy thud.

Stricken, I looked up into Devin's eyes.

Helplessness. That was all. The hunger, the ambition— all of it, gone. This is what he had to do. This is what he'd been sent here for. Not to protect me. Not to study me. Not to control my powers. To kill me.

He'd been fighting it all along.

"I'm so sorry, Skye. I had no choice," he said, his voice rough with emotion. "And falling in love with you was one more thing I couldn't help."

Devin pulled the blade from me. I was surprised at how sudden the pain was when it came on.

I was floating, cold, feathers brushing my cheek and hair. My eyes were closed, but I could feel the wind rushing past me and smell the winter sky. When I opened them, it was like a newborn opening her eyes on the world for the first time. In the clearing far below me, a wall of fire rose from where I'd fallen next to Devin. But the Guardian and his Gifted superior were gone. A black spiral of smoke curled into the air. I could smell the acrid burning of pine and sap.

The scene grew smaller with distance, but whether it was moving farther away or I was, I couldn't tell.

Sounds came in and out of focus, like someone was turning the volume on my car stereo up and down too quickly. I heard my name.

It was Asher's voice, that much I knew.

"Stay with me, Skye," he implored, his voice cracking. As we flew higher, he grasped me tightly in one arm and pressed a hand over my wound with the other. "Don't die. You *can't* die. Not yet."

I couldn't answer. I wasn't there, but somewhere else, somewhere not of this world. I realized that the hand that was grasping me was grasped in my own.

"I can't heal you." His voice was thick, shaking. "You know I can't. I wish I could. I'll find someone to do it. I swear."

The wind rushed past me, harder.

"No matter what."

The air grew thinner, the world below me, smaller, until

everything disappeared, all sound ceased to exist. All I could hear was Asher's breathing as I clung to him, and the sound of my own faintly beating heart.

We were past the clouds, into the beautiful dark.

Acknowledgments

I OWE THE HUGEST debt of gratitude to the following people:

My brilliant editor and friend, Maria Gomez, for believing in this project—and in me—from the beginning. Thank you from the bottom of my heart for all that you tirelessly did for ABD.

Barbara Lalicki, for your guidance, insight, and knowing exactly what needed to be fixed, when.

The whole team at Harper, but especially: Elise Howard, for the inspiration and the leap of faith; Susan Katz and Kate Jackson for your support; the powerhouse marketing, publicity, and sub rights teams; Erin Fitzsimmons, for the unbelievably gorgeous and thoughtful design. Also Ray Shappell, for spending a whole day with me waiting for the perfect lighting.

My publishing families at HarperCollins and Penguin, for inspiring, conspiring, listening, encouraging, understanding, commiserating, and jumping for joy with me on a daily basis.

Rachel Abrams, for talking with me about this book more than any reasonable person should have to.

My endlessly talented, amazingly supportive (not to mention witty and charming) writer friends in New York.

The Elevensies, and all of my new online friends, for sharing the journey with me.

Micol Ostow, for first making me realize I could be a published author.

Jessica Regel, for believing in me and being so, so patient.

Kari Sutherland and Shelby Trenkelbach, for your creativity, imagination, and brainstorming prowess (for which I'm endlessly grateful)!

My friends—near and far—for providing hugs, meals, bus trips, distractions, wine, big blue to crash on when I needed to get away, dancing, laughing, Lloves with two Ls, and being the very best of people, always, no matter what.

My sister, Shelby Davies, for things too numerous to list, and too important to try. That's for the book we'll cowrite.

And my parents, Jody and Lee Davies, with love and gratitude and everything else that can't be put into words.

SKYE'S CAPTIVATING STORY

continues in

*T*he first thing I noticed when I opened my eyes was the gray light surrounding me like a film of gauze. I winced and squinted, trying to focus my vision, but the light was so bright that my head began to throb. I closed my eyes again, and I took a deep breath.

That was good. I was breathing now, at least. It meant I wasn't dead.

When I opened my eyes again, I tried harder to focus, struggling to make sense of where I was. The cold seeped in around me, and I tried pulling my cream-colored jersey-knit comforter up around my chin. A threadbare fabric brushed my skin instead.

This isn't my blanket. Panicked, I looked for something familiar, some touchstone to show me that I was in my bedroom. But everything around me was strange and unknown.

I'm not at home.

Slowly things began to crystalize. Images and shapes snapped into place; lines sharpened and space defined itself. The light was falling softly through an open window. I could just make out a couple of brushstrokes of color, brown and green smudged against a white sky. Treetops. Colorado in winter.

A stray slant of light fell across the faded quilt that covered me. I wiggled my toes and watched the movement cause ripples in the light thrown across the bed. So I wasn't paralyzed. I tried my fingers, too, and then my neck. I blinked several times and then opened my mouth, stretched it wide, and closed it. I could move, but my muscles and joints felt stiff and unused. How long had I been lying here?

As I turned my head, I caught a glimpse of something metal on a wooden nightstand next to my bed, and my body tensed. Instantly my mind flashed to the woods in the darkening gloom of evening, to the glint of metal hurtling toward me. My heart was pounding, and my throat was suddenly dry. I didn't know if my reaction was caused by my memory or my imagination.

What happened to me?

"Wake up," a female voice whispered, using the hushed tone meant for hospitals and libraries. "Come on. Go sleep downstairs on the couch. You must be exhausted."

Straining to see where the voice was coming from, I honed in on a young woman standing in the far corner of the room. Long chestnut hair hung in a thick, glossy braid down her back. *She isn't talking to me*, I realized.

Then a second voice yawned in response. A guy's voice. "Mm-hmm. How long was I asleep?" I tried to see around the woman without moving the muscles below my neck, but that was harder than I'd thought it would be, and I gave up. I could just make out a battered snow boot splayed out behind her. Whoever she was talking to was sitting in a rocking chair in the corner. Something about his rough, scratchy voice was familiar. I felt a spasm in my chest.

"Has anything changed?" His voice was hollow, like he already knew the answer.

"No," she said. "And if you want her to get better, you have to let her rest."

"I'm not bothering her if I just sit here, am I?"

"It's not just her I'm worried about. You need rest, too. How are we supposed to protect her if we're exhausted? Come on, I just slept. It's your turn."

"But I . . ."

"You're not doing her any favors if you fall asleep again.

With all that's coming . . ."

"I don't care about what's coming, Ardith. I care about what happened. If I could just go back to that night—"

"Asher, listen to me—"

Asher. At the sound of his name, something silvery and light coursed through my veins. My face felt hot and cold at the same time.

"You can't," the woman said.

I wished I could sit up and call to him across the room. But my body wasn't cooperating.

"I just want her back," he said quietly, and I was struck by how different he sounded. So serious and somber. I couldn't detect the smallest hint of the usual sly wink in his voice.

Thousands of tiny stars pricked across my vision. Something terrible must have happened to me to make Asher this worried. But what?

"We all do," the woman said. "We can't win this without her."

"Not because of the *fight*, Ardith."

"I know." The woman's shoulders tensed. "Once upon a time someone said that about me. He risked his life to get me back. And look what happened." Even from my bed in the corner, I could tell these words were full of meaning. I wondered what the story was. They'd clearly known each other for a long time.

"That was different," said Asher darkly.

"It was the same. Passion is our way, but love can drive an angel mad, Asher. It can disrupt the heavens, change the outcome of a war."

"Isn't that the point?" Asher exhaled loudly and kicked his boot out in frustration. He was hundreds of thousands of years old, but he looked and acted just like a seventeen-year-old guy. "I thought we're all about falling in love and changing the world. Isn't that what makes us Rebels?"

"Ordinarily, yes," she said. "But these are strange and dangerous times. The truce between the Order and the Rebellion ended the minute Astaroth destroyed Oriax. Now we have to look out for ourselves first."

"A little hypocritical, isn't it?" He snorted.

Ardith stared at him. "Maybe," she said. "But there are repercussions now that we couldn't have known. We're not the Gifted. We can't divine fate."

"I won't let go of her," Asher said, his voice hard. "When she wakes up, she'll join the Rebellion. You'll see. She'll help us."

"Yes," she said. "In the meantime, go to bed. I started a fire down in the fireplace."

Asher sighed, dropped his head into his hands. "I hope this works."

Ardith placed a hand on his back. "Me too," she said.

She moved out of the way then, and I could see him perfectly. I was reminded instantly of the first time I saw him, leaning up against the wall outside of Love the Bean on the night of my birthday. His hair was so dark, his eyes such a magnetic black that he didn't just look at ease at night—it seemed as if he were a part of it. The moonlight shone on his high cheekbones, and he had a playful, arrogant glint in his eye.

Now his eyes were sad, serious. There was no hint of moonlight, no cocky challenge. His long-sleeved thermal shirt and jeans looked wrinkled and slept-in, like he'd been wearing them for days. His dark hair had grown a little longer and looked wild, like the worry was causing it to stand on end. Something had changed him.

Wind rattled the window frame, and I swallowed back a lump of jealousy when Ardith turned around. She was stunning, with dark brown eyes and flawless olive skin. I closed my eyes before she could see me awake.

"I want to stay here tonight," Asher said. "In this chair. You take the bed."

Ardith sighed. "Okay. But if she wakes up, remember what they said. Don't talk about what happened. She's going to be in a precarious state, and it could be dangerous if the memories come rushing back too quickly."

"Yeah, yeah, I know." He let out a long breath. "What are we going to do? Even if this works, we can't take her back to the Rebel camp."

"No," Ardith agreed. "If she does wake up, her powers will be much too unstable. They'll collide with so much chaos. It could destroy us. Or her," she added.

"They were right. She's a ticking time bomb. A weapon waiting to happen."

"But eventually"—Ardith paused—"*soon*, I hope, she'll be more controlled. Asher, the memory will trigger powerful emotions in her. You know what she's capable of in that kind of state. You were there. You have to stave off those memories for a while. If they come rushing back suddenly, it may be too much."

"She can handle it."

"I mean for us."

There was another pause. I was dying to open my eyes, but held back. My heart was in my throat, and I was so afraid that in the silence they would be able to hear it beating faster, hear my breath coming in short, uneven gasps.

"I remember when I felt the way you do now," Ardith said quietly. I pictured her putting a gentle hand on Asher's back.

"It wasn't your fault," Asher said. "What happened to Gideon. It was mine." He took a breath, and everything in the room seemed to breathe in with him. "I love her."

"I know," she said. "And there's nothing I can say to stop it from happening." I heard the swish of material, and a door squeak on rusty, ancient hinges. The sound of footsteps going down the stairs. And then, suddenly, it was quiet in the room. So quiet I really could hear the beat of my own heart. Not Asher's, though. That didn't exist.

I opened my eyes.

Asher was still sitting with his head in his hands. His back rose and fell softly with each breath.

I couldn't get his words out of my head. *I love her.*

I couldn't pretend to sleep anymore. I couldn't just lie there and not say anything. *I love her, I love her, I love her,* coaxed my heartbeat. I struggled to sit up.

The rickety bed creaked under me.

Asher's head snapped up at the noise.

And our eyes met, a flash of darkest lightning, blinding me to everything but the only two things in the world that mattered:

I was alive.

And Asher loved me.

e opened our mouths at the same time. I closed mine immediately, but Asher's remained open. I felt tears spring to my eyes. *Be strong, Skye. You're alive. You can do this.*

Asher let out a strangled noise and jumped out of his chair.

"Skye!" he choked, pushing his hair out of his eyes. And then he was beside me, around me, scooping me up in his arms and pressing me tight against him. "It worked," he said into my hair. "I thought—I didn't know what to think. It's my fault. I . . ."

My face felt wet, and I realized tears were streaming down my cheeks.

"Did I die?" I asked. My voice came out croaky and hoarse.

He laughed, a soft murmur that sent a thrill through me. "No, you didn't die. Just scared us for a bit, that's all." He pulled away and looked me square in the eyes. "I knew you'd make it."

"Aunt Jo always says I'm nothing if not a fighter," I said croakily.

"Too true," he said, a grin spreading slowly across his face. He let his thumb slide across the freckles on the bridge of my nose. "You're a lot of awesome things."

I put my hand over his, and it slid down to cup my cheek. He was staring at me like I was something precious he had almost lost.

"What . . . what happened to me?" I asked.

"We can talk about all of that later."

"But—"

"Right now, just rest," Asher said soothingly. "We'll talk when you're feeling up to it."

"I'm feeling up to it," I argued, struggling to sit up straighter in the bed.

He put a hand on my shoulder to steady me and looked at me seriously. "You really don't remember?"

I shook my head, wincing a little at how stiff I felt. Asher pulled back so that he was looking down at me.

"You're alive, Skye," he said. "You're safe here. Those

are the important things."

"Way to avoid the question." My gaze swept past him, to the open window. "Are we in Colorado?"

"Yes," he said. "But, Skye——"

"What is this place?" I asked.

"We're in a cabin. But listen, once you start asking questions——"

"What kind of cabin? How did you find it?"

"Let's talk about it when you've got all your strength back," Asher said. "I don't think the Order will be able to find you here."

I paused. *The Order.* How could I forget that group of angels who could control fate and the Natural Order of the world—including human lives? They believed in living by rules no matter the cost. Their messengers were called Guardians, sent to Earth to carry out their master plan. They had no free will.

According to the Order, no one did.

Asher grinned at me and raised an eyebrow. "And if all else fails," he said, "they'll have to get through me before they can lay a finger on you." The familiar flash of mischief crept back into his eyes. "Only *I* get to do that."

I grinned at him challengingly. "Oh, yeah?" It was hard not to feel safe with Asher. He exuded confidence, and in that moment, I believed him when he said he wouldn't let anything hurt me.

I wondered if my mother had felt the same way with my father. If that was what had led her to believe he was worth risking everything for. My parents had been angels, something I'd only just found out on my seventeenth birthday. My mother was a Guardian, and my father, a Rebel. But by the time they'd given birth to me, they'd already been cast to Earth as mortals—the punishment for loving each other. Now they were dead, and I had powers raging within me that no one seemed to be able to understand. Least of all me.

You'd think the Rebellion would be dangerous, with their staunch belief that revolutions and destruction led to rebirth and renewal. But, as I looked into Asher's dizzying black eyes, I knew that he was right—being safe from the Order was the better option. Something about the Order's calculated control felt even more dangerous. I had an eerie feeling that there was a specific reason I was scared of them now, too. It had to do with why I was here, with how I'd ended up in a coma in the first place. I could almost remember. . . .

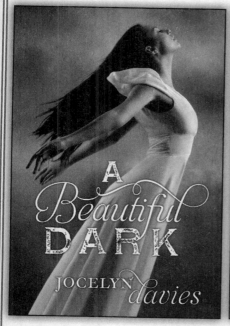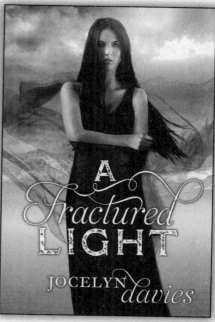